Song of the Sphinx

Book 2 of

The EGYPTIANS! Trilogy

Jay Palmer

Books by Jay Palmer

The VIKINGS! Trilogy:
    DeathQuest
    The Mourning Trail
    Quest for Valhalla

The EGYPTIANS! Trilogy:
    SoulQuest
    Song of the Sphinx
    Quest for Osiris

Jeremy Wrecker, Pirate of Land and Sea

The Magic of Play

The Seneschal

Viking Son

Viking Daughter

Dracula – Deathless Desire

The Grotesquerie Games

Cover Artist: Jay Palmer

Website: JayPalmerBooks.com

Jay Palmer

ACKNOWLEDGMENTS

Thanks to those researchers and authors who provide the rich source material to indulge enquiring minds!

Bibliography (and recommended reading!):

- "The Ancient Egyptian Books of the Afterlife", by Erik Hornung, translated by David Lorton
- "Dictionary of Ancient Egypt", by Ian Shaw and Paul Nicholson
- "Book of the Dead", by E.A. Wallis Budge
- "Egyptian Magic", by E.A. Wallis Budge
- "Bulfinch's Mythology", by Thomas Bulfinch
- "Dictionary of Occultism", by Lewis Spence
- Marvel Comics, by Stan Lee
  Special thanks to Edith Hamilton, author of "Mythology", for introducing me to the intricacies of my favorite subject!

To a sweet, gentle lady, a marvelous dancer,
and a true friend, Cindy French.

Chapter 1

The Nile River

NATE

Tired of the heat, and unused to his skin feeling so dry, Nate stepped to the far side of the ship, and there he found Sister Aspertine hiding in the small corner of their sail's shadow, which covered their aft rail. She sat wearing her habit again, although it was ruined, wrinkled and stained, and her wimple lay upon her head like a limp, crumpled scarf. She looked up at him with red eyes; *she'd been crying.*

"I never got to thank you," Nate said softly, and he sat beside her, close, but not too close.

"Thank me ...?" Sister Aspertine asked.

"For getting us out of Prince Fernando's palace," Nate smiled.

The corners of her mouth upturned slightly.

"I was so ... scared," Sister Aspertine said. "That ... cardinal ... angered me ..."

"You should get angered more often," Nate said. "May I ask ... how the cardinal ...?"

"God must judge him, and I fear that His punishments won't be kind," Sister Aspertine said.

"Your strength inspires me," Nate said. "This mission … I've never been at ease with it …"

"Yet you follow …," Sister Aspertine began.

"I'm a squire; Karl's my liege," Nate said.

"God's the liege of all," Sister Aspertine said.

"Lord Sir Rafe, whom I would do anything for, is a man of great faith," Nate said. "Eric and the Seer were both men of faith, willing to die for their pagan deities. But Karl's not … deep; he believes what's placed before his eyes … and doesn't go looking for mysteries."

"This … doorway that we seek… is it not a mystery?" Sister Aspertine asked.

"Karl would rather be back in Castle Bristlen, drinking beer and playing with his kids," Nate said. "He couldn't care less about any 'crack in the world'; if not for Roselyn, he wouldn't saddle a horse to see it."

"He's ensorcelled by that demoness," Sister Aspertine said.

"Roselyn's no demoness," Nate said. "She's certainly betrayed her faith in God, and learned to fight under immortal sword-masters, but she's a woman, susceptible to their weakness."

"Weakness …?" Sister Aspertine asked.

"Love," Nate said. "Of course, being a nun, you know nothing of love …"

"The Brides of Jesus know eternal love!" Sister Aspertine hissed, giving Nate a nasty glare.

"I stand corrected," Nate said calmly. "I meant love in the physical sense; nuns don't share the … carnal … intimacy … that everyone else does. I've seen you shiver in your sleep …"

"Nuns don't always sleep alone," Sister Aspertine said. "When it's cold, we become bedfellows, and God's always with us."

"Never would I disrespect God," Nate said, "but His love warms the heart; a different kind of love warms the toes."

Sister Aspertine looked away.

"I'll not speak of such things," she said.

"I'm sorry if my speech offends you," Nate said.

"No, I ... I just wish that these women would ... try to pray," Sister Aspertine said. "It's blasphemy!"

"They probably think the same about you," Nate said.

"That's more blasphemy!" Sister Aspertine snapped.

"I don't think so," Nate said. "To anyone who practices one faith, another faith must seem blasphemous. I'm not justifying them ... or their faiths, but I've known them since I was eight, and I couldn't ask to meet more honorable people."

"What of your faith?" Sister Aspertine asked.

"God sent an angel to keep my faith strong," Nate said.

"I'm glad to hear that," Sister Aspertine said. "You can help me guard against these pagan obscenities."

"Help you ...?" Nate gave a soft chuckle. "Sister, you're the angel that God sent me."

Sister Aspertine startled, but then she blushed.

"I'm no angel," she mumbled.

"You certainly look like one, and besides ... an angel's what we need most," Nate smiled. "The last thing that we need's another Valkyrie."

Sister Aspertine laughed sweetly, and suddenly a shadow moved; Phil came around the sail to look at them.

"Hello," he said with a suspicious look. "What have we here …?"

"Something you wouldn't understand," Nate said to his brother. "Intelligent discussion."

Phil looked doubtful.

Sister Aspertine instantly stood up.

"Squire, what're you implying …?" Sister Aspertine challenged. "May God forgive your soul for even thinking such filth!"

At the tone of her voice, Henry, Samuel, and Elaina peeked around the sail. Phil stared agape, unable to reply.

Without another word, Sister Aspertine walked fore, out into the hot sunlight, stopped by the rail, made the sign of the cross, and bowed her head in silent prayer. Nate gave Phil a nasty look, but inside he was laughing.

Pretty Sister Aspertine was starting to think that they were friends, perhaps even conspirators, which meant that Nate could expect more private meetings with her … and who knew where they might lead?

He grinned at Phil; *his dumb older brother was losing to him again, and that was all he cared about.*

They shared an evening meal as they sailed past another Egyptian city with uncounted ships crowded at its many docks. Eloise asked if this was Alexandria, but Henry said no; Alexandria was far larger. He'd visited Alexandria once, long before; that's why Rafe had chosen him to go. Yet he'd never been far beyond it, although he'd heard many stories about sailing up and down the Nile.

Rain fell that night, and the only extra canvas that they had was small, so they stretched it across the deck and held it up with ropes and spears that they'd plundered from the pirates. They had to squeeze under the canvas and sleep crowded, side-by-side; Nate tried to get a place

beside Sister Aspertine, but Phil got there first, and Nate
was forced to sleep against the other side of the ship.
However, this ship was long and narrow; they slept with
their feet touching, and having removed his shoes, Nate
smiled when his toes touched the stockings of Sister
Aspertine.

Alexandria was a huge city, so vast and bright that, to
Nate, it looked like Eloise's description of Asgard. The
scorching sun beamed upon the city, and within an hour
of dawn all were damp with sweat, but they shielded their
eyes and stared at the crowded streets and buildings,
unable to turn away. Nate was amazed; he'd assumed
that London was the largest city in the world, certainly the
biggest that he'd ever seen, although the city in Italy was
definitely huge, and they hadn't explored it completely.
Alexandria stretched out over a vast track of shoreline,
with many tall towers and palaces. The buildings here
were of strange styles, of an architecture that Nate had
never seen, walled and roofed with thick tan stones,
probably to protect them from the relentless sun and
oppressive heat.

Yet life grew abundantly. In the distance, outside the
city, they saw thick date-palm orchards, which Henry
described as a delicious, exotic fruit. Along the shoreline
grew tall, long-leaved green reeds, with brown tufts
shaped like sausages on top, and many colorful flowers.
The waters beneath them shined a brighter blue than any
waves striking England. Despite the hot air, which
seemed to evaporate their every breath, they stared at the
beauty of Egypt as much as they stared at the baked land,
strange buildings, and even stranger ships and sailors.

The Egyptian sailors stared at them just as much;
sailing by on ships of odd configurations, some just wide

barges with ornate sides, and even the poorest sailor wore a short shift of purest white, and jewelry sparkled against their sun-bronzed skins. Some sailors were Moors, with very dark skins, and as they saw the companions, the expressions on their faces became the looks of a person assaulted by an unexpectedly rancid smell. Many pointed at Roselyn, who was wearing Hel's armor, and these sailors either laughed or made gestures to ward off evil.

Henry suggested that they discuss how they should proceed, and how they hoped to purchase more supplies, since what was left of their food was mostly fish going bad. Karl counted their supply of coins, which wasn't enough to last them all summer, and suggested that they try to sell the pirate's weapons, but their last ship had been stolen while they were attempting that, so little enthusiasm for it showed.

Elaina suggested that they look for an expert on Egyptian lore, as their quest might require knowledge of the lost gods that they didn't have, but Nate insisted that they needed a translator, as without one, every attempt to communicate would fail. However, they had no idea how to find a translator. They tried shouting to passing ships in all the languages that they knew, but none seemed to understand anything that they said, and most sailed past shaking their heads.

That night, Elaina tried to dance, to fall into a rhythmic trance, and find what they needed. Her dance aboard their new ship was amazing, and some Egyptian ships sailed closer, the foreign sailors straining to watch the exotic performance in the bright moonlight, and their smiles could be seen even across the waters. Phil watched as if mesmerized. Nate sat, entranced by Elaina's dance, and wondering if his harmless flirtations with pretty Sister Aspertine might not be better targeted to this older, more-available woman.

With melodious ease, Elaina swayed from side to side, even dancing upon the narrow rails, often with her eyes closed, and always with the constant rocking of the ship. Despite being their eldest, her balance and dexterity were amazing, and she flexed and bent in ways that even Roselyn would have difficulty matching, with a grace and fluidity that warriors lacked entirely. Her slender arms trailed her body like veils, or led her into spins and turns, and Elaina could kick above her own head, her toes pointed to the stars, without bending her knees or back in the slightest. Her fingers flowed as she did, waving like magical fans wafting spiritual energies, or twitching as if playing the world on invisible flutes. She swayed with mesmeric fluidity, and her statuesque beauty enhanced her performance so magnificently that Nate felt lustful stirrings rise.

Sadly, when her dance ended, Elaina's shoulders slumped; the universe had shown her nothing. Elaina refused to complain; her connection to the universe had reached its fullest, but no revelations had come of where they must go.

Roselyn scowled, and then walked to the back of the ship, alone, staring out at the countless stars reflecting off the dark waters. Nate wondered if she was angry; she'd promised to give up her quest to find the Seer by the end of summer, and her immortal life would end if they failed.

He'd only seen the Seer once, when he was a little child, and after all of the stories of him that he'd heard, he'd wanted to meet him, to talk to him, and try to worm some magical secrets out of the legendary mage; perhaps he knew a spell to seduce rich women, which would allow Nate to arise to a status even higher than that of a squire.

Yet, after traveling all the way to Egypt, it appeared that their quest was already over; they had no idea where to find a second 'crack in the world'.

The next morning, they sailed into the mouth of a huge river; the widest waterway that Nate had ever seen, and Samuel explained that this was only one of several tributaries which emptied into the Mediterranean Sea. They didn't sail in easily; the current of the river pushed strongly against them, and Henry and Samuel were hard-pressed to manage both the sail and the rudder. To sail upstream in the wide but crowded river, they had to carefully tack with the wind and avoid colliding with other ships. Their progress slowed. However, just as they began to make a steady headway, a large golden ship, gleaming with fresh paint and many carvings, with colorful sails and ribbons blowing about in the strong breeze, came floating downstream, carrying someone shouting at them. Aboard the gold-painted ship stood many warriors, and all of them had bows with arrows noched.

"Halt!" cried a short, rotund man with only a single thick lock of black hair hanging to the side, which was tied with many blue ribbons. *"Surrender my ship, thieves!"*

At Karl's signal, Henry and Samuel released their lines, and their progress against the current faltered. The gold ship turned toward them.

"Surrender!" the short man shouted again, and soon they could see his glare.

"Hail!" Karl called to him. "Wherefore do you demand our surrender?"

"Wherefore' ...?" he asked. "You stand upon my ship, my stolen ship, and ask 'wherefore'?"

"It's his ship!" Henry whispered.

"We didn't steal this ship!" Karl shouted back, and everyone noticed that many ships were slowing to witness the exchange. "We were attacked by pirates, and we took this ship from them ... after we slew them."

"You slew ...?" the rotund man demanded, for their ships were quite close. "A few men ... and women ... slew pirates? *You lie ...!*"

Roselyn stepped forward and buckled on Hel's helmet, and Phil donned a pirate's helm, and Nate stepped beside him wearing armor; he tried to draw his sword, but Eloise laid a restraining hand upon his arm.

"Sir, we don't lie," Karl said. "Please, allow us to come aboard and discuss ..."

"That's *my ship!*" the short man shouted.

"And we've rescued it from a band of bloodthirsty pirates, and expect payment for our services," Karl shouted, and the short man started to reply, but Karl cut him off. "I don't mean that you should buy back what's yours; hear us out, and you may learn something to interest you."

The rotund man rubbed his chin, considering Karl's words, and then gestured to his men, who lowered their bows.

"Bind my ships!" the strange man ordered.

In short order, the ships were lashed together, red and gold, and all of their sails were lowered. The current of the Nile swept them both back toward the Mediterranean Sea, but no further gestures of hostility evidenced.

Roselyn held her heavy sword and eyed the Egyptian archers, who seemed delighted to stare back at her. Karl and Eloise introduced themselves, using their royal titles, and told Al-Hassim, the short, rotund man, where they came from, and described their need for a master of Egyptian lore.

"Why?" Al-Hassim asked. "What does England care for the history of Egypt?"

Karl and Eloise exchanged nervous looks, which Al-Hassim noted suspiciously.

"I'm a Norse Seeress," Elaina spoke up suddenly. "I seek an entrance to the realm of the gods of Egypt."

Al-Hassim glanced at her warily ... and then laughed.

"I've no time for jokes, woman," Al-Hassim said.

"I don't joke," Elaina said. "My friends have come here for me, at my request. I intend to find a ... a doorway to the forbidden lands ... and enter it, in the name of Odin, God of Battles."

Al-Hassim smiled, and then laughed again, and finally shook his head, rustling his blue ribbons. He turned to his guards.

"My boat has been stolen by madmen!" Al-Hassim shouted, and they all laughed.

Eloise covered her face with her hands; at first, Nate thought that she was ashamed, but he'd known her since he was a child. Her posture was stiff and rigid, as it always was when she healed. While Karl grimaced and Roselyn gripped Hel's sword tightly, ready for the fight to begin, suddenly Eloise lifted her head and extended her arms, waving her fingers at the dozen archers on the golden boat.

As one, all of Al-Hassim's archers closed their eyes, lost their smiles, and slowly collapsed onto their deck.

Al-Hassim gasped, his eyes wide as full moons, as Karl jerked his head to glare at Eloise.

"They're only asleep," Eloise said warningly. "But, if I'd wanted them dead, then they would be."

Al-Hassim stared at Eloise, and glanced at all of the others, and suddenly he drew a gleaming dagger and brandished it threateningly.

"There's no need for that," Karl said, waving for him to lower his blade. "We don't want trouble, and we'll gladly return your ship, but our quest is of vital importance. Once we're done, we'll need your ship no longer."

"Are you serious?" Al-Hassim asked. "Do you really seek a doorway to the lands of our gods?"

"We do," Karl said.

"Do ... do you think that you ... that you can find such a door?" Al-Hassim asked.

"We've already found one ... in the Norselands ... and returned from it," Karl said.

"I've found three," Roselyn corrected Karl, "but one was barred by a gate of flames."

"We carry representatives of the Norse gods and the Lady of the Druids," Karl said, gesturing to Roselyn and Eloise.

"And of the True Christian God," Nate added, and he nodded to Sister Aspertine, who looked terrified, hiding beside the mast.

Al-Hassim glanced to see Sister Aspertine, and then looked carefully at each of them in turn.

"This ... doorway ...," Al-Hassim said. "When you enter it, would you mind ... if I came with you? Just for a bit ...?"

"If you'll help us, then your company is welcome," Karl said.

"I've a friend, several days sailing from here, who knows much about our ancient mysteries," Al-Hassim said. "Why don't we join companies ... and share some of my drinks ...?"

"Is it strong drink?" Roselyn asked.

"Al-Hassim drinks only the best!" he assured her.

Both smiled brightly.

Chapter 2

The Choice

PHIL

The intense heat was delightful and invigorating. Phil had always hated the constant rain and chill of England, and while he was quickly learned that his skin reddened painfully under the bright Egyptian sun, he'd never be cold here.

"You seek our gods … and none of you are Egyptians …?" Al-Hassim laughed as he talked with Karl and Roselyn. "You hope to travel the paths of our dead … without dying! That doorway must be well-hidden, if it exists, but there's no need to seek our gods; look up … and behold the divine!"

Confused, the companions looked up in the blinding brightness of the Egyptian sky.

"Ra is my God, and there he is, shining upon us," Al-Hassim said. "Ra drives the golden sun-disk, which shines light upon all the Earth. Some call him Re, and others call him Helios, but there he sails … across the sky each day. At night, Ra travels the Underworld, through a great

tunnel filled with demons, and at its exit lies the
monstrous demon Aapep, the most ferocious of
adversaries. Aapep would kill Ra and devour the sun, and
thus end daylight forever. But Ra is stronger, for he
knows the name of Atum, and Osiris gave to Ra his
Amsu-staff, powerful enough to fight the great demon
each morning. Ra drives the immortal terror back, and
his victory is our golden dawn."

"We deny no man their beliefs," Eloise said. "We see
Ra, but have you no other gods …?"

"Indeed!" he said. "Thoth is the Judge of Souls,
whose wisdom excels all. Nut is the Sky, and upon her
dark skin shines all stars. Isis is the great wife, the
cleverest of all the goddesses, who can restore the dead to
life. Osiris is the Dead God, the Ruler of All, reborn by
his wife after he was murdered by Set, the God of
Darkness and Evil."

"Tell us all you can," Karl urged. "We must know
everything …"

"I'm no lore-master, but my friend is," Al-Hassim
said. "The Ptah knows more about Maat than any living
man."

"Maat …?" Karl asked.

"Maat is All," Al-Hassim said. "Maat is Order and
Civilization, the Heart of the Cosmos. Maat is the soul of
creation, and the advisors of Osiris, which distinguished
the lands from the chaos of the Nu. Maat begets proper
behavior, dominates good-hearted nature, and makes life
and happiness possible. Maat is all gods and pharaohs,
that which maintains order and sustains life."

"Is Maat a … truth … or a god?" Karl asked.

"Both," Al-Hassim said. "The Maat gods are the
hidden ones who live on truth, whom no mortal has ever
seen. But deny not the power of Maat! Always treat

Maat as gods ... or goddesses, lest you would tempt the anger of all things."

"Praise to Maat," Karl said, bowing slightly.

"You're wise, but you're also strange," Al-Hassim said. "I'll take you to Ptah Shabaka, for he knows the answers you seek, if any does. Your presence may amuse him ... and ingratiate me in his valuable favor."

"We thank you, and gladly accept your invitation," Karl said.

Phil didn't trust Al-Hassim, although the short, rotund man seemed both friendly and generous, providing them with excellent and ample foods and drink. Each dish was heavily spiced with cumin, coriander, or cinnamon, and some were sprinkled with toasted nuts, salt, or dried garlic. However, Phil thought that Al-Hassim looked untrustworthy, and looked askance at his painted face, thick with black eyeshadow, and his single lock of black hair tied with blue ribbons, as if his whole head was a gaudy decoration. Phil declined the heady drinks offered to him.

"Drink less ... and keep your sword ready," Phil whispered into his brother's ear.

"Why?" Nate asked, holding a frothing ceramic cup and seeming oblivious as always.

"We've made truce with a man about whom we know nothing," Phil replied softly, wary of anyone listening. "He has armed guards, he's taking us upstream to who-knows-where, and he could have his men turn upon us without warning. We're Karl's squires, sworn to defend our company ... and we can't do it drunk!"

Slow as always, Nate looked about as if seeing their situation anew, and then he frowned.

"You worry too much," Nate scowled.

"I doubt if Sir Rafe would agree with you," Phil said.

Nate shook his head. Frustrated, Phil left him beside the rail, and moved closer to Karl and Eloise. He silently abused his little brother with disappointed stares. However, he noticed that Nate stopped drinking in big gulps and rested his hand upon his hilt.

"You must be exceedingly polite and respectful of Ptah Shabaka," Al-Hassim said to Karl. "He's the wisest man in Egypt, and nothing exists in the desert that he doesn't know."

"We'd be honored to meet him," Karl said. "Is he a king?"

"Ptah Shabaka is not a pharaoh," Al-Hassim said. "However, he has held the posts of both Tjayty Sab Tjaty, the Royal Vizier, and Imy-Rkat News, the Overseer of Royal Works. Both are lofty positions, and only the pharaoh ranks higher."

"Perhaps he'd like to join us, too," Eloise suggested.

"It's possible," Al-Hassim said. "Although he's no longer young, Ptah Shabaka thirsts for wisdom, and he's studied more of our ancient writings than any other in Egypt, even our priests. But you must be careful in his presence; he's proud, and subtle, and thinks deeply. Despite his years, but he can strike as deadly as a pale scorpion … when he chooses."

"I, too, seek wisdom, as part of my service to my Lady," Eloise said.

Sister Aspertine scowled and looked away.

Resting under a tan sunshade, they sailed both ships, red and gold, against the strong current of the Nile River, and in some places the sails failed and the guards took up long oars and rowed them along. The vast, amazing city that hugged the river banks slowly fell away, replaced with irrigated fields and crops, and trees appeared in specific spots, as if planted more than naturally grown, often in ordered rows, and they passed another wide orchard of palm-dates. In some places, the flora stretched wide across the valley on both sides, but in other places it neared the river so that only a narrow swath of trees, bushes, and grasses separated the river from the sand. Phil wondered where their forests were. The lush foliage of England seemed to be missing entirely, as if baked out of existence by the cruel southern sun.

"Beer ...?" Al-Hassim asked, lifting his wide cup. "This is henket, made by repeatedly pouring water over the finest barley and emmer cakes, until they dissolve, then are left in a warm place to ferment. This one is spiced with dates and honey. The poor make henket with stale bread, which tastes bitter and bland. I told you; I drink only the best."

Karl thanked their host again, and Roselyn drained her wide cup and handed it a servant to be refilled.

A man came forward with a wide, white-stone tray laden with treats. The white stone gleamed so translucent that the bright sunlight shone through it. Al-Hassim was served first, and the others accepted the fig-filled pastries.

"What a beautiful dish!" Elaina said. "What stone is that?"

"The finest alabaster," Al-Hassim said. "It's a stone sacred to our goddess Bast ... mined from limestone caves. Many sculptors use it for divine statues, as well as for vessels, jewelry, and perfume jars. In our tongue, we call it a-labaste. Please, accept it as my gift."

"You're truly generous, but we must decline," Karl interjected. "We've a long, hard journey ahead of us, and it would be a shame to break such a treasure."

"But we thank you for the offer," Eloise said.

In the distances between the cities, they saw tall hills that looked like sand piled against rocks. When they did sail past a city, they found more tall trees growing thickly beside the river. Inside the crowded cities, and the strange, sand-colored buildings, with their perfectly smooth sides, gleamed as if polished, countless people walked, with peculiar skins and unusual clothes that would appear alien in du Harmonn.

No attack came.

Day after day, Al-Hassim sailed them upstream, delighted to listen to the tales of their adventures through the Norse 'crack in the world', although appearing very doubtful of its validity. Karl had tried telling it, then let Eloise take over, but neither were great storytellers. Finally Karl asked Nate, and he retold their tales with dramatic voices and gestures, so much that they let him describe the whole rest of their adventure.

While Nate talked, Phil grew bored, and asked Roselyn if she'd continue their fighting lessons, but she refused; to teach them now would share her wisdom with guards sworn to Al-Hassim, and she was loathe for the training methods of the einherjar to extend beyond their company.

Phil was also bothered by Nate; twice he found him whispering with Sister Aspertine in the late evenings, and both looked irritated when they spied him watching them. Perhaps he should warn the naïve nun about his brother's lewd intentions, but ... *why should she believe him?*

Phil also noticed that Eloise and Roselyn no longer seemed to be speaking to each other. No words of animosity were voiced, keeping up an obvious presence for their host, who chatted incessantly ... until Phil wished that he could throw Al-Hassim overboard just to comfort himself with a few minutes of quiet. Yet Phil was mindful of his place and his duty; he stayed close to the Karl, Eloise, and Elaina, ever aware of where each was, and he stayed sober and kept his sword loose in its scabbard.

Three hippopotamuses surfaced, their bloated bodies floating underwater, exactly as Samuel had described them on their knarr as they'd sailed from England. While the companions stared, Al-Hassim, and all the other boats, gave the monsters a wide berth.

That evening, all of the companions stood, crowded to the rail, and stared in mute amazement. Three tall, sharp-peaked structures, which they'd first thought were mountains, rose on the far side of a city. Phil couldn't believe the immensity of them.

"Those are pyramids," Al-Hassim said. "Tombs of our pharaohs of old. These three aren't our only pyramids, but they're the biggest. This is Giza, an ancient and sacred city."

"Before we leave, I must dance there," Elaina muttered, and the rest of the companions stared speechless.

After a few more days of easy sailing, which was pleasant, the number of ships that crowded the river slowly diminished, and they arrived at their destination.

The city of Beni Hassan was large, perhaps as big as Madrone, but they didn't explore it. Upon arrival, they tied up both ships and disembarked. Al-Hassim paid a messenger-boy to run ahead and tell Ptah Shabaka that he was bringing guests, and they proceeded into the early afternoon heat, in the hottest part of the day, sweating their path through the long, straight, even streets of the ancient city, whose inhabitants stepped back to allow Al-Hassim, with his many guards and strange companions, to pass by uninterrupted.

After over a mile of walking, they arrived at guarded gates flanked by mammoth statues, both of which were of women, one of which had the head of a monstrous vulture, and the other resembled nothing that Phil had ever seen, but looked like a bloated sea otter with the mouth of a donkey. The guards at the gate must've been expecting them, for they opened the gates as they approached, and Phil was unnerved at the resemblance of these gates to the sturdy portcullis of Castle Bristlen before it was broken by Eorl Sir Aledard. Gates this strong served two purposes: *to keep people out … and to keep people in.*

Al-Hassim led them into a hall decorated with intricate paintings, including countless weird symbols, like a strange pictorial writing in long rows, full of images of men, women, strange beasts and birds, and in some places the shapes of the people and animals were combined into creatures so bizarre that Phil was strongly reminded of the tales of the Wolflord and the Wolfqueen. Amid the paintings lay colorful images of the mammoth statues flanking the gate, sitting on thrones, with many subjects bowing before them. No huge tapestries hid the walls, as were hung in Castle Bristlen, but every inch of these walls, and many of the thick stone pillars that upheld the high ceiling, bore countless masterful carvings and paintings.

Al-Hassim ushered them inside, past several more statues and huge vases carved from alabaster, and bowed deeply before an elderly man sitting on a huge pile of gold-silk pillows, who sat close to the far wall under a painting of the gleaming sun shining down upon a huge triangle … one of their pyramids. Many servants stood behind Ptah Shabaka, and he responded to Al-Hassim's deep bow with a royal nod. Phil wondered if he was indeed Egyptian royalty, as instead of a crown, he wore a thick cloth headdress, pinned with a dark-red jewel set in silver. His face was painted, especially around his eyes, which bore thick bands of dark cosmetic smears, which seemed to be the custom of every member of his household, even the servants. He and Al-Hassim spoke freely in their foreign language, in which Phil clearly recognized him introducing each of the companions by name, and when he was done, Ptah Shabaka nodded his greetings to Karl, and gestured to the many large, empty pillows set upon the floor in a long row beside him.

Al-Hassim had them all bow before Ptah Shabaka, and then had them sit on the pillows, which were incredibly thick and soft, but had no backs, and Phil had to struggle to remember to not lean back too far. Unfortunately, he had to sit on the farthest end, next to Henry and Samuel; Al-Hassim sat next to Ptah Shabaka, followed by Karl, Eloise, Roselyn, Elaina, Sister Aspertine, and then Nate; in order of precedence, Nate should've been last, except for the sailors, but Phil was loathe to start an argument when they were obviously guests.

"Ptah Shabaka calls you forth," Al-Hassim said to Karl. "He has a gift for you."

Karl rose, stepped before the seated elder and bowed deeply. Ptah Shabaka held Karl long with his wizened eyes, and then he lifted up to him a small, gold trinket shaped like a fat beetle. Ptah Shabaka spoke, and Al-Hassim translated.

"O Breathless one, let me live
and be saved after death.
Thou Bearer of Peace Offerings, who openest
thy mouth for the presentation of tablets,
for the acceptation of offerings,

> *and for the establishment*
> *of Maat upon Her throne.*
> *Let the tablets be brought forward,*
> *and let the Goddess be firmly established.*
> *I am a noble Sahu. Grant that I may become*
> *one of those who follow the great god.*
> *I am the Son of Maat,*
> *and wrong is what I execrate.*
> *I am the Victorious One."*

Karl remained still, listening, and then he glanced at Al-Hassim.

"I don't have any … tablets," Karl whispered.

"It's a prayer to Maat, one of many," Al-Hassim whispered back. "No reply is expected, but to bow is required, and to kneel is to show great respect."

Karl bowed deeply, and then kneeled before Ptah Shabaka, whose nod of acknowledgement needed no translation. Then Ptah Shabaka and Al-Hassim shared a whispered conversation, glancing often at their guests. When finished, Ptah Shabaka leaned back and assumed his regal bearing, and Al-Hassim turned to Karl.

"He has given you the gift of a scarab," Al-Hassim said to Karl. "Gold is the color of Khepera, and the scarab is our most-sacred symbol of immortality."

"Khepera …?" Karl asked.

"Ra, the Sun-god," Al-Hassim explained. "Ra has many names; Khepera means 'to arise, to become'. Khepera is the God of the Rising Sun, Ra, who emerges triumphant, as the glorious dawn enshrines his honor with the defeat of Aapep. Khepera wears a golden beetle helmet, as he ascends into Shu, the sky, victorious and immortal."

"I thank you for sharing this wisdom," Karl said, and Al-Hassim translated his reply.

"Worthy guests respect the beliefs of their host ... especially when that host commands a whole city and a hundred guards," Al-Hassim said, giving Karl a warning glance. "Khepera is the father of all men and women, for he once visited all lands, and wept tears upon the dirt, and his tears became the first mortals."

Karl nodded, and then he turned to Ptah Shabaka and bowed deeply again. Ptah Shabaka spoke again, and Al-Hassim translated.

"In the beginning, there was only Nu, water and darkness. From the Nether came an egg arising from the water, and from the egg came the God Ra. From Ra came Maat, or Thoth, the divine intelligence, and from Thoth was born the four elements of women: Nu, Nut, Heh, and Hehet, and the four elements of men: Kek, Kehet, Nen, and Nenet."

"So ... Ra was your first god?" Karl asked.

"Speak that not!" Al-Hassim hissed. "Ra is the most beloved god of Ptah Shabaka, so I worship him, too. Other gods were once worshipped in these halls, but we don't name them now. Names are important, for all gods hear them, and all names are power. Ra only survives his battle against the Great Devil Aapep because of a secret name that only Isis and Horus share.

"Khepri, Kheperi, Khepera, Ra, Re, Helios: all are different aspects of the great Sun-god, before whom all in this house bow ... if they would keep their heads."

Karl bowed deeply a third time, and Ptah Shabaka nodded again, then gestured to his side.

"He invites you to join him for dinner," Al-Hassim whispered. "Come and sit; it is death to refuse."

Karl held up the gift, bowed a final time, and then returned to his huge pillow.

Beautiful young girls, clad only in skin-tight silks and sheer veils, exposing naked breasts, came forward and brought to each of them an ornamented brass cup with silver trim, filled with a very tart wine, which they called irep, and then they brought plates of breads, cheeses, and small, cooked fowl which Phil couldn't identify, although he ate them gladly. There were flat, soft breads, rich, tiny slices of sweet fruits spiced with honey and fiery peppers, and the heady irep was so powerful that it made Phil's head spin. They also provided oxen and other roasted meats, food which Phil assumed only the rich ate in abundance, as well as fresh dates and dried fish.

After their plates lay mostly empty before them, or cleared away by the beautiful serving girls, they called for 'shemayet' and 'khner', which Phil didn't understand. However, then a troop of women musicians stepped out and took seats to the side. They began playing instruments that Phil recognized; harps, lutes, lyres, cymbals, bells, tambourines, drums, flutes, and trumpets, but also wind instruments that Phil had never heard before, high and whiney, yet loud and capable of amazing artistry.

Then dancers emerged. Lovely, exotic woman shook and gyrated in unison, some covered with jingling jewelry, while others were quiet as an unconscious whisper, dancing as pairs with a grace and symmetry that only Elaina could match. Each was young and muscular, and performed cartwheels, handstands, and amazing backbends with skills to widen even Elaina's eyes, and each performance seemed to mesmerize her. Phil wondered if these dancing girls were somehow communicating with the universe, as Elaina did, but soon he swelled with the pure entrancement of the spectacle.

Hours later, after the sun had set and moonlight shined through the high windows, conversation began. Al-Hassim translated between Ptah Shabaka and Karl, and what little Phil could hear involved a quick retelling of their Norse adventures. Translating made this tale very difficult, but not one other voice spoke during their conversation, and few even walked across the floor, as if even the barefoot serving girls dared not allow their quiet footsteps to disturb their lord's concentration.

Finally, almost an hour later, everyone stood and bowed, and two servants helped Ptah Shabaka to stand, and he was escorted by a line of young women out of the hall.

The sense of rigid formality ended with his departure; many visibly relaxed, and one man coughed loudly, as if he'd been holding it back for some time. Led by servants, Al-Hassim preceded the companions across a wide courtyard filled with a beautiful fountain spraying water in three directions, and then into a whole building set aside for them. A spacious common room with a firepit dominated the center, with a round hole in the ceiling, surrounded by many doors, each leading to a small guest room. Servants placed ceramic cups, bottles of irep, and baskets of breads and fruits upon their tables, and then bowed their way out.

"Here you shall rest in peace and comfort," Al-Hassim said to the companions. "You mustn't rush Ptah Shabaka or repeat your request; he'll finish his prayers and consult the stars every night, and not one word will he answer you until he chooses to reveal his decision. I can't say what he'll decide, but he's a fair man, a wise ruler, and, if I may say so from my previous visits, I believe that he was favorably impressed with your tale … and interested in your quest. Soon, perhaps tomorrow, we'll know his mind."

"We must complete our quest before the end of summer ... with his help or without it," Roselyn said.

"And we hope," Karl added to Al-Hassim, "that you continue to accompany us, and that we may rely upon your ships to transport us to our next destination."

"That depends upon your destination," Al-Hassim said. "If a man can see the lands of the ancient gods and live, then I'd be such a man. But such an honor can't come without a price, and I'd hear that price before I'm required to pay it."

Al-Hassim departed, leaving the companions alone. At once, Karl sat and poured a glass of irep, and drank it entirely before he spoke.

"So we wait," Karl said to the companions. "At least, we're on the right path."

"Ptah Shabaka knows more than he says," Elaina said. "Whatever his response, we must judge it carefully and quietly."

"If I had my Valkyrie strength then I'd make him talk," Roselyn said.

"We must act peacefully," Karl said. "We don't need enemies on both sides of the 'crack in the world'."

"Enemies ...?" Elaina asked. "Are the Egyptian gods our enemies?"

"Why are these entrances hidden?" Karl asked. "Gods don't like mortal visitors."

"We have three months before we have to think about turning back, so we have plenty of time," Elaina said. "I suggest that we all get some rest ... and enjoy the hospitality of Ptah Shabaka."

Sister Aspertine led them in a bedtime prayer, and then she entered a bedroom and closed the door behind her. Nate watched her intently, then chose the room beside hers, smiling as he wished everyone good-night. Phil shook his head and headed for a door on the opposite wall ... when the words that he feared most were spoken.

"Come, husband; let's sleep."

Phil glanced back. Eloise had risen to stand before Karl, but as she finished her last word, Roselyn rose suddenly, her expression furious.

"I'm his immortal lover," Roselyn snarled.

"We're married," Eloise met her challenge.

Before either could speak again, Karl held up a palm to each, motioning for silence.

"I'll sleep alone ...," Karl started.

"You will not!" Roselyn shouted.

"I'm your wife!" Eloise shouted.

"I've waited for you for eight years!" Roselyn shouted back.

The two women lunged at each other, and Karl jumped between them, knocking them apart. The strength of the Valkyrie had indeed left Roselyn; both she and Eloise were knocked back by Karl's gentlest shoves. Yet both stood glaring, eyes burning into each other. Nate's door creaked open as he peered out to stare at them, and Phil and Elaina said nothing.

"We can't afford this," Karl said. "We'll insult our host ...!"

"You insult us both," Roselyn said to Karl. "We're no maids to abide indecision. Choose."

"Yes," Eloise said. "Choose, husband, your wife ... *or her.*"

"Please ...," Karl started.

"This quest goes no further ... until you choose," Eloise said. *"Husband ...!"*

"Choose ... for the last time ... *and forever!*" Roselyn said.

Neither girl spoke again, save by glares, and Karl glanced from one to the other, swallowing hard. The longest moment of their lives passed, and finally Karl sighed.

"I love you both," Karl said. "Equally. No matter who I choose, I'll always love the other. I can't choose ... but this can't go on. Yet, if I choose ... is our quest over ...? Consider what you're asking; *this isn't the time or the place ...!*"

Neither Eloise nor Roselyn spoke. Karl stared at both of them, and the moments crawled.

"Go to bed," Karl ordered. "I ... need to think ... alone."

Karl walked into an empty bedroom, without looking back, and closed the door behind him. Eloise and Roselyn stood glaring at each other, but Phil shook his head and closed the door to his room.

"You seek a grave risk," Ptah Shabaka told Karl three days later, with Al-Hassim translating. "Powerful curses protect the tombs of the old gods, and I would not awaken evils to doom the peoples of Egypt. When the gods answer my prayers, then you'll know. Until then, patience."

Phil and Nate followed Karl as guards escorted them from the royal presence. Endless waiting was infuriating, especially since Eloise and Roselyn had escalated their rivalry to threats, and Karl had to shout down both of them several times, fearful of insulting their host.

Egypt's growing heat cooked them, even inside the cool stone buildings of Ptah Shabaka's palace. Only Elaina welcomed the gossamer, sheer white outfits that were offered to them, and she alone wandered about, with three young servants assigned to her, exploring the palace of Ptah Shabaka and bathing in the wide, cool baths with the other women. Henry and Samuel kept quiet; days passed without them saying a word, and Sister Aspertine led the men in prayers every morning and evening; she seemed to be enjoying the daily arguments between Eloise and Roselyn.

On the fifth day, Roselyn threatened to end the matter by killing Eloise, at which Karl objected angrily. However, as Karl was shouting at her, suddenly Roselyn swooned; she fell forward onto the table, unconscious.

"*Eloise!*" Karl shouted angrily.

"*No one threatens a Druid priestess!*" Eloise shouted.

"What do you think she's going to do when she wakes up?" Karl demanded.

"Nothing," Eloise said, "*if you choose your wife ... as you should.*"

When Roselyn did awaken, Karl had to physically restrain her, and he called upon Phil, Nate, Henry, and Samuel to help. Elaina stole Hel's sword and ran off with it before Roselyn could reach it; otherwise things might've gone badly. Yet Roselyn had her Valkyrie-strength no longer; the five men held her with ease, and she cursed them all in Norse.

Only one comment stopped Roselyn.

"*I have to choose, don't I ...?*" Karl asked, and no one answered him.

Karl signaled for the others to release Roselyn, and he walked away slowly, looking thoughtful.

"Give him time," Henry said to Eloise and Roselyn, who were still glaring at each other. "He's a man of honor; he'll do as he must."

Late that night, after the moon had risen into the cloudless starry sky, Karl slowly wandered back into their hall, walking as quietly as he'd exited. Everyone sat frozen; although late, no one had shown any interest in sleeping.

"Once before, we were forced to make a choice," Karl said clearly, so that all could hear, but obviously looking at Eloise and Roselyn. "We could've betrayed Eric, and left him in Hel's domain, but instead we betrayed Hel ... and stole Eric from Niflhiem. None of us liked that decision, even though it proved for the best. Now I'm being forced to make another decision. However, no good will come from this. Before I choose, I want to know your intentions ... if you don't hear the answer that you want."

After a long pause, Roselyn spoke.

"I must find Athelwynne, alone ... if no other will accompany me," Roselyn said.

After another long pause:

"The Seer is a fellow Druid and servant to my Lady," Eloise said to Karl. "Your choice only determines my reason for finding him."

"Are you threatening a Valkyrie?" Roselyn demanded.

"You're not a Valkyrie!" Eloise shouted.

"I'm Reginleif ...!"

"You're Roselyn ...!"

"Silence!" Karl hissed, and his seething tone quieted them both. "I didn't fall in love with a Valkyrie ... or with a Druid priestess. Neither of you fell in love with a baron; I was a homeless farmer ... and right now I'm sorry that I ever accepted a coronet. I wish that the Seer was here; he'd put an end to this." Karl sighed. "We can't go on this way. I'm giving you both one last chance: don't make me do this ... *one of you won't like it!*"

Both Roselyn and Eloise sat unmoving, and neither looked away.

"I'm not happy with either of you, and in no case is that a first," Karl said. "If you're chosen, then you must accept that I'll continue to love you both, even when neither of you will speak to the other."

No one spoke. Karl swallowed hard, but he seemed determined.

"Eloise … Roselyn …"

Both women stood.

"You made me do this," Karl said softly. "Eloise, you'll always be my wife, but we were married with the intention that I'd eventually go to Roselyn … I was willing to wait for death, but you're forcing me …," Karl bowed his head, but spoke very firmly. *"It's time I went to Roselyn."*

No one spoke, but all eyes turned to Eloise. She burst into tears and ran from the hall. Elaina ran after her daughter, the silence broken only by their running footfalls. Phil stood to go after his baroness … to see that she didn't harm herself. He glanced at Nate, whose confused expression looked comical, and realized that he'd best take him … to keep him out of trouble. Without a word, Phil bowed to Karl, grabbed his brother's arm, and pulled him toward the door.

"Hell awaits those who betray their marriage vows," Sister Aspertine said.

Pulling Nate outside, Phil scowled; *Karl's sufferings would come far sooner than his death.*

Chapter 3

The Clue

ROSELYN

Nights passed in languid ecstasy. Once in their bedroom, Roselyn gave Karl no chance to regret his choice, but their days were torments; Eloise and Elaina didn't return, and twice each day, either Nate or Phil would appear to report on Karl's wife and mother-in-law, who'd secreted themselves in a remote corner of the palace. Both whispered that Eloise was still sobbing and cursing Karl. The only good news was that Elaina had refused to let Eloise use magic against Roselyn. The palace servants had found them and were offering them what foods and comforts they could.

Sister Aspertine made herself insufferable; she assumed a pious, haughty air, and repeatedly condemned Karl for abandoning his Christian wife for a pagan demoness. Her morning and evening prayers were attended only by Henry and Samuel, since both of Karl's squires were quietly guarding Eloise, despite her commands for them to 'go away'. Sister Aspertine wouldn't let Karl join her for prayers unless he repented.

Roselyn felt sorry for Eloise; before the Gates of Valhalla, she never should've suggested that Eloise marry Karl. She'd created the animosity between them, which would now last forever. Yet Karl had chosen her ...

She didn't have to kill him!

Roselyn wished that Elaina would just dance and discover the location of the 'crack in the world'. That was the only purpose that Roselyn could imagine for dancing, which she disdained, although she envied Elaina's physical control.

Elaina danced like a fairy, which deeply troubled Roselyn. Although she tried to deny it, memories of Alfhiem stabbed her. Her transformation had shown her a gentler form of existence, as opposite as she could imagine to the rough seriousness of a Valkyrie. She longed to feel again the unequaled happiness of being a fairy, the pure joy of being light, free, and one with all nature. As a Valkyrie, she would never experience happiness such as existed in the Mere of Mab, and regretted that she'd never again know infinite peace.

She'd made the right choice; she'd never be free of the responsibilities that she'd accepted, and she'd never know peace until she knew that her friends were no longer in danger. However, she'd never stop missing having thin, flapping purple wings, the intimate sensitivity of total sharing, or the bubbling effervescence of the waterfall of blue light delighting her every passion, excelling every sensation that she'd ever known ... as a human or a Valkyrie.

Yet, as moisture gathered in her eyes, she pushed it all away. As a Valkyrie, her duty was to scorn weakness ... even that which she secretly desired.

Three days later, the Ptah summoned Karl to his hall early in the morning, and Roselyn walked at his side.

"Last night, I dreamed of a sandstorm," Ptah Shabaka said, Al-Hassim translating. "It consumed my city, and approached my palace, but here it halted. Out of the deadly clouds of swirling dust walked a white camel with golden wings; upon it sat a warrior-woman of fearsome aspect; she was small and thin, black-haired, but her complexion was pure white, which only those from the farthest north wear. Her face was pale, angular, and her teeth, when she snarled, gleamed like summer clouds. She reached into her armored breast and lifted up a golden key, holding it out to me, as the sandstorm behind her raged with potent fury; I awoke sweating and trembling, certain that I and my palace were about to be destroyed."

"Sire, I'm no prophet," Karl said, "but I fear that this wasn't a dream."

"You describe my shield-sister Róta, our wisest and most-cunning," Roselyn said.

"No woman threatens me," Ptah Shabaka said. "You must leave."

"As you command, Sire," Karl said.

"Please, Lord; we need your wisdom," Roselyn said.

"The doorway you seek opens in the Temple of Osiris," Ptah Shabaka said and Al-Hassim translated. "Only one mortal knows the sacred words to unlock it: the Mad Hermit ... in the Valley of Thieves."

"Thank you, great Ptah," Karl said. "We'll leave at once ..."

The expression on Al-Hassim's face stopped him.

"We can't enter the Valley of Thieves!" Al-Hassim said.

"We've no choice," Karl said.

"We'll be murdered, our throats cut in savage ritual …!" Al-Hassim argued.

Karl shook his head with a bitter smile.

"Every road to a 'crack in the world' is lined with death," Karl said.

Al-Hassim hesitated, then spoke to Ptah Shabaka, who seemed displeased, but neither Karl nor Roselyn understood their language. At last, Al-Hassim sighed.

"I'll sail you upstream to the Valley of Thieves," Al-Hassim said. "Once there, we part company. I do this at the bidding of Ptah Shabaka; my boats remain with me."

"I thank you," Karl smiled.

Al-Hassim looked surprised.

"But … you'll have no ship to sail you back to England!" Al-Hassim said.

Karl laughed.

"Once we find the Seer, we'll need no boats," Karl said. "He's the most powerful wizard ever born on Earth … and our friend."

Ptah Shabaka treated them to another meal, at which all of the company was required, but no entertainers performed, so it was their shortest meal in the palace. Eloise and Elaina sat by themselves, apart from the others, and only evil looks exchanged between the groups. Yet Ptah Shabaka seemed eager for their departure, and as the sun rose to its zenith in the hot, cloudless sky, the companions walked with bowed heads out of the palace, through the city, and boarded the boats of Al-Hassim.

"You robbed me," Al-Hassim grumbled to the companions. "I'd hoped to see the land of the ancient gods, but if you enter the Valley of Thieves, then their blades are all you'll find."

"That's what the pirates thought … before we slew them and brought back your boat," Roselyn said.

"Would that you'd sailed it home to England," Al-Hassim said. "I'd rather lose three such ships than the favor of Ptah Shabaka."

"He's angry with you?" Karl asked.

"Ptah Shabaka doesn't like taking orders from a woman … not even in a dream," Al-Hassim said.

"He's a fool," Roselyn said.

"All friends of the pharaoh have enemies," Al-Hassim said. "His foes will claim that Ptah Shabaka's strength is failing."

"Better one bad dream than the wrath of the Valkyrie," Roselyn said. "This is our first sign of hope; Róta hasn't abandoned me."

"The Lady of the Druids couldn't enter Yggdrasil unaided," Karl said. "Róta might be able to lead us to the 'crack in the world', but beyond that, we'll be out of her reach."

Roselyn scowled; *was Karl truly trying to frighten a Valkyrie?* In Valhalla, she'd once killed a man for such words, but she had to restrain herself; she was only Roselyn. She insisted to the others that she was still Reginleif, but Hel's armor was her only protection against swords … her mortal body ached from wearing it … and she had no protection against Eloise's sorcery; an ex-Valkyrie was pitifully weak compared to a Druid priestess.

Karl's choice hadn't ended their rivalry, only escalated it to open warfare. If not for Elaina, Eloise could've already killed her. If she got in sword-range, her skills could easily kill Eloise, but this wasn't Valhalla; *Roselyn had once considered Eloise her only friend on Earth, as close as a sister. Could Roselyn truly kill her?*

Strangely, Roselyn felt sure that she could ... *but what would Hel say ... when Roselyn had to tell her that she'd murdered Eloise ...?*

Roselyn rested her hand on the silver Garm-pommel of Hel's sword and leaned onto the ship's rail, looking out at the hot, barren plains of the desert away from the scrub brush near the river. Soon they'd be entering that arid land, whose death and misery wouldn't end with the sunset. Roselyn hated deserts, and had scowled whenever Valhalla had transformed itself into baking sands. The others didn't know what awaited them; traversing a desert would be a nightmare, like walking through a roaring fire in black plate armor ... and trying to not get roasted.

Four days they sailed south up the Nile, and Al-Hassim's generosity shrank each day. In places, they sailed past villages, trees, and planted fields, all crowded close to the riverbank; only parched sand and rocks colored the distant hills. At last, tall, stony hills rose into the oven-like sky, and only Al-Hassim smiled.

"Over those peaks lies the Valley of Thieves," Al-Hassim said. "There's a cleft not far from here, where you may enter easily, but if you do, then Isis protect you."

"Glad to hear it," Karl smiled.

"Glad ...?" Al-Hassim asked.

"If you're not approaching certain death, then you're not headed to a 'crack in the world'," Karl said.

For the first time in days, Al-Hassim laughed.

"We repay our debts," Karl said. "If we do return, we'll try to bring you something, or send a message to you."

"Send the message to Ptah Shabaka, and then he'll summon me to hear it," Al-Hassim said. "Perhaps that'll mend the rift that you caused."

Left on the shore with a large sack of food strapped to Phil's back, and fifteen bladders of water, half over Nate's shoulders, the companions waved good-bye to Al-Hassim as he unmoored his beautiful ships and let the current flow them back downstream.

Without a word, the companions began their hot march. The cleft into the Valley of Thieves opened before them, but by the time that they reached it, they were already broiled and tired. To each of them, Nate shared a mouthful of henket, this one sweet and strongly fermented, from their meager supply, and then they sat in a narrow shadow inside the cleft, feeling the dry, dusty air steal the moisture from their mouths.

Inside, the Valley of Thieves extended a wide, low range. Scrub brush thrived in great abundance, but all of the low bushes looked old and gray, showing no trace of leaf or flower. They could see no end to the valley; the rocky hills angled away from them on both sides, which reminded Roselyn of the glowing 'V's, the tracks left by Eric's ghost that they'd used to follow him to Castle Bristlen after the death of Svenson Two-Sword. Yet not one living thing showed itself, not a bird, snake, or mouse, and Roselyn wondered how they expected to cross the desert on foot ... and how long it would take ... and if their pitiful supply of water would last.

Although Karl was anxious to move on, Roselyn cautioned him that it was best to travel at night. They spent the evening resting in the growing shadow, waiting for nightfall. As the sun lowered, Phil handed out some food sparingly, and by the time that the sun neared the horizon, they stood, ready to begin.

Even though the evening was cooler than the day, walking in Hel's plate armor kept Roselyn overheated, yet she was loathe to let her weakness show. She needed the exercise to keep up her strength, but the healing effects of the Water of Life had ended, and her stomach was still sore from the wound she'd received in the gladiatorial pit. Karl, Phil, and Nate also wore their pirate-stolen armor and weapons, and they all had hidden daggers that Roselyn had insisted that they carry. They headed straight into the valley, Karl leading, with Samuel and Henry walking behind, trailing Elaina and Eloise. As it was named the Valley of Thieves, Roselyn assumed that they'd soon find brigands, whom they'd have to fight. Phil again suggested that Roselyn resume instructing them, but Roselyn refused.

"Desert is our worst enemy," Roselyn said. "The more we exert ourselves, and the more that we perspire, the sooner our waterbags will be depleted … and thirst kills more-assuredly than daggers. However, when the sun rises, I'll share with you the wisdom of the einherjar."

As the dawn rose, they kept walking, until an hour after sunrise, when the heat of the day suddenly increased, and breathing became difficult. Al-Hassim had given them one parting gift: a large white cloth. They stabbed their every sword into the ground, and threw the tarp over them, and then weighted its edges with rocks. Inside this pathetic tent they crawled to escape the blistering sun, but it seemed even hotter inside.

"We must keep watch," Roselyn said. "One on each side; we mustn't let enemies sneak up on us."

"We want them to find us," Karl said. "We'll never find this Mad Hermit by wandering blindly."

"Yes, but we want our swords in our hands as they approach," Roselyn said. "Elaina, would you keep watch behind us … please?"

All eyes turned toward Elaina, who sat stiff-lipped under the white awning; neither she nor Eloise had spoken to Roselyn since Karl had split their company with his decision. Yet Roselyn had asked politely, something which she seldom did.

Exchanging glances with her daughter, Elaina said nothing, but she crawled to the back edge, lifted the thin fabric, and peered out.

"Henry, watch in the direction that we're headed," Roselyn said, and he nodded.

Henry crawled to the edge opposite Elaina and peered out.

"Nate, share water with everyone," Roselyn said. "Just a little, to wet our throats, and slow the coming thirst that the day will bring. But attend, while you do your duty; this is the wisdom of Valhalla."

Roselyn took her turn at the waterskin that Nate passed around, and then waited until he'd shared with everyone before she said another word.

"Who's the feeder, and who's the food?" Roselyn asked, and she glanced at each of them, but no one spoke.

"Who's the feeder, and who's the food?" Roselyn repeated.

All of them looked at each other uncertainly.

Slowly a dry, raspy voice, harshened by the desert, came from behind Roselyn.

"That's how animals think," Sister Aspertine said.

"Correct," Roselyn glanced at her. "For a warrior, victory is life, and all life must feed; to be an einherjar, you must learn to think like an animal, simple, direct, without question, and hunger for the deaths that you must cause … to prevent your own death from feeding those who hunger for you."

A general agreement was murmured by the men, and a few stole glances at Sister Aspertine, crouching under a low section of their primitive tent.

"The mind, body, and spirit must fight in unison," Roselyn said.

"I understand that one, begging your pardon," Samuel said. "Being ready to fight isn't enough; mind and spirit must be equally prepared."

"Prepared how?" Roselyn asked. "How do you prepare both mind and spirit to fight?"

To Roselyn's delight, their conversation quickly became animated. Only Eloise and Elaina kept silent, but the rest of them discussed these topics so freely that Roselyn could've mistaken them for newcomers to Valhalla. None of the companions spoke with the expertise of an einherjar, but when any topic seemed to be failing, she voiced another tidbit.

"Disorder the flesh, reorder the fight."

"How one perceives their opponent determines how one fights."

"The deadliest fighter seldom fights."

"The easiest victory seldom is."

"Downhill, your enemy is likely to die."

"Uphill, you're likely to die."

"Mud slips."

"High grasses hide enemies."

"Thick forests prevent escape, but their edges defend against foes in the open."

"All terrain talks, if one is wise enough to listen."

This phrase evoked only silence, so Roselyn expanded upon it.

"Sight along each horizon," Roselyn said. "Memorize the horizon's pattern of rises and falls; if it ever changes, then you're being spied upon."

Conversation exploded among the companions, and led to other topics without Roselyn having to provide prompts. Eventually, as they talked, Roselyn began adding in more wisdom common among the einherjar.

"Fight only to win. Ambush whenever possible. Surprise usually wins. Against lesser odds, overwhelm. Fight as wall when odds are even. Fight back-to-back when outnumbered. Never forget why you fight. Never doubt your need to kill. Obey your commander, even if they order you to certain death; victory in battle isn't a solitary achievement."

"But what about while you're fighting?" Phil asked. "What do you think about while your enemy is stepping into range?"

"Forget your victories," Roselyn said. "Remember your defeats. Stay on your toes. Keep a springy step about a balanced stance, rocking forward and back: that which stands still is a target. Know and push your limits. No blow is too dirty if it kills. Of equal ability, the overconfident fighter always loses. Don't get cocky."

"It takes faith to be a true warrior," Karl finally smiled. "...and there are Valkyrie to impress."

Roselyn smiled at him.

Eloise scowled.

Despite their dry throats, when evening came, they ate some bread, folded their awning, and resumed their trek. They met nothing but rocks, sand, and an occasional small snake or scorpion. The next day was the same. They all took turns watching for attackers, but none came. Disdaining their irep, Roselyn openly worried about their water supply, of which two of nine botas were already dry. Then, on the third day, Roselyn eyed their horizon, and stepped out of the awning to look at it closely.

"We're being watched," Roselyn said.

"Why?" Karl asked. "We're a small threat."

"Every fight's a risk," Roselyn said. "They can just wait us out, let the desert kill us, and scavenge all we have."

"What should we do?" asked Phil.

"Find them," Roselyn said. "March into their camp ..."

"I'll find them," Elaina said, mopping her brow. "Anything to get out of this heat."

"Desert camps move quickly," Roselyn said to Elaina. "Dance at sunset, and then we march directly toward them."

"The only Christian way to find anything is prayer," Sister Aspertine croaked, her once-smooth voice almost gone.

"Pray," Karl instructed her. "If God informs you of where the thieves are hiding, then we'll go where you direct."

All day Sister Aspertine prayed, while the others tried to rest under their sweltering tarp. With the first lessening of the dusk's heat, a relief to their painfully reddened skin, Karl politely asked Sister Aspertine if she knew where the thieves were encamped. Sister Aspertine scowled and looked away.

After they broke camp, they sat in a wide circle. Elaina took off her shoes and stood alone in the light of the setting sun. Everyone fell silent, and Elaina began to dance.

It was eerie; in the desert, away from most sounds, the soft wind seemed to take on a new pitch, as if rising in response to Elaina's steps. Roselyn was strongly reminded of that little waterfall, barely a puddle, where Glororil and Silvana had taken her, where the water-fairies had made music in the tinkling waterfall, and where she'd clapped hands and joined in their song; *Elaina heard that music.*

When her dance ended, Elaina faced a set of nearby hills. The look on her face was ecstatic. They all stood and looked at the rise lit by the last light of evening and the growing brightness of the moon. Soon they heard a bird's cry that was obviously only a poor imitation. Karl smiled and cried out to the thieves.

"We know that you're here!" Karl shouted. "Show yourselves; we come to talk."

Receiving no reply, they started marching toward the hills.

As they reached the closest incline, suddenly ten men rose up from the summit of the hill, and a thudding roar was followed by eleven camels charging out of a ravine, each with a rider shrouded in black and wielding a drawn blade. The companions halted, watching the riders circle around them to block their exit.

"There's no need to surround us," Karl shouted to the men on the hilltop. "We've come on an urgent quest and must speak to those who live here."

"None enter the Valley of Thieves except to die," someone shouted back to them, but it wasn't a man's voice; it was a woman's, yet her tone was harsh and snarling.

"We seek the Mad Hermit of the Valley of Thieves," Karl shouted.

Several of the men startled, and a few made gestures with their hands, as if warding off evil.

The woman upon the hill stepped closer, stopping at the edge of the slope. In the moonlight, they could see that she wore a black shift under bands of black leather armor, like all of the men, but underneath she wore a wore a woman's dress, decorated with sparkling beads like the dancers at Ptah Shabaka's palace, but her clothes weren't scanty or revealing. Hanging from a thick leather belt, she wore a long, slender-curved sword like Henry's, a khopesh. On her head rested a furred helmet with a spike, and she walked like a warrior, with firm, measured steps. Her thick hair looked black, even in the moonlight, and her features were that of an attractive young woman, but her heavily-painted eyes held a fire which only the Valkyrie possessed.

"Why do you seek the Mad Hermit?" she demanded.

"For wisdom, for which we'll trade," Karl said. "Ptah Shabaka sent us."

"What wisdom have you, and what do you seek?" she asked haughtily.

"We carry wisdom of the legendary lands of Yggdrasil," Karl said. "Wisdom of meeting with northern gods, and speaking with them, as I'm speaking with you," Karl said. "We seek a doorway to the lands of the gods of Egypt."

The desert woman stared at them, her black-painted eyes unfathomable, and she examined each of them individually, but without speaking. Finally, she turned to her men and sneered:

"Seeking a Mad Hermit … comes a company of madmen!"

All of her men laughed, and many lifted and shook their weapons.

"No," she said, waving them back. "Why drag their corpses home? Tonight they'll be my guests, and when the sun shines high tomorrow, then I'll enjoy their screams ... as you enjoy their women."

The men's laughter rolled across the desert flats, and they were still laughing when the echoes of their laughs returned.

"This way, mad-folk," she gestured.

Roselyn alone stood unmoving as the others began walking, surrounded by the armed and mounted men, but she quickly matched their pace; *something wasn't right.* Like Eric Bjornson, and all of the other einherjar after centuries of learning, Roselyn could read an opponent by sight alone, and size up their potential threat. This black-haired desert woman was obviously a warrior; she stood, walked, and talked not only like a warrior but as a leader of men, and by the way that her arms moved as she walked, she bore thick muscles upon her bones. She had fearless eyes; she could be a potential Valkyrie, if she were a daughter of Odin. Yet her reaction when Karl had mentioned the Mad Hermit was childishly obvious, although Roselyn was certain that only she'd noticed it.

This woman knew more than she wanted to say, but she also believed that the companions were no threat to her, and she wished to keep that knowledge secret from her men.

From that moment on, every movement that the female desert-leader made, even the tone of her voice as she spoke in Egyptian, screamed that she was being deceptive. Roselyn wondered who she really was ... *and why she was trying to deceive everyone.*

Jay Palmer

56

Chapter 4

A Wife's Fury

ELOISE

Karl deserved to die!

Never before had Eloise wished for Karl's death. Several times she'd risked her life and everything that she had to spare him, but all in vain; now she wished only to hurt and humiliate Karl ... *as he'd done to her!*

He'd regret his choice; *Eloise didn't have to accept shame and disgrace!* Karl would be hers again, and if he refused, then she'd force him to reconsider, and Roselyn ... *she'd never interfere again, even if Eloise had to summon Death to hunt her!*

Eloise plodded behind the others, hiding her fury. She wasn't worried about these thieves; between her magics and the company's fighting skills, Eloise was sure that they could handle twenty filthy desert ruffians.

The walk wasn't far; the ravine that the camels had ridden out of led to a series of deep rents in the earth, and finally to a large, torch-lit area. There they stopped; over a hundred thieves rose to leer at the companions. Eloise felt a pang of fear; *her magics could never defeat this many!* Yet something troubled her more: all of their assailants were men, led by one woman; *why?*

This didn't make sense!

Escorted to a colorful blue tent surrounded by flaming torches, they were given places to sit. The leader-woman sat before the door to the tent, behind a burning brazier, and at a snap of her fingers, henket was brought for all of them. Around them crowded the desert thieves; dirty and crude, with eyes that fixated upon her, Roselyn, her mother, and even Sister Aspertine. Every mouth dripped with lustful depravity, and their gazes roved across the women like the lurid tongues of rapists.

Finally, she pulled off the black scarf that hid her face, and Eloise startled: *their host was a woman about her age ... with a stern but lovely face, dusky skin, and dark eyes ... another beauty to tempt her lying husband's attention!*

"I am Alarika, Queen of the Army of Thieves," the woman said. "Share your wisdom with me, if you'd meet the Mad Hermit."

"You've promised to kill us," Karl said with only a small attempt to conceal his sarcasm. "Why should we share anything with you?"

"Tell her ...!" Eloise and Roselyn said together.

Both rivals glanced at each other; they hadn't spoken to each other for almost a week, and only bitter enmity burned in their eyes. Eloise knew why Roselyn wanted their story told; *their wisdom might be all that was keeping them from being raped!* Yet a Valkyrie could never admit fear; *they'd have to kill Roselyn ... and Eloise couldn't stop them.* Her magic, if it worked, might be able to delay a dozen of these desert rats, perhaps two, but without the fighting skills of Reginleif, they'd quickly be overwhelmed.

"Squire Nate, you tell our story best," Roselyn said. "Share with our host the tale of the birth of a Valkyrie."

At a wary nod from Karl, Nate rose and began the story of Eric Bjornson and his quest for Valhalla. Nate improved his storytelling, and spoke with dramatic gestures, clever voice-impersonations, and pointed at each of the companions as he named them, and described their challenges as heroic adventures, stories deserving to be cast into song.

As Nate spoke, one of the thieves translated for the men, trying to mimic Nate's gestures and voices, which he did poorly. Yet the thieves made a good audience, and soon they were laughing, gaping, or shocked, hanging on Nate's every translated word. Nate went into far greater detail than he usually did, and often referenced parts of their tale which only Rafe and Seren told. He often had to drink some henket, to keep his dry throat from rasping, and finally begged for water, to keep his mind clear, as the henket was quite strong.

To Eloise's amazement, Nate went on hour after hour, even describing her kidnapping and first transformation into the Wolfqueen in such realistic words that Eloise winced; luckily, Nate didn't know about who'd slept with who during their travels, in England or on the dragonship, or she would've blushed even more than she did when he'd described her and Roselyn riding naked to save Karl and Eric.

For over three hours Nate talked, and the moon was setting before he described their final battle against Loki, and all of the thieves cheered and applauded when Eric entered Valhalla.

When Nate finished, he bowed like a Saxon minstrel to all of the thieves, then to the translator, and lastly to Alarika, to whom he'd directed his speeches during most of the tale. Alarika had sat listening to all of it, but she frequently glanced at the others, and especially at Karl, and her every glance at him twisted Eloise's stomach; *for all of his good qualities, Karl had never once resisted the charms of a pretty woman.*

"A wonderful tale," Alarika said when the applause died. "Worthy of a last meal, I'd say." She gestured to the men closest to her, and they nodded and hurried off. "However, the ending of your tale stripped you of every proof: you have no treasure, no Seer, no gods or half-goddesses; why should we believe it?"

"Roselyn wears the armor of Hel, Goddess of Death," Karl said.

"I've been admiring it … it will fit me well," Alarika said. "A pity that it's dented and scratched. But that's not proof; have you any proof that you're more than a company of madmen and whores come to pleasure my men?"

Eloise startled at the insult, and Sister Aspertine started to object, but Karl waved her silent, and then, with a deep sigh, he said:

"Eloise …?"

Eloise glared at Karl; *how dare he?!?* It was the first time that he'd spoken to her since he'd betrayed her, *and he calls upon her to save them?!?*

"Eloise … *what?"* she asked.

Every eye turned toward her, and all of the companions glared. Eloise smiled falsely just to annoy them, but then she stood, walked over to the brazier before Alarika, and looked down into the tiny red, orange, and yellow flickering flames. She didn't have her tools, only the Seer's moonstone, or she'd show them some really impressive false magic, but she'd practiced this spell many times; it was one of the first that she'd truly mastered.

> *"Lady of glory,*
> *Lady tall,*
> *Lady I worship,*
> *Lady all,*
> *Lady beautiful,*
> *Lady divine,*
> *Lady of wisdom,*
> *Thy will be mine."*

On her third recitation, which ended with her tenth trip circling around the brazier, Eloise felt the magics rise within her. She felt the schisms that she'd first learned about while reading the Seer's personal notebooks, but she forced his image from her mind and concentrated on feeling the subtle forces around her, the elements wafting upwards from the brazier.

Slowly she reached out … and the small fire rose to welcome her. As friends they greeted each other, priestess and flame, mortal and element. The fire didn't burn her, but leapt into her hands like a playful kitten, and then it nuzzled and caressed her, like a loving pet.

Eloise played with the dancing flames, which jumped and frolicked all over her, and she shared with the fire her real love for it, and her gratitude for its nature, which heated her when she was cold, and cooked her food until it was delicious. She wrapped her arms around herself as if hugging the rising flames, which now covered her, and she felt it return her hug with gratitude, cherishing her like a friend.

Then Eloise held out her hands, allowing the friendly fire to return to its source, the fuel which fed it. The tiny tufts of flames jumped back into the brazier, leaving

Eloise free and unlit, unburnt, and then the fire returned to normal.

With a smug grin, Eloise went back and sat in her place with calm demureness.

Reactions to her display were mixed; some cheered and applauded, but even more looked horrified, and half of the thieves seemed shocked beyond words.

"*Heka …!*" many muttered, all with fearful glances.

Alarika watched, fascinated, but then her expression grew cold.

"Why should we trust those who perform heka, which you call 'magic'?" Alarika demanded.

"We never asked for your trust," Karl said. "We've told you our tale; now, where's the Mad Hermit?"

The food arrived, carried on wide platters, but no answer was given.

"Eat well, and drink your fill," Alarika ordered with a cruel smile. "Enjoy your last meal."

Piled on one side of each platter was a thick brown paste, brimming with many different minced vegetables, fava beans, and cooked grains, and the other side held flat circles of bread. More platters came out, shared among the thieves, who took circles of bread and dipped them liberally into the paste, then ate both with gusto. Following their example, the companions liberally dipped their bread. The paste tasted like a spicy oat gruel that'd been overcooked, then set to dry, and it had many odd flavorings which Eloise couldn't identify. Alarika alone didn't eat, but sat staring at the companions in silence, as if she'd devour them with her eyes. She waited until they were finished, and then ordered her servants to bring more henket. However, as soon as they were done, Karl suddenly stood up.

"We thank you for this meal," Karl said. "Now, where's …?"

"Tie them to face the dawn," Alarika said to her men. "After the sun tenderizes their skins, they're yours."

As the sun rose over the distant horizon, the companions found themselves tied wrist to wrist in a long line, between two large boulders, facing the rising sun. Ten guards stood watching them. One of them had dared to walk up to Sister Aspertine, Eloise, and finally Elaina, and he'd reached out his filthy hand and fondled their breasts, leering, until their screams summoned Alarika. She ordered the guard back, and commanded that the companions weren't to be touched until noon, when, after the sun had seared their pale skins, they'd be more-prepared to answer her questions … and willing to enter their tents. Then, she promised, the women would be theirs to indulge themselves upon. The guard grudgingly obeyed, and Eloise silently hung between Elaina and Henry, wondering if they'd escape.

To everyone's surprise, Roselyn had cooperated in their capture; when Phil had started to draw his sword, Roselyn had stopped him, drawn Hel's blade, and stabbed it into the dirt, then allowed herself to be bound between Phil and Karl. Eloise didn't know why Roselyn had allowed herself to be tied up without a fight, but Roselyn refused to comment upon it, and the guard that had translated for Nate was standing too close for them to talk without being overheard.

The sun rose in all its brightness, blinding them, making them avert their eyes. The dry heat of the day quickly flamed; by noon their already sunburnt skins would be completely seared.

Alarika appeared only an hour after dawn, just as Eloise was certain that her skin would never recover. She walked down the line of the bound companions and stopped before Eloise.

"The rest of my men are asleep ... mostly drunk," Alarika whispered to Eloise. *"Can you take out these guards ... quietly?"*

Eloise looked up at her in surprise, then slowly nodded.

Alarika nodded back, then continued down the line, stopping at the end to glare at Karl, and then marching back. Eloise lost track of her movements, reaching inside of herself with a short prayer to The Lady, feeling for the darkness within her soul, the absence of the Lady, and preparing to share that darkness with these thieves, as the Seer had once felt for the light in his soul to spark a candle aflame. Yet Eloise felt no light, only her loss of Karl tearing at her soul, as if a part of her body were being cut away.

An eternity later, Eloise bit back a scream, fighting to deny her pain; these thieves were far more difficult to reach than the archers of Al-Hassim, whom she'd dropped onto their deck with ease. Yet she was successful; as one, all ten guards toppled over and collapsed upon the hot sands.

"Excellent!" Alarika whispered, and she drew a knife and severed the rope between Nate and Sister Aspertine, and then she gave the knife to Nate. "Free yourselves; I have camels ready, packed with your things, and I scattered mad-weed into the fodder of the others; they'll carry no riders today."

"Why're you doing this?" Karl demanded.

"I'm the Mad Hermit's daughter," Alarika whispered. "Be quiet! We must flee before my army awakens!"

Riding a camel was far less comfortable than riding a horse, but Eloise clung to her reins and urged the huge beast onward. Camels were taller than horses, and Eloise feared that she'd fall off, and the greater height was certain to increase the likelihood that she'd get hurt.

Camels had long, hairy legs, thin, with bulbous knobs for knees, and their hard, boney humps seemed designed to tip riders off, rather than secure them. Their twisted-cloth saddles did little to soften their bounces, and their ugly faces bore perpetual frowns. Their pace swayed more, and felt stilted and jarring, not the smooth, familiar gait of horses. Yet worst of all was their stench; without frequent rains, these camels never washed, and they stank worse than mixtures of burning offal, which was the required incense for many Druid curses.

Alarika provided each companion with a black cloth to cover their heads and faces, and she led them straight west, away from the rising sun. They didn't stop until noon, by which time they were exhausted, overheated, and dehydrated.

Alarika led them into a large cave, big enough for their camels and them, and much cooler. Yet she insisted that they could only rest briefly.

"By now, my men know that I betrayed them," Alarika said. "Even on drugged camels, or afoot, thieves travel fast, and they'll follow our tracks."

"What about a sandstorm?" Roselyn asked. "It could hide our trail."

Alarika stared at her.

"Are you so powerful that you can command the desert to rise?" she asked.

Roselyn glanced at Eloise, and all eyes followed hers.

"What's a sandstorm?" Eloise asked.

"A wind," Roselyn said. "A mighty storm of air ... strong enough to blow the sands."

Eloise paused; wind was an element, and she'd heard of such spells before, but she'd never cast one.

"I can try," Eloise said.

"We can't stay here," Alarika said. "All desert dwellers know of this cave ...!"

"Where's the Mad Hermit?" Karl demanded.

"Dead," Alarika said. "My father knew that he was dying, and so he prophesized that I must be made leader of the thieves ... or that all of them would die. After that, every few days, another leader of the thieves dropped dead; soon the thieves begged me to be their chief. Yet my father promised me that someday strangers would take me away, and that they'd succeed where he'd always failed."

"Succeed ....?" Elaina asked.

"To awaken the Guardian," Alarika said. "Father spent his whole life trying, but died unfulfilled. I've been the leader of the thieves for three months, praying each day to be rescued before they get over their fear ... and do to me ... what they'd do to you."

"In God's name, why did you have us tied ...?" Sister Aspertine interrupted.

"My hold over them was failing, and their lusts wouldn't be delayed long," Alarika said to her. "I had to quietly drug their henket, collect your weapons, gather supplies, and pack our camels. Now, enough talk! Drink sparingly, and breathe the cool air; we must venture back out into the heat at once ... unless you can raise the sands."

She looked at Eloise, and all fell silent. Eloise stared at all of them, and then she walked back to the tall mouth of the cave, looking out at the scorching sands.

A wind! Eloise was now the strength of their company; not Roselyn. If she could summon a strong wind, then she'd prove her leadership to all of them ... especially Karl.

Eloise forgot their plight. She forgot their pursuers, the hundred and twenty thieves that would rape and torture them, if they couldn't escape. She forgot everything, and concentrated on the Lady ... and the wind. It shouldn't be difficult; wind was an element, just like fire, water, and earth; Eloise just had to reach out to it, to befriend it, as she'd done with the tiny flame, and beg it to rise at her command. She called to the Lady, and repeated the chant that she'd used to animate fire, to become one with the wind.

Eloise reached out toward the vast, roasting expanse outside the cave; the smothering air over the desert, its baking vastness, the open winds that dried away the clouds and seared dusty lungs, sapped moisture from the skin, and left everything as barren as death. She recited her chant a second time, and then a third, each time reaching out further, feeling for the subtle element, the intimacy of air, and the playfulness of breeze. She extended her arms, closed her eyes, and let her senses drift, wafting about for the slightest contact. She could sense the wind, but unlike fire, which always remained with its source, or water, which always flowed to fill the lowest place, or earth, which remained still, the spirit of air moved freely and quickly, and seemed to dart about as if avoiding her.

Eloise expanded her range, extending her fingers, reaching deeper into the endless sky. *She had to do this, to find the wind, and prove who ruled this company!* Yet the farther that she reached, the faster the wind seemed to dodge, always just inches beyond her grasp, and Eloise opened her senses even more.

The sway of reality tipped her; Eloise had to hold onto reality, to keep one foot in the real world, an anchor to balance between her birth-world and the universe beyond imagination. If anyone wholly fell into magic then they'd never make it back. Only a mad shell, identical, but soulless, would remain. The Seer had risked this danger more than any other, but she was no equal of his; she clung to the dark lessons that his memoirs and ledgers had taught her, methods that even her Masters on the Magic Isle didn't know, and Eloise pushed herself even farther into the distant vapors. She could feel the spirit of the wind; *if only she could reach it* ...

Suddenly the wind swarmed over her, engulfing and encasing. Eloise screamed. The desert wind was no gentle friend like the soft breezes over England; this wind blew viciously, ravenous and sadistic. It bit like the teeth of rusty saws, cutting off life, and blasting with heat so unbearable that Eloise faltered, off-balance, and tried to push it back. Yet no mortal could shove heat away, especially not dry desert gusts which murdered without caring and left bones to bleach in the sun.

Barely Eloise clung to consciousness; *she'd once defeated Death!* She couldn't let a hateful wind devour her; she forced herself to stay calm and determined, and called upon the Lady for strength. The wind rose before her, towering and omnipotent, ever-shifting, unseen; Eloise couldn't strike anywhere without it being elsewhere. She reeled, feeling it repeatedly bite at her, a great invisible mouth filled with teeth of hate. The desert wind had drawn her out, lured her into its realm, and sought to extinguish her.

Karl; thoughts of Karl had strengthened her against Death, but as she brought his image to her mind, all that she could see was her ultimate betrayer. She couldn't shield herself with Karl; the wind's dry claws tore through his image and stabbed into her mind. Eloise couldn't relent; she had to remain focused, stalwart; but where Karl's image had stood, Roselyn's face appeared, taunting and tormenting.

The hot southern wind was all-powerful, too strong for her, *but Roselyn wasn't,* and Eloise couldn't let her husband be stolen.

If I die, my death will free Karl ... to marry Roselyn!

Focusing on anger, propelled by jealously, Eloise drove her way back to her world, back to the reality from which she'd come, and tore free from the deadly claws.

Behind her, the desert wind rose in murderous fury.

Painfully, the rocking sway of a camel tilted her dizzy, hanging head and nauseated stomach. Eloise awoke retching onto a hairy camel's side. She heard no sounds, and felt nothing but agony. Then hands seized her, distant voices mumbling, and she sensed that she was being carried.

"We can't stop here," Alarika's voice echoed from somewhere. "We must move on."

"Water ...," Eloise croaked.

Some liquid, like a blessed relief, dribbled into Eloise's mouth, but far too little.

"More ...," Eloise said.

"Just a little," Karl's voice said. "If we can't preserve our water, we'll die."

Drops trickled inside Eloise's parched mouth, but not even a mouthful. She forced open her eyes, despite an intense headache.

"Hold on, daughter," Elaina said. "We've got you."

"Where ...?"

"Lost in the desert," Elaina said. "Well, Alarika knows where we are. You've been asleep for two days."

Two days ...?

"We're very proud of you," Elaina said.

"That was the fiercest sandstorm that I've ever seen," Alarika said. "If we hadn't been inside the cave, it would've killed us."

Eloise choked, tasted grit inside her mouth, and tried to spit, but no spittle came.

"I ... I didn't raise it," Eloise finally said, gasping in the hot air, trying to make sense of what'd happened. "The desert air tried to kill me, and when I escaped ... it grew angry."

"It was magnificent," Alarika said. "Her Sekhem is strong."

"Her ... Sekhem ...?" Elaina asked.

"Her immortal life-force," Alarika explained.

"That's her God-given soul!" Sister Aspertine snapped.

"I know not what you mean by 'soul'," Alarika said. "Which part of her spirit do you mean?"

"Part ...?" Elaina asked.

"Thoth protect me from ignorance," Alarika scowled. "Your Ka is your spark of divinity, your most vital essence. Within our bodies, the Ka is our image, our genius, our character, disposition, and mental attributes. The Goddess Heket, sometimes called Meskhenet, creates the Ka, breathing it into each child as they emerge from their mothers. The Ka requires food and drink, and thus, after death, when the body can no longer feed itself, Egyptians leave offerings of food and drink upon the graves of those whom they loved. If no foods are left on their graves, then their Ka starves, and may lack the strength to journey to Nephthys, to rejoin with the Ba.

"The Ba is your personality, your heart-spirit, noble and sublime, the height to which any mortal can aspire, if they strive for it. It's our Ba which measures our true worth. After death, the Ba lingers with the body, while the Ka flees at once. Before the final rites of burial, the priests perform the 'Ceremony of the Opening of the Mouth' to free the Ba of its link to the body. Then the Ba can fly out of its body to join with its Ka in the House of Nephthys.

"The Khaibit is our shadow, which contains the Sheut, our dark side. The Sheut walks in the shade of the person, and holds our darkest fears. It's where the spectral servants of Anubis hide from all light. When you die, your Sheut leads your Ka and Ba to the House of Nephthys.

"The Khu is our glorious, shining intelligence; our Khu fires our desires. Yet it is Sekhem, our inner power, from which comes every Egyptian's strength; Sekhem is the might of our will. Last, and most important, is our Name, for it is by our name that we will be recognized by the gods."

"What part of the soul is our name?" Eloise asked.

"Name is not a part of our ... soul, as you call it," Alarika said. "Name is what unifies all five parts, the Ka, Ba, Khaibit, Khu, and Sekhem, that all may someday be rejoined with the body, and our lives restored."

"Egyptian dead return to life ...?" Nate asked.

"Few are reborn, for the dead can't restore themselves," Alarika said. "If they could, then mighty Osiris would've done so."

"Osiris ...?" Roselyn asked. "Odin knows of him!"

"Osiris is the true ruler of all lands," Alarika said. "Osiris was murdered by his brother, Set, the Infernal Darkness, who cut apart and hid the pieces of Osiris' body in many lands. But Isis, Osiris' loving wife, gathered all the parts of his body, and his Ka, Ba, Khaibit, Khu, and Sekhem, and spoke his Name, and so she restored Osiris to life. This resolve is most-important to all Egyptians, to safeguard the lightness of our hearts, allow no impurities to enter and take root, and to have our bodies meticulously prepared after our death, that we may someday be reborn. It is for our rebirth that we leave behind loved ones who desire our return so greatly that they may take the pains to someday awaken us."

"If we hadn't been inside that cave, someone would've had to rebirth all of us," Elaina said. "You did wonderfully, daughter."

"The storm covered our tracks, but they're sure to be seeking us by now," Alarika said. "We purposefully crossed a rocky plain, where thieves travel to hide their route back to the Nile River. There's a straight path to a nearby oasis, and I suspect they they're upon that road already, rushing to ambush us as we attempt to reach water."

"We circled back," Karl said. "We're headed to someplace called the Valley of the Kings; that's where the Mad Hermit told Alarika to look; where the instructions are written to awaken the Guardian."

"We must cross open desert, and today's our last riding during the day," Alarika said. "Tonight we ride until dawn, and then camp in the daytime. It'll be a hard trek, but at the Oasis of el-Daklha, we'll find water."

"Then all of the pieces can come together," Elaina said. "With the instructions to awaken the Guardian, we can sail north to him, and he'll give us the words to open the 'crack in the world' at the Temple of Osiris. Alarika will take us all the way … if we let her join us."

"Don't assume victory," Alarika said. "My father knew the ritual, but he never succeeded."

"Never …?" Karl asked. "How will we …?"

Alarika shrugged, and Eloise's head hurt too much to care.

"Don't waste your strength worrying about awakening the guardian yet," Alarika said. "We're about to enter the desert, and I doubt if all of you will survive."

"Isn't this desert?" Roselyn asked, looking around.

"The Valley of Thieves borders between the two lands of Egypt," Alarika said. "Foremost is the Kemet, the black lands, where the seasonal floods of the Nile cover the growing lands with dark, rich soil, and the other is the Deshret, the red lands, where Ra bakes the sands. We will soon be entering the Deshret."

Chapter 5

Brutality

HENRY

The Deshret cooked them. Every morning they crammed themselves underneath their white awning, between their smelly camels, which they staked in a circle about them, and used their heads and tall humps to uphold their meager tent. Yet shade was little help; the sun shone mercilessly, right through their thin canvas, and soon only Alarika had skin that wasn't bright red and swollen.

Henry suffered in silence, determined not to be the first to complain. Like Samuel, he knew better than to speak above his station. He'd accepted that this journey could rival the fantastic tales of the gossips of Demril. Originally, he hadn't believed that Karl, Eloise, Roselyn, Seren, and Rafe had visited Yggdrasil. Fighting giants and meeting pagan gods was ... unbelievable; Henry had smiled along with everyone else just to avoid arguments, and to show his loyalty to Baron Karl ... until he'd seen the Valkyrie descend upon Castle Bristlen.

Henry had marched to the Siege of Castle Lasky, fearing a dangerous battle when he, with a single spear and a pitifully-small shield, would be charging a thirty foot crenelated wall manned by enemy archers. His odds of survival were small, almost hopeless. Then, with the dawn, came the unexpected opening of the castle gates: Baron Karl stood holding a bared knife against Sir Lasky's throat; that'd been the greatest relief of Henry's life; *they'd won without even needing to fight.*

Henry had helped loot the castle after all of Sir Lasky's guards had been disarmed, and then Baron Sir Karl had executed Sir Lasky for crimes against the Barony du Harmonn. Then, to everyone's surprise, Karl had called out Sir Lasky's only son, a mere boy of fourteen, and placed his dead father's coronet upon his young son's head. With many warnings, and promises of friendship, and hopes that he'd grow to be a wiser baron than his father, Karl had patted the stunned boy's shoulders, and then led his whole army away peacefully; the war was over, the castle plundered, and only one death had resulted.

On the long march home, Henry had followed Karl gladly, carrying a sack full of plunder over one shoulder, proud to be a soldier du Harmonn … and a loyal subject of Baron Sir Karl the Brave.

Yet their recent adventures, since they'd sailed from England, dwarfed the tales of Yggdrasil … and he'd seen magics to make him no longer doubt.

Amid all those heroic tales arose countless sufferings; freezing in the North Sea, burning under Loki's stare, and the magical bindings of the mad Goddess Heid. Their journey across open desert excelled any pains that he'd heard from the lips of bards. Henry couldn't imagine that a worse torment existed than being cooked alive.

While they could, the others spoke of the cool, wet forests of England, but Henry tried to remain silent. Alarika accused them of making up stories; she couldn't believe that any place existed where it rained every day, and finally she sneered and claimed that their wetlands had made them soft.

"The Deshret keeps Egypt strong," Alarika said.

"True strength comes from God," Sister Aspertine argued.

"We have many gods, and all are mighty," Alarika said.

"There's only one God," Sister Aspertine said.

"As a Valkyrie, I choose the honored dead for Odin's army," Roselyn said.

"Your god prizes warriors," Alarika said. "They wouldn't endure the Judgement of Thoth."

"What's that?" Elaina asked.

"A judgement that none born of England could survive," Alarika said, and she took a small drink of henket to wet her throat. "The gods of Egypt praise neither wealth nor power. Before their greatness, pharaohs and slaves stand equal. Strength avails nothing, and courage is irrelevant. To Thoth is revealed all mortal words and deeds, and his scales decide all fates.

"All who die face Thoth's judgement. The Ibis-headed One leads the Ka, the foremost part of each soul, to the Throne of Osiris, who sits forever wrapped in mummy-cloths, wearing the Uraeus Crown, and holding the Scourge and the Crook crossed upon his breast. Before him stands a huge balance, the Scales of Justice, and jackal-headed Anubis, the God of Darkness, escorts the Ka to its judgement.

"Before the Weighing of the Heart, each dead man's Ka must speak in its own defense. Then Anubis draws his knife and cuts the heart out of each Ka and places it upon the Scales of Thoth, which is balanced only by the Feather of Truth. Heavy is the heart of every evil-doer, and it drags down the scale ... so low that Ammit, the Devourer of Hearts, can catch the sinner's beating blood-pump in his jaws. Then is the evil-doer driven forth into the darkness of the Duat, to dwell forever with Aapep the Terrible in the eternal Pit of the Fire River."

"Sounds like Hell," Nate said, glancing at Sister Aspertine, but she scowled and looked away.

"Yet, if the Feather of Truth and the heart balances, then the good man rejoices," Alarika said. "Thoth cries aloud to Osiris and the gods:

True and accurate are the words this man has spoken. He has not sinned; he has not done evil. Let not the Eater of Souls devour him. Grant him the eternal bread of Osiris, and a place make for him here in the Halls of Peace with the followers of Horus.'

"This is the Judgement of Thoth," Alarika said. "The Final Judgement."

"Your gods praise a good heart above all things," Elaina said. "What great gods you have! Small wonder why your civilization has lasted so long."

"The Maat of Egypt lives still, and will endure forever," Alarika said. "If we can awaken the Guardian, then you'll witness the power of our gods."

"I've seen too much of gods," Karl said.

"Master, may I ask a question?" Henry asked.

"Of course," Karl said.

"Forgive me, desert queen," Henry said. "But ... I've heard all the stories of Yggdrasil, but of the gods of Egypt, I know little. If we do arrive in their lands, what shall we find? What is true about your gods?"

"The gods of Egypt are described in writings four thousand years old; in this lies both our strength and our weakness," Alarika said. "Our strength is that Egyptians have dwelt long upon the mysteries of our gods, and achieved understandings of which your infantile faiths are yet unaware. Our weakness is that our stories have been wrongly retold and repeated, and altered by pharaohs and fashions, so that we're no longer certain which of our stories are true."

"My young race doesn't suffer that weakness," Roselyn said. "Yet knowing isn't always a blessing. Gods are as fallible as mortals ... and some gods lie."

"Maybe that's the purpose of Winter, as the Lady of the Druids described it," Eloise said. "Deprived of direct contact, which culminates in Summer, even the most devout follower must doubt."

"Alas! Many Egyptians now deny our gods, Anubis curse their souls," Alarika said.

"Tell us what you can," Karl said.

"Three gods created themselves," Alarika said. "Primordial gods, we call them. First came Atum, the Father. Then arose Ra, the Creator. Last came Thoth, the All-Seeing, who knows all. Atum fathered Shu, who is Air, and Tefnut, who is Rain. Being the first son and first daughter, Shu and Tefnut married, and they bore Geb, who is the Earth, and Nut, who is the Sky. Geb and Nut also married, and they bore four children: Osiris, the King of All, Isis, the Just and Merciful, Set, the Evil One, and Nephthys, the Queen of Death. There are many other gods, including some primordial goddesses who came later, such as Wosret, Atum's first wife, and Amunet, Atum's second wife."

"Inbred ...," Sister Aspertine murmured.

"Don't insult my gods!" Alarika warned.

"We mean no disrespect," Karl said quickly, glaring at Sister Aspertine.

"If he was alone, then how did Atum father anyone?" Sister Aspertine demanded.

"Atum mated with his shadow, and spat his children from his mouth," Alarika said. "This I know, for I've read it on temple walls."

"The Bible …!" Sister Aspertine began, but Karl cut her off.

"Rest now," Karl said to everyone. "Try to sleep. The hottest part of the day is coming, and we need to travel from dusk to dawn … without killing each other."

Henry laid down upon the hard sands, resting his arm over his eyes to shade his face from the sunlight, which glared right through the fabric of their awning. The fables of the Egyptian gods sounded as crazy as the fables of the Norse gods, but Henry felt certain that, if any gods existed, then, very likely, they all did.

Desert nights were a thousand times better than the days, but they were so tired, burned, and thirsty that no one felt relieved, even in the deepest part of night when an occasional breeze would chill their cooked skins until they shivered, yet no wind could draw the fire of the merciless sun from their flesh, an inferno that seared them even as their teeth chattered with the night's cold. Under the brightest starlight that Henry had ever seen, night after night, they arose before sunset and mounted their camels with increasing despondency. As the stars brightened, Alarika would point out some prominence on the distant, bleak horizon, and then they'd ride toward it … until the cruel rising sun blinded them.

The Deshret was the most hateful place that Henry had ever imagined, even worse than the legendary Lakes of Fire, which he'd assumed would kill you quickly, yet which seemed preferable to the slow torture of being baked alive.

Alarika was fanatical about saving water, and refused to waste it even when Phil cut his hand on a sharp rock. The only ones who drank more than they did were their camels, but even their portions were limited, and slowly they emptied two waterbags every day. Alarika had provisioned them well, and after their supply of henket was depleted, she produced four waterskins that she'd hidden for their last days. Yet she gave most of it to their camels. While they ached, she kept promising them that more water than they could ever drink waited for them at the Oasis of el-Daklha.

More than a week passed, and still they crossed open desert.

Their skins were scarlet with white blisters, and the slightest touch stung like barbed hornets, yet they had to keep moving. Pain exhausted them. In some places, nothing lived this far out in the Deshret; no raiders, insects, not even the cries of birds. In other places, swarms of gnats and other flying insects descended to feast upon them, while sand fleas bit their scorched skins, making every moment miserable. Every few days a snake hissed at them from under a rock, or Alarika spotted and circled an area infested with scorpions, some large and dark, but the deadliest small and pale. Each delay meant that they'd be trapped out here even longer, and the companions groaned. All armor, burning hot in the sun, had to be removed, along with any unneeded garments. Elaina put away her chemise, unable to bear its weight upon her burned arms, wearing only her red outer dress.

Silently Henry wondered if they'd soon die and be lost, unknown bones bleached by the merciless sun.

Days blended together in a miasma of pain, until Henry was no longer certain if he was awake or enduring the worst of nightmares. Days proved too hot to sleep, and in the nights, the monotonous plods of his camel's wide hooves, and exaggerated sways of his back, kept Henry from sleeping at all. Consciousness became a punishment, a curse, and awakening only intensified its obscenity.

As they watched, parched and suffering, Alarika surrendered the last of their water to their camels.

None could talk except Alarika, and she could only hoarsely croak, and her dark skin looked as baked as theirs.

The next morning, as the sun rose, Henry gave up, glad that they could finally die, yet Alarika suddenly waved to them all frantically, and then pointed to the distant horizon. Miles away, eclipsed by the rising sun, rose a stand of tall, thin shadows.

Their camels turned toward the shadows and increased their speed, such that Henry doubted if he could halt them. The sun rose fully, and through the blinding light, the tall, thin shapes coalesced into a blessing beyond words: *trees*.

The trees stretched high like sacred benedictions, and under them lay the first shade that they'd seen since leaving the cool cave after the sandstorm. The first trees that they passed stood on a rise. From that high vantage they looked down upon a wide, sparkling lake; to Henry, it seemed a magical paradise. The rising heat of the day, which fanned their vision, was countered by the sudden moisture in the air, and they rode their camels right to the lake's edge and splashed into the shallows. They dropped off their mounts into the water: it was real, drinkable water, and the companions splashed in with relish, drinking, and letting it soak through their clothes and cool their burned and blistered skin.

The sudden cool stung worse than any pain he'd ever felt, but Henry didn't care; he drank as deeply as he could, uncertain if he could still claim sanity; power and wealth meant nothing beside precious water. He sank into its shallows and only arose when his need for air forced him to surface.

One bath couldn't ease their pains; they camped beside the lake for five days. Karl insisted that they needed to heal and recover their strength before they moved on, and even Eloise agreed, when her voice returned on the third day. They camped under their canvas shade, strung between trees, and sat unmoving among tough grasses and bushes.

They made few fires for cooking; firewood carted from the riverside was extremely expensive, and cutting down a tree near el-Daklha was forbidden; to waste wood in an area where so little existed was a crime.

They weren't alone; a large city existed on the far side of the lake, but they only visited it once. They desperately needed supplies, oils for their skins and ointments for their sores, liniments to prevent infection, a dozen skins of strong henket and bottles of irep for their pains, and an ample supply of bread and dried fish, as all of the food that Alarika had packed was eaten ... mostly by their camels. Yet everything at el-Daklha was expensive. They had no choice; they had to sell their camels to afford new supplies, but Alarika assured them that they could walk the rest of the way. Nate suggested that they buy more waterbags, but Alarika insisted that they wouldn't be needed; their trek across the Deshret was over.

The locals obeyed an unspoken truce at the Oasis of el-Daklha; no one fought. Enemies camped side-by-side and shared their supplies rather than violate the truce of el-Daklha. Yet Alarika seemed wary and doubtful, and she watched every newcomer to the oasis with her hand on her khopesh, certain that her army of thieves was still hunting them.

Finally, they left the Oasis of el-Daklha, walking for two days to the Oasis of el-Khraga, which wasn't nearly as comfortable as the Oasis of el-Daklha, although far more crowded. No lake graced this tree-covered oasis, only many deep wells, whose greedy owners charged them for every bucketful. They spent only two days at the Oasis of el-Khraga, and then they marched onwards, sharing the crowded road with travelers, camels, and many carts, all steering toward the Valley of the Kings.

Soon, to the south, the Nile River appeared, and their road led beside it. Many boats floated on the river, but they had no money left for passage. To the north, they saw only barren, rocky hills, dominated by the peak of As Ta Dehent, which was naturally shaped like the pyramids that they'd seen at Giza.

When they arrived at the Valley of the Kings, all of the companions stared in stark amazement. A relatively narrow valley yawned, with brightly-lit sheer rock walls. Built into the walls were stone temples and palaces, and almost every stone surface was decorated with runic carvings, each reeking of antiquity.

"Behold the Royal Necropolis!" Alarika said, gesturing toward the crowded valley.

Statues taller than ten men abounded, and four great figures seated on thrones sat around the entrance to one tomb, while a series of carved steps and long paths led up to other ornate doors opening into the side of hills. Many pillars simply stood, ornamentations of kings, and some walls were covered with the Egyptian's strange writings. Monuments abounded, all in the same style, gigantic, as if the gods themselves had chiseled them.

The valley seemed crowded, like all the cities of Egypt, and if people packed together to escape living in the Deshret. Most of the Egyptians seemed busy, leaving sacrifices, seeking blessings, or merchants selling offerings. Many beggars just sat in the few shadows and held their hands out, praying that someone would take pity upon them and give them food. Alarika led their way directly through the crowd and stopped before the largest temple of all; their destination was deep inside the temple.

Sister Aspertine refused to enter the pagan temple, and Nate looked askance at the strange stone figures outside it, and suddenly offered to stay and guard her. Frowning, Karl ordered both squires to stay and guard Sister Aspertine. Henry and Samuel offered to join the squires, but Karl insisted that they stay close to him, that after the desert, they deserved to see this. Together they entered the open doorway into the cool, hand-carved temple.

The decorations inside were even more impressive. The rock walls and pillars boasted many bright colors of paint and dye, less worn by the elements than the monuments outside. The wonderful coolness inside the temple eased his pains and reminded Henry of the cave that they'd hidden in while the sandstorm raged, but as always, he and Samuel kept quiet. Some of the men inside the temple looked like strange priests, and they came and spoke with Alarika, and accepted a thin silver bracelet from her in place of coins. One priest gave her a torch, bowed, and stepped back, allowing them to pass deeper into the bowels of the temple.

Alarika led them on a winding passage, and took turns with unerring certainty through a labyrinth of tunnels in which the rest of them would've gotten hopelessly lost. Out of sight of the priests, she opened a secret door that looked like a flat section of wall. They passed by shelves of small earthen and alabaster vessels, all tightly sealed, and several sarcophagi, which Henry knew were coffins of the rich.

Henry stared at the indecipherable writings on the walls, the vessels, and the sarcophagi, which looked like stylized pictures that local children might draw … if they weren't so masterfully-crafted. The wavering torchlight seemed to make the images and writings move, and Henry prayed that it was just his imagination, but a creeping fear tingled up his spine; these tunnels were obviously older than anything he'd ever imagined, and many of the painted figures confused him.

"Forgive me, Alarika, if I ask out of ignorance," Henry said. "I understand decorating the dwellings of the living, but why decorate inside a tomb?"

"Decorate …?"Alarika asked. "Where …?"

Henry pointed at all of the hieroglyphs and drawings.

"Those aren't decorations," Alarika said. "Art enforces our existence, evokes contact with our gods, and supports worlds both seen and unseen. These writings continue our presence beyond our mortal lives, and carry our names, our stories, and our beliefs into days that our eyes won't live to see, and thus keep our Bas alive, that someday we may live again."

"But … these fancy vessels …?" Henry asked, pointing to a wooden box of ornate, sealed jars that had the heads of people or half-animal gods, all of polished stone or ceramic.

"Those are canopic jars," Alarika said. "Canopic jars contain the body's organs … removed during mummification."

The companions exchanged horrified glances, and Elaina looked disgusted.

Finally they came to a large engraving on a back wall, and their torchlight revealed a tall, resting lion painted in gold, above it a strange symbol: a cross with a loop atop it. Alarika paused and studied the markings on the walls beside and beneath it.

"This is the Guardian, our symbol of the lion," she said. "This is ankh, the sandal-strap, our symbol of life. Here is the chant to unite them ..."

She ran her fingers over the pictorial markings and read them carefully.

"It ... it can't be ...!" Alarika said.

"What is it?" Karl asked.

"I know this incantation," Alarika said. "It's one of the many songs that father made me learn as a child; I've known this all my life!"

"What does it say?" Elaina asked.

"It's the lament of two lovers torn apart forever, and their undying love for each other," Alarika said. "They refer to each other as brother and sister; that was common in old songs. There must be more here ... wait a minute ..."

She knelt and long examined the strange writings beneath the golden lion.

"It says that Hor-em-akhet, the Guardian, was so moved by the sad tale of the lovers that he came to life and roared," Alarika said.

"The Guardian ... is a lion?" Karl asked. "I've never seen a real lion ... only heraldic depictions of them ... like a big cat."

"Hor-em-akhet is a sphinx," Alarika said. "A giant statue of a lion that guards the pyramids. Legends say that Khafre, an ancient pharaoh, desirous to speak to the Guardian, had its face recarved into the likeness of a man, specifically, himself, so that when he brought the Guardian to life, he could talk to it."

"A giant statue …?" Karl asked. "How can a statue talk?"

"It's one of our oldest legends," Alarika said. "Part of the core beliefs of the Egyptian faith."

"Does it say anything else?" Elaina asked, closely examining the complex pictographs.

"It tells of the history of Pharaoh Khafre," Alarika said. "He was a cruel, brutal ruler, who barred his own people from entering their temples. It is said that he was greedy, jealous even of the gods, and that he brought the sphinx to life to draw from it knowledge that no mortal knew."

"That's what we're trying to do," Karl said.

"The rest tells of his greatness, and how Pharaoh Khafre's spirit finally arose and was praised by the gods, but all of the pharaohs claim that," Alarika said. "There's nothing else about the sphinx here."

"So, you already knew the chant to awaken the sphinx?" Roselyn asked huffily.

"Yes, but why should it work?" Alarika asked. "Father knew this song … he taught it to me … and yet Hor-em-akhet never awoke for him."

"We have to try," Roselyn said. "Where's this sphinx?"

"Hor-em-akhet rests a few hours' walk from the Nile River, far downstream, past Cairo, at Giza," Alarika said.

"We sailed past there already!" Roselyn complained.

"We must go back," Elaina said.

"We need a boat," Alarika said.

"I'll get …," Roselyn began.

"We buy, not steal," Karl said.

"We've no coins left," Eloise said.

"We could purchase passage to Giza aboard a ship, but even that's expensive," Elaina said. "If Eloise could perform some simple magics for …"

"We can't draw attention to ourselves," Alarika said. "My army of thieves knows that we escaped them, and they must be ranging about, looking for us."

"We could sell the gold scarab that Ptah Shabaka gave me," Karl said.

Alarika asked to see the gold scarab, and Karl pulled it from its hiding place, where Alarika's thieves hadn't looked, and passed it over, letting her examine it.

"It's a meket, also called a nehet, or a sa," Alarika said. "All those words mean 'to protect'."

"An amulet," Eloise translated. "Druids use those, too."

"Let's hope that it works," Elaina said.

"We should keep it, if we can," Alarika said. "We need all the protection we can get."

"But …," Karl began.

"I'll earn our passage," Elaina assured them.

After a very brief tutoring, they walked out into the center of the hot, crowded Valley of the Kings, and each person, especially Elaina, drank water from their skins. Then Elaina had them spread out, form a wide circle around her, and each companion began clapping their hands in unison.

Elaina began to dance.

To the rhythm of their clapping hands, Elaina spun with her arms outstretched, and then she kicked above her head with one foot, then the other, and unexpectedly performed a back-flip almost effortlessly, as skillfully as any acrobat. Many Egyptians paused from their unknown purposes to stare at her, and soon a crowd gathered.

Henry enjoyed watching her dance as much as any man, even Phil, who stood with his mouth agape and seemed mesmerized. Despite her age, Elaina danced better than any woman that he'd ever watched, and she danced differently than when she'd been seeking communion with the universe. Now she seemed to dance for the pure joy of movement, smiling brightly, spinning her arms freely and waving her skirt with her hands. Men made up most of the crowd, and Elaina obviously knew which dance moves men liked to watch. Elaina gyrated amazingly fast, shook her limbs in rhythm with her skipping feet, and flounced her immense natural beauty at the Egyptians, careful to focus her attentions on those who were well-dressed and carried large purses. All smiled, and many joined their hands in the rhythm of the companion's cadence, clapping and applauding.

Elaina put on a dazzling show, executing twists and back-bends that would snap the spines of most of her audience, yet which she did with ease. She made certain to smile at every watcher ... and wink at the rich ones. Henry smiled; Elaina knew what she wanted from her watchers, and her years of dancing had given her the youthful appearance and vitality that she needed to attract any man.

Finally she wove her way to Roselyn, snatched Hel's helmet off her head, and held it out as she traversed the circle of onlookers. Many dropped a coin or two into Hel's helmet, and Elaina then danced into the crowd, circling outside of the companions, holding the helmet out to everyone watching ... especially the rich. When she was done, she returned to the circle, thrust Hel's helmet back into Roselyn's hands, and danced to a frenzied pitch, then ended with a dramatic flourish that left her audience cheering and applauding.

As her dance ended, Roselyn pushed into the crowd and thrust Hel's helm at as many onlookers as she could, and many gave her another coin even though they'd already donated. Yet the crowd quickly dispersed, and Roselyn emptied her helm into Karl's hands.

"Is it enough?" Karl asked.

"Barely," Alarika said. "Let's head to the docks and see."

It wasn't enough, but at the docks gathered an entirely new crowd of men, and Elaina performed again. While fewer coins were donated, soon they had enough to buy passage aboard a ship to Giza. Alarika found a willing boatman; he steered a wide, flat-bottomed barge. Its elderly owner had already sold his wares and was about to sail downstream with his three sons. He took their coins eagerly, and they climbed aboard his barge and relaxed; the companions had left the cruel, hot desert and returned to the cool, soft river.

Henry tried to keep from smiling. He was still sore, his once-tough skin, hardened by years at sea, had been no protection from the savage Deshret sun. Tiny white flakes still covered his face and arms, and shed whenever he moved, but he felt like he was in a dream, traveling on an adventure like the tales that he'd once refused to believe in.

He felt lucky; Eloise and Roselyn had repeatedly demonstrated miracles like he'd only seen once in England, when thirteen women warriors had descended from the heavens on winged horses to save Castle Bristlen. Once they'd returned, he and Samuel would spend the rest of their lives trying to convince their friends and family that these miracles had actually happened ... and that he and Samuel had witnessed every one of them. Who could doubt them, when the Baron and Baroness du Harmonn could verify everything that they said?

No sunshade protected the deck, so Henry suggested that they tie their awning to the mast and rest in its shade, as all of their skins were newly-healed, still pink, and sensitive to direct sunlight. The owner of the barge had no objection, so they affixed the awning, and then they poled out into the main stream. Their sail billowed wide, and they let the northern current do most of the work.

Henry relaxed; the whole land of Egypt seemed centered around this huge, slow-flowing river, against which most of their cities were built. He eyed the shore on both sides, watching as they drifted past fishermen and workers, men riding camels and horses, and others, probably slaves, pumping water into irrigated fields. He didn't like the heat anymore; compared to England, where he'd always been too cold, Henry recalled the comforting heat of his one previous visit to Egypt, when he'd seldom left his boat and never ventured this far south, but out in the Deshret, under the oppressive and blistering Egyptian sun, which baked everything to brown sands, he'd longed for his cold northern homeland.

They were approaching a 'crack in the world'!

Henry worried to think that he and Samuel might soon be exploring another world, perhaps even a whole other universe, full of unknown threats and challenges. Most in Demril, at the Bent Hook, had envied Eloise and the others' adventures, and wished that they'd seen Yggdrasil, but secretly Henry feared to leave this world. Eric, Roselyn, and the Seer had failed to return from Yggdrasil …

Would they succeed in finding another mystical doorway?
If they did, should he enter it?

Would he ever get back …?

Of course, they had survived the desert … and nothing could be worse than that!

Bored, Henry and Samuel helped the elderly owner and his three sons pole, and miles swept past them. Nate passed around a waterskin, and Phil shared with the companions two large, hard loaves, which was all that they had left of their food from el-Daklha. Even that would've been lost, had the heat of the desert not made swallowing too difficult to manage for days. Yet more food could be bought, and Elaina had no objection to dancing for coins.

Suddenly Samuel cried out. He fell hard and limply onto the deck. Sister Aspertine screamed, and her high-pitched wail stung their ears. A long, deadly arrow shaft lay sticking out of Samuel's bleeding back.

"Thieves!" Alarika cried.

Henry fell to his knees beside Samuel; they'd been boatmates for fifteen years, and protected each other's backs many times, but Henry saw the arrow sunk deep into his best-friend's skin, right through the center of his back, and bright blood spewed from beneath Eloise's hands. His friend was dying; the arrow was pointed at his friend's heart, and it looked deep; *even if they could get it out, his chances of survival were slim.*

As the others screamed, Henry glanced back to see the arrow's shooter. Along the bank rode five scruffy desert-men in black robes, three with bows, and as Henry looked, two more arrows flew at them. One slashed the air past one of the boatman's sons, and the other shot a hole through the awning right over Eloise's head. Henry clutched Samuel tightly, shielding him with his body; the riders were galloping their camels, coming closer, and noching more arrows. Eloise began chanting, but the blood was still spewing, and Sister Aspertine screaming.

"Faster!" Karl shouted, and he jumped up, grabbed a pole, and tried to help them sail faster.

Roselyn slapped on her helmet and jumped to the back edge of their barge, standing between Henry and the others. Hel's black armor and Roselyn's impressive shape made her an obvious target. The thieves aimed their bows at her, but Roselyn was best-trained; while she no longer possessed the strength of her shield-sisters, as the deadly arrows flew at them, Roselyn expertly blocked them, letting their metal tips graze against Hel's vambraces just enough to deflect them harmlessly away. Nate and Phil jumped to stand behind her, to somehow help, but she ordered them back, insisting that she needed all of the room that they could give. At her command, they brought her Hel's sword, and so great were her fighting-skills that she used the flat-edge of the sword to block the arrows entirely, letting them *'plink'* off and fall into the river.

While Roselyn protected them, Eloise continued chanting her mystical incantation, but her expression was pale and fearful. Henry lightly gripped the feathered arrow and pulled; its wooden shaft was firmly lodged in Samuel's bones; *they'd have to cut it out.*

The pursuing thieves aimed directly at Roselyn, but uselessly; she deflected every one of their arrows into the shining blue waters … or onto the raft at her feet. As they sailed faster, poled by Karl and the boatman's sons, the sweating camels of the thieves eventually tired and fell behind, trapped on the shore. Henry knew that he should be helping them pole, but he couldn't leave his oldest friend to die alone. Samuel was gritting his teeth, cursing when not gasping for breath. Then he looked up into Henry's eyes ... and his breath failed.

Soon the arrows of the thieves could no longer reach the barge, and suddenly the thieves turned and rode off, separating into two groups, one following the shore, the other two leading off into the desert.

"They're going to summon others," Alarika said. "Soon my whole army will be chasing us."

"How's Samuel?" Karl asked.

Henry looked up; even in the dry heat, tears were running down his face. Eloise met his eyes with tears in her own; *Samuel was beyond the healing skills even of the greatest Druid priestess.*

"Dead," Henry said, and the anguish in his voice couldn't have been greater.

Eloise lowered Samuel's eyelids: *no hope remained.*

"Sister Aspertine, Samuel was a good Christian," Karl said softly. "Will you lead us in prayer for him?"

Sister Aspertine looked horrified, and tears leaked down her face to equal Henry's, but she slowly composed herself, and then crawled forward to kneel before Samuel, made the sign of the cross, bowed her head, and prayed.

Elaina and Roselyn both took up poles, pushing their barge faster, while Karl and his squires knelt beside Henry and prayed for Samuel's soul. As they prayed, they sped down the Nile, passing other ships, where many sailors paused to stare at the strange sight, and some called to them, but most recognized that one man aboard their barge was dead, even from a distance, and they allowed the barge to pass in silence.

Why am I here? Henry wondered.

For the first time since this quest had begun, Henry considered abandoning the company. Karl had said that every route to a 'crack in the world' was a path toward death, but not until now did he realize how truly he'd spoken. With the passing of Samuel, now three of their starting company was dead, and all had been sailors. Their fourth, poor Rishard, was hospitalized in Italy; only Eloise's magic had kept his wounds from being mortal, and he was also a sailor. That arrow could've hit any of them, or one of the barge-owner's sons, but no; *another sailor had died.* Now he, Henry, was the last sailor: *the sole expendable companion.*

Was death his fate?

For the first time, Henry felt sure that, if he entered through any 'crack in the world', then he'd be entering his own grave. From this moment on, he'd have to take his role in this party more-seriously, watching for every danger, and do all that he could to prevent any deaths, since the next dead companion was likely to be him. He needed to take a more-active role, to encourage Elaina to dance whenever she could, so that she could hopefully perceive all dangers before they stumbled upon them.

Why was he staying with these people?

Henry knew that Karl had once faced a moment like this: the stories said that, when Eric had first come to Castle Bristlen, Karl had to decide between certain death upon the battlements or fleeing his duty and saving his life. Karl had chosen to save his life; *shouldn't Henry choose the same?*

Henry's oath to Sir Rafe had been no different than Karl's oath to Eloise's hated stepfather. Henry should follow his baron's example; he should jump overboard right now ... swim away ... and never see these fool companions again ... not continue on their path toward death.

Then he looked at Samuel ... and guilt welled. Samuel and he had been delighted when Lord Sir Rafe had chosen them, and gladly determined to see this undertaking through.

Henry bowed his head and continued to pray.

When it opened, would he enter the 'crack in the world' and honor his oath to Lord Sir Rafe, the most honorable Christian that he knew ...... despite that it would probably end his life ...?

Jay Palmer

Chapter 6

The Guardian

ELAINA

Why must the innocent die?

For the first time, Elaina considered joining Sister Aspertine in serious prayer. *Three of my companions have died, and Rishard and Roselyn almost died, and we still haven't found the 'crack in the world'. I must do all I can to insure that no more lives are lost, even if it means praying to God ... as I haven't done since Skafti's predictions stole my daughter.*

Despite being helped by the current, poling their raft northward seemed to take forever. Sailing was vastly more comfortable than the Deshret, but Elaina would gladly face torture again rather than ride beside the corpse of another fallen companion. Nate and Phil helped Henry wrap Samuel's body into the half of their awning, and they folded the last half of it over him like a shroud. Kneeling on the deck beside Samuel, Sister Aspertine whispered The Lord's Prayer many times. She paused only when Elaina handed her a waterskin, and then she resumed praying.

Elaina knew why Sister Aspertine was praying so ardently, which had little to do with Samuel. Never before had Sister Aspertine doubted her faith, but she was weakening, succumbing to the madness around her. Elaina had felt similar doubts before Skafti had taught her to communicate with the universe.

Sister Aspertine had failed her promise to Sir Rafe; her companions were no closer to God than they'd been on the morning they'd left England. Now her soul was in mortal jeopardy; traveling with 'a witch, a demoness, and a seeress', Sister Aspertine had witnessed powers that every precept of her faith told her God wouldn't allow. Living too long surrounded by 'evil and heretical' practices, Sister Aspertine was bonding with them, becoming part of the company, and accepting beliefs that her faith denied.

Elaina hadn't considered that they might not succeed, that they might die trying to find a second 'crack in the world' ... or never return, should they pass through it. Skafti had often murdered in the practice of his arts, but she'd refused to kill, preferring wisdom and understanding. Yet she was finally reunited with her daughter, and despite any risks, she'd never be parted from her again.

Long after the sun set, Elaina curled up beside the others and fell asleep on the hard boards of the barge. Exhaustion claimed them all ... except Henry, who kept silent watch over Samuel.

She awoke with the sun on her face. Samuel's body was still by the mast, Henry beside him, and the others were gathered in the fore, eating. Nate, Karl, and all three of the boatman's sons were poling, and their barge plowed through the water, leaving only a peaceful wake trailing behind them.

Eloise approached her mother and knelt beside her, holding out a handful of smoked meat strips and a wineskin.

"Where are we?" Elaina asked softly.

Eloise glanced back, as if worried that she might be overheard, and then bowed close to her mother's ear.

"In grave peril," Eloise whispered. "We'll be at this Guardian tomorrow, but what good that'll do, I can't see. Alarika's thieves are only a few hours behind us, and they know where we're going."

"How long will it take to awaken the sphinx?" Elaina asked.

"Alarika doubts if it will work," Eloise said. "If the thieves arrive before we awaken the sphinx, then we'll likely never get away. Mother, maybe you should …"

"I'm not leaving," Elaina said firmly. "Being back with you … it's like returning to life."

Eloise hugged her mother tightly, and Elaina smiled; *even death was worth this!*

Elaina ate her breakfast and drank deeply, but declined when Sister Aspertine invited everyone to join her in morning prayers. Only Nate dropped to his knees beside her, and Sister Aspertine scolded everyone else, saying that they owed Samuel all the prayers that they could say. Finally Karl, Henry, and Phil joined them, handing their poles to the women. Elaina took one of the long poles, helping the three sons to push their barge downriver as best she could.

After their prayers, Nate and Phil took over helping pole them downstream, and Henry assisted the elderly owner of the wide barge with no less skill than that of his sons. As Elaina sat beside Eloise, the elderly barge-owner argued with Alarika, apparently demanding more payment for the danger that she'd brought to his family, but her only answer was to draw a dagger and hold it to his throat.

At dusk on the second day, they held a funeral for Samuel, and everyone set down their poles out of respect. Sister Aspertine led the ceremony, but everyone took a turn, speaking of how much they treasured his help and friendship, and Henry spoke long of his fondest remembrances. The boat-owner and his sons stood and bowed their heads in respectful silence. Finally, when tears filled most eyes, they released Samuel to the Nile, and Nate and Phil took up the poles and pushed them away.

The afternoon sun was glaring when they poled within sight of Giza and its three tall pyramids. Quickly docking, the elderly captain and his sons wished them no farewell, shoved back out into the current as soon as the last companion's feet hit the dock, and they quickly poled away. The companions were left standing on the riverside of Giza, a huge town, and Alarika led them straight into the heart of the city.

"The Guardian's four miles inland," Alarika said. "We'll have to walk quickly."

"We don't have time for walking," Roselyn said. "Your thieves'll catch us."

"We don't have enough coins to rent camels … and no time for dancing," Karl said.

"We can't risk not finding the Seer," Roselyn said, and she drew her sword.

"Roselyn, no!" Karl shouted, but she ignored him.

Many people were crowded about, townsmen busy with their labors, women dragging children about, and several large carts being driven by men.

Roselyn jumped aboard the back of a cart, climbed to the front, and as the driver objected, she kicked him with such force that he reeled, and she held the sword of Hel near his face. He looked both terrified and startled, and shouted many complaints, but only Alarika understood Egyptian; she spoke with him, and finally he nodded.

"He'll drive us to the sphinx, but only if we promise not to harm him or steal his grain," Alarika said.

Karl held out his hand, showing his last two coins.

"Tell him that we'll pay for his service with these," Karl said, and after Alarika translated, Karl placed the coins in the driver's hand, and they all climbed aboard his cart.

At Alarika's insistence, the driver hurried his camels, and they rolled through the crowded city with angry pedestrians shouting at them and jumping to escape being trampled. The city was vast and beautiful, with that bare, square architecture of which all the stone and dried mud buildings seemed to be constructed, and populated by an industrious, strong people. In many ways, these foreign cities were much like Madrone and the large cities of England, except that houses in England were mostly built of wood.

Eventually a great shape arose before the three huge pyramids. Elaina gasped, stunned by the size of it.

The Guardian sat, immense, as big as Castle Bristlen main keep. It looked like a stone hill shaped like a lion, but bearing the face of a man, and its ever-open eyes stared forward, imposing wonder and dread upon all. The driver stopped his cart before it, beside carved paws bigger than his cart, its camels, and them. The companions dismounted in silence.

"You … you want to awaken … *that?*" Karl asked.

Elaina stared up at the monstrous sphinx. It looked like a carved mountain, and the idea that it could come to life left her flabbergasted; it could leap over the Nile River … or devour them all in one bite. The face was smooth and cultured, and it looked wise, and Elaina wondered what it'd be like to communicate with it, and if this was how her companions had felt when they'd faced the Norse gods.

"We must start," Alarika said. "We haven't long; when my army of thieves rides in here, we'll all be slain."

"Awaken it," Roselyn ordered.

Alarika led them toward the narrow gap between the massive front paws, under the huge face, until they had to tilt their heads back far to look up at it. It loomed over them, still and silent, and Alarika raised her hands and chanted.

Elaina couldn't translate her words, but Alarika recited a long incantation, in a broken cadence, a chant which seemed to be a song, if recited by someone with a better voice. Her shouted chant filled the courtyard, but was quickly lost in the hot, dry air. The companions waited in silence, watching for any sign of awareness, any movement or glow, but the sphinx remained unaltered, devoid of life. Her incantation had as little effect upon it as words had upon any statue.

Sister Aspertine smiled, but it was a troubled, bitter grin. Elaina wondered if Sister Aspertine wished that the giant statue wouldn't come to life, as that'd be another blasphemy, although success alone might save their lives. The rest of the companions looked apprehensive; if this didn't work, then their quest would end upon the blades of a hundred thieves.

Finally Alarika turned away, shaking her head.

"Did you recite the chant correctly?" Roselyn asked.

"I verified every word of it in the Valley of the Kings," Alarika said.

"We missed something," Karl said.

"Perhaps a sacrifice ...," Roselyn suggested.

"My father tried that," Alarika said. "He sacrificed children: that's why they called him mad."

"Let me try," Eloise said.

"You don't know the incantation," Alarika said.

"I've communicated with God, the Lady of the Druids, and the Norse God Loki ... although that didn't work out ... favorably," Eloise said.

"It can't hurt," Karl said, and he motioned everyone else back.

Out of a pouch, Eloise drew the blessed moonstone, which she held up, as if showing it to the sphinx.

"Use this, too," Roselyn said, and she held out the sword of Hel. "It's divine, at least ...."

Eloise glared angrily at Roselyn, and Elaina feared that her daughter would hurl her moonstone at Roselyn, but instead Eloise took the sword, whose weight pulled down hard on her shoulders. She set its point upon the ground, gripped its handle firmly, raised the moonstone in her other hand, and closed her eyes. Softness shrouded her features, and she looked at peace.

> *"Blessed Lady, glory divine,*
> *Hear now this request of mine.*
> *Grant to me, my heart fulfill,*
> *My one request, be it Your will.*
> *Awaken this beast to speak to me,*
> *Be it Thy will, so mote it be."*

Long Eloise waited, but no evidence came that the monstrous sphinx was anything but a statue. She tried other chants, and waved the moonstone in several unique patterns, holding it beneath the great stone nose, but garnered no effect.

"Nothing," Eloise finally lowered her head.

With stooped shoulders, Eloise handed Hel's sword back to Roselyn, and then she returned the blessed moonstone to the pouch on her belt. The companions all glanced at each other, but no one knew what to say.

"I can try," Elaina said. "I can't bring it to life, but perhaps I can communicate with it … or discover why Alarika's chant didn't work."

No one objected, and all moved farther away, giving her room to dance. Elaina lifted her head as far back as she could, looking up at the huge statue, and then she walked forward, all the way up the narrow passage between the paws, and placed her hands splayed against the beige-yellow stones of its base. She could feel prodigious power within it, as if she were touching the mightiest talisman on Earth, and she strove to hear any sounds within it. Yet the loudest sounds came from the crowd of strangers that'd gathered behind them, who were watching them with undisguised curiosity, and conversing in amused whispers.

Elaina ignored them; the dry winds pressing against this mammoth statue told of endless centuries of resistance, which even the fierce, angry desert wind couldn't hope to topple. Strength such as Elaina had never imagined flowed within this great monument to the Egyptian faith, which would certainly overwhelm her if she couldn't become one with it.

She tried to dance, but the stillness of the sphinx overwhelmed her. She became a statue herself, frozen, trapped inside a rigid, stone body. This ancient amulet of the gods had watched over countless generations that had lived and died in its shadow. Her limbs and mind seemed to stiffen with a solidity unknown to her.

Slowly her mind clouded over and her thoughts grew dim. This task was beyond her, a puny mortal trying to join with an immortal icon, a testament to a people that had struggled under the weight of civilization while her homeland had been only primitive tribes. This was the essence of antiquity, born with the birth of humanity, a witness to eternities long forgotten, a token of gods that'd roamed the Earth before Odin was born or Heimdall traveled its lands. Before such supremacy, Elaina stood insignificant and powerless.

Yet ... slowly ... creeping like a thief, a sensation that Elaina had never felt before tingled on the edge of her perception; time itself remained, and time back then was the same as today, an eternal link to this ageless tribute to the Egyptian gods. Elaina grasped at time itself, and felt it reach back endlessly, beyond mortal comprehension, into channels of wonder and pathways that never ended. In those tributaries flowed movement, the most-subtle sensations, and Elaina felt more than heard the music she desired most.

With a slowness never before attempted, Elaina began to dance. She was nothing before eternal time, but her weakness aided her, for her connection to the vast centuries of the past was so frail and dim that she instantly felt a oneness with it. She moved in cadence with seasons ever-cycling into years, sliding into centuries, until she felt every movement of the sun creeping across the sky, again and again, as her thoughts and memories faded.

She danced back, emerging from between the massive paws, out from the restricted space into the court before it. Her arms became moving sundials, her steps crossing eons, and her fingers flexed with moments that flitted by, never to come again. She kicked high, stepping into time immemorial. In communing with time, Elaina felt an enormity before which even the universe felt small; all the ages of the past, before human memory, flowing to the unknown beginning. Wholly lost, Elaina spun adrift in a cosmic reality of which she'd never considered. The enormity of time swallowed her.

Then, slowly, she heard distant sounds, and recognition dripped upon her, as a rare rainfall in this arid land; her own bare footsteps slapped against the stones beneath her feet. Elaina stumbled, tripped, and fell; she hit the ground painfully, shocked more than hurt; it'd been decades since she'd last tripped and fallen. Elaina heard gasps and exclamations; she was on the ground before the massive paws of the sphinx; she'd slipped out of her dance.

Running feet approached, and hands that belonged to her daughter seized her.

"What ... happened?" Eloise whispered.

Elaina didn't know. She'd managed a new communication with an old and eternal universe, and seen a side of reality, past, present, and future, greater than she'd ever witnessed ... but she'd returned without the knowledge she sought.

"I ... failed," Elaina said, although she couldn't have imagined a greater triumph.

Eloise helped her to rise, and assisted her as she limped back.

"Well, that's it," Karl said. "We'd best leave while we can."

"We've one other hope," Nate spoke up, and he looked directly at Sister Aspertine.

"*Me …?*" Sister Aspertine asked. "Surely … you can't expect …!"

"When all else fails, there's prayer," Nate said.

"No, it …. *I can't …!*" Sister Aspertine said, looking up at the giant sphinx. "I can't pray to God to bring this … monster to life. Better that we all die than unleash this …!"

"We've no choice," Karl said. "I'll pray, if you won't."

They all stared, and finally Sister Aspertine bowed her head.

"I'll pray," Sister Aspertine said. "There's never an excuse for not praying. But I'll pray for our souls as well, that we may meet our ends in His sight."

Sister Aspertine turned to face the sphinx, made the sign of the cross, and knelt in silent prayer.

Roselyn scowled at Sister Aspertine, strode forward, and stood before the great sphinx. She lifted her eyes and shouted to the sky, holding high the sword of Hel.

"*Róta!*" Roselyn called. "*Róta, help me! Help us fulfill the need of Odin, our master! Odin, hear me! Send to me my wise shield-sister, loremaster, Wrecker of Plans! We stand at the door to restoring our connection to the Elysian Fields, needing only your wisdom to continue! Hear me, my sisters! Prudr, Göll, Herfjötur, Hlökk, Randgríðr, Geirahöd, Hrist, Mist, Skeggjöld, Skögul, and Hildr; I stand before you, your sister still! Help me!*"

Long Roselyn waited, glaring upwards in challenge, as if she had the power to command the statue of the gods. Yet no answer came, no beat of powerful wings, no whisper of a voice from Yggdrasil. Finally Roselyn cursed in Norse, and she turned away in disgust.

"Master," Phil said to Karl, "time's passing. The thieves'll be here soon. We don't know how to awaken this Guardian. We should flee ... and live to try again."

"He's right," Alarika agreed. "We can lose ourselves in the city ..."

"We've tried everything," Phil said. "There's nothing left to try."

"There must be something," Karl said. "Ptah Shabaka said that if we spoke the sacred words then the Guardian would come to life ..."

"That's ... not what he said," Roselyn said. "When dealing with prophecy, you must listen carefully to every word."

"What'd he say?" Karl asked.

Roselyn paused, as if recalling every detail.

"It was our ... last private audience ... with Ptah Shabaka," Roselyn said. "He'd dreamed of a Valkyrie coming to him, and threatening his city with a sandstorm; he was angry. He didn't like being threatened ... especially not by a woman. He said ... he said that we had to *'speak the sacred words, from deep inside our hearts, to enter'.*"

"But we're not trying to enter here ... are we?" Elaina asked.

"Not here," Alarika said. "Entry must be done in the Temple of Osiris, near the Valley of the Kings. These words tell us nothing."

"They tell us a lot," Eloise said. "Words don't evoke magic; chants and incantations are just ... guides, tools to align our thoughts and emotions ... from deep inside our hearts."

"Perhaps we're just not saying it ... *'from the heart'*," Elaina said.

"I'll try again," Alarika said, but doubt and worry marked her features.

Once again, Alarika approached the massive sphinx, and this time she paused, and when she spoke, chanting in Egyptian, her voice was deep with emotion. She effused sorrow and loss, such that any could hear her regret. A great reaction came from the crowd gathered to watch. Alarika fell to her knees and wrenched out each word, and some in the crowd applauded, as if watching an entertainment, with no idea what was happening.

Alarika recited her chant fully; seven distinct stanzas, while the companions waited expectantly ... but nothing happened. The sphinx remained stone and evidenced no sign of life.

"It didn't work," Karl scowled.

"She's faking emotion," Eloise said. "You can't pretend to have emotions that you don't; to work the magic, your emotions must be real."

"How can I evoke real emotions?" Alarika asked. "The poem is about two lovers separated forever ... by death ...!"

The companions startled and exchanged glances. Elaina's eyes widened with comprehension.

"*No!*" Eloise shouted.

"*You promised!*" Roselyn said, a hint of threat unhidden in her voice.

"*He's my husband!*" Eloise shouted.

"Alarika's tribe is coming!" Phil said warningly. "We need to try or flee ...!"

"Tell us what to do," Karl said to Eloise.

Eloise's face reddened ... and her eyes became steely. She focused her stare upon Roselyn ...

"*Daughter, stop!*" Elaina ordered. "*We've no choice!*"

Eloise hesitated, then turned her glare upon her mother.

"Kill me, if you will," Elaina said to Eloise. "I won't fight my daughter. But if you can't set aside your jealousy now, we all die!"

Eloise stared at her mother, and the intensity of her eyes never lessened, but she spoke through gritted teeth.

"Gods don't hear words," Eloise said. "Gods feel emotions."

Elaina met her daughter's stare with a gasp of realization; *they could do this!*

"Alarika, remember the story that Nate told you about Yggdrasil and the Valkyrie?" Elaina asked. "Karl and Roselyn were lovers separated by death; tell them the words …"

"They don't speak Egyptian …," Alarika said.

"Gods don't need languages," Elaina said. "Translate; they'll provide what's needed."

Karl and Roselyn exchanged worried glances, neither willing to comply.

"Hoofbeats!" Phil startled. *"The thieves are coming!"*

Elaina paled; a thunder of many rapid hoofbeats approached. These savage heathens cared nothing for their quest; *Alarika's thieves would kill them all!*

"Delay them, if you can," Alarika said suddenly. "Karl, you must start; repeat after me …!"

Karl listened closely, then turned to face Roselyn, and recited each line.

> *"Sister without rival,*
> *most beautiful of all.*
> *She looks like the star-goddess,*
> *rising at the start of the good new year.*
> *Perfect and bright, shining skin,*
> *seductive in her eyes when she glances,*

sweet in her lips when she speaks,
and never a word too many.
Slender neck, shining body,
her hair is true lapis,
her arms gather gold,
her fingers are lotus flowers,
ample behind, tight waist,
her thighs extend her beauty,
shapely in stride when she walks the earth.
My heart is stolen in her embrace.
She makes the neck of every man
turn round at the sight of her.
Whoever embraces her is happy.
He is the head of lovers,
and she is seen outside
like the One Goddess."

Alarika waited until Karl had finished, and then she faced Roselyn, who repeated her words reluctantly ... as the hoofbeats grew louder.

"My brother overwhelms my heart with his words.
Sickness seizes hold of me.
Now he's near the house of my mother,
and I can't even tell that he's been.
It's good of my mother to order me like this,
'Give out of your sights'.
See how my heart is torn by his memory.
Love of him has stolen me.
Look what a senseless man he is
but I am like him.
He realizes not how I wish to embrace him,
or he would write to my mother.
Brother, yes! I am destined to be yours,
by the Gold Goddess of women.
Come to me, let your beauty be seen.

Let my father and my mother be glad.
Call my people together in one place.
Let them shout for you, my brother."

The clatter of individual hooves on stone became district. Alarika turned back to Karl and fed him each line:

"My heart thirsts to see her beauty,
as I am seated at home with her,
but I found Mehy on horseback
with His men, the seducers.
I don't know if I should hold myself before Him,
or if I could pass by freely.
River and road looked alike:
I couldn't decide where my feet belonged,
blissfully unaware of my passion.
Why did you stroll in, Mehy?
Look, if I pass Mehy,
I'll tell Him my circuits,
'I am yours' I would tell him,
and He would clamor my name,
appointing me to that inner palace,
the one with his followers."

As Karl spoke, Phil grabbed Nate's arm and drug him away. The roar of hooves filled the patio, and the nervous crowd began to anxiously break apart.

Alarika's army of thieves came pounding around the buildings. The crowd tried to run in different directions, but the thieves came at them from all sides, pouring in. Merchants and townspeople fled before their foaming mounts. Dozens of thieves hemmed them in and drove them together, cowered and trapped.

Swords scraped from scabbards, and were brandished threateningly, but Phil held up both hands and surrendered, and the thieves halted to glare at him and

Nate. Henry walked up beside them, raised his hands, and surrendered.

They're sacrificing themselves, Elaina thought, but then she reconsidered her brief flair of hope; *these lowlifes won't be satisfied until all of us are dead.*

Sister Aspertine kept praying softly, then raised her hands, and walked up to join the men.

"Continue ...!" Elaina whispered to Alarika, and then she walked up to stand beside Sister Aspertine, her arms raised in surrender.

Behind them, Alarika fed Roselyn the next lines:

> *"My heart bares itself*
> *at the memory of your love.*
> *I can't walk like a person.*
> *It has strayed from its shelter.*
> *It doesn't let me put on a dress.*
> *I can't even wrap my scarf.*
> *No kohl can shade on my eye,*
> *I'm not anointed with oil.*
> *'Don't stand there - go in to him'*
> *it tells me at each memory of him.*
> *Don't, my heart, be stupid at me:*
> *why are you acting the fool?*
> *Sit, be cool, the sister has come to you,*
> *but my eye is just as troubled.*
> *Don't make people say of me*
> *'she's a woman fallen by love'.*
> *Be firm each time you remember him,*
> *My heart, do not stray."*

As Roselyn spoke, her voice changed. Her strong Valkyrie tenor softened, and Elaina recognized the longing filling her voice; *even when angry at each other, true lovers can't exchange such words without being affected.*

Karl's voice took over, and the same emotions filled his deep voice. Despite misgivings, Elaina suddenly knew why Karl had chosen Roselyn over her daughter.

"I worship the Gold Goddess.
I sing of her Presence.
I raise up the Lady of Heaven.
I give adoration to Hathor.
Praise to the Mistress.
I report to her, and she hears my pleas.
She ordered a Mistress for me,
and she is come herself to see.
What a great thing has happened to me!
I feel overjoyed, ecstatic, great,
when told 'she is here',
Look, she has come, the amorous are bowed,
so great is my love of her.
I send my prayers to my goddess.
She gave my sister as a gift.
Three days to yesterday since my pleas,
in her name; since she left me the day is five."

The thieves glared at them, clearly hearing their emotions, if not understanding their words, and they glanced at each other, unsure. One of them called out to Alarika, but she kept feeding the next lines to Roselyn, who spoke, suddenly flooded by tears.

"I passed by the front of his house,
and found his door was open.
Brother was standing beside mother.
All his brothers stood with him.
Love of him steals the heart of any wayfarer,
perfect youth, none like him,
choicest brother, a miracle.
He looked at me when I passed by,
but I am too alone to cry out.

How my heart races for joy,
Brother, when I can see.
If only mother knew my desire,
then she'd accept me at once.
Gold Goddess, yes! Put it in her heart,
so I may rush to my brother.
I would kiss him before his staff.
I would not cry tears.
I would be happy that they realized,
that you are the one who knows me.
I would make festivals for my goddess.
My heart has escaped to go out,
to let brother see me in the beautiful night,
fully, in passing by."

The lead thief said something to his companions, a harsh command, although Elaina couldn't understand his words. His fellow thieves grinned evilly ... and raised their swords.

Nate whispered to Phil, and suddenly both drew their swords. Two against four dozen; *the squires had no hope of winning.* Yet, to Elaina's disbelief, both squires freely set their swords upon the ground. Then they knelt, their empty hands again in the air. Henry glanced at both squires, and then he knelt beside them. With a glance at each other, Sister Aspertine and Elaina also knelt; *every second that they could delay the thieves mattered.*

Behind them, Alarika fed the last lines to Karl, whose voice cracked with sorrow.

"Seven to yesterday I haven't seen sister.
Sickness has entered deep into me.
I've grown heavy in my limbs.
My body has lost sense of itself.
When the chief physicians come,
my heart finds no relief in remedies,

and the ritual-readers; there is no way through them.
My sickness can't be uncovered.
Just tell me 'here she is' is my cure.
Her name alone can raise me.
The coming and going of her messengers,
is what can cure my heart.
Being her brother is better than any medicine:
more important to me than any prescription.
My health-cure is her visit.
As she gazes, then I am well.
As she opens her eyes, then my body is young.
As she speaks, then I am strong.
When I embrace her, she banishes harm from me.
She is left me now seven days."

With these last words, looking at Roselyn, a single tear slowly streaked down Karl's face.

The snarling thieves dismounted and started forward, raising their swords to slay the companions, evil leers on their dirty, scarred faces.

A strange noise filled the sky, a soft, distant whistle and countless grinding scrapes, as if every grain of sand in the desert were scratching against its neighbor. The baking-hot air suddenly cooled, and a chill wind blasted down upon them, and a shadow passed over the sky, darkening the morning blue to twilight purple. Only inches from the companions, their blades raised to kill, the thieves glanced upwards with fear-filled eyes.

Every man, woman, and child gasped and looked up.

A sudden loud, rocky crunching reverberated. Elaina glanced up and behind, and for the first time in twelve years, the universe seemed suddenly alien, as if she'd never communed with it. Disbelief filled her eyes; the massive, statuesque face just above her trembled ... and moved. Stone eyelids slowly closed, raining dust upon them, and then opened again. Stone pupils lowered to view them. Rocky cheeks rose and puffed out, massive eyelids blinked again, and then a monstrous mouth opened, and a terrible, horrific roar deafened the entire city to the shore of the Nile and beyond. The deep, vicious cry of a killer beast echoed across the lands, and then the stone face lowered to look at them.

"Greetings, faithful," growled the feral voice of Hor-em-akhet, the Great Sphinx of Egypt.

Every eye in the courtyard stared at Hor-em-akhet, the living sphinx, the immense monument ... *alive*. Most of the Egyptians fell to their knees and pressed their faces to the dirt, some fainted, and the mounted thieves dropped to grovel upon the ground.

"It speaks English," Karl gasped.

"No, it's Egyptian," Alarika said.

"I ... hear Norse," Roselyn said.

"Great Guardian Hor-em-akhet, I hear you," Eloise said, looking up without fear. While almost everyone else cringed, Eloise rose to her feet and gracefully bowed before the living statue, calling up to it. "I am Baroness Eloise, a servant of the Druid Lady, my deity of a distant realm, far to the North. Forgive me if I fail in customs unknown to me, but we've journeyed far, over sea and desert, to beg a boon of you."

"I know ... whom you seek," said Hor-em-akhet the Guardian. "He whom you love, the Messenger Between Divinities, has brought new light to those doomed to darkness eternal, Lords Lost To This World. For them, no hope remains, only memory and sorrow, and of the one you seek, nothing remains. Yet your pathway is open, if you would brave death beyond death."

"How can we enter, Most-Sacred One?" Eloise asked.

"Only the dead may pass freely to the lands of the dead," Hor-em-akhet said. "Yet the life of an innocent, shed in the holy place, may open a portal where the living may enter. Recite his prayer, call upon Osiris, and jump into life."

The head of Hor-em-akhet the Guardian rose slightly, and focused upon all of the kneeling Egyptians cowering before it.

"Descendants of my children, Blood of the Nile," Hor-em-akhet the Guardian said loudly, and his voice rolled like a fevered thunder. "Fear not, and celebrate; while light shines in the Lands Divine, in the Kingdom of Osiris, hope brightens. Aid these strangers; their quest brings great hope to He Who Has Lost All."

With these words, the loud rumble of massive stones repeated, deafening every ear in the city of Giza, and a savage, reverberating growl came from the nearby desert that stretched to the horizon, as if every grain of sand suddenly shifted, or a great jungle beast roared across an entire landscape. A fierce, cold wind from the North blasted upon them, billowing garments and sending veils flying. The sun turned crimson, and orchid clouds flashed black against a scarlet sky, and the Egyptians screamed.

Then ... all fell silent. The cool wind restored itself to a hot, gentle breeze, the yellow sun again beat down brightly, and the southern sky resumed its endless, eternal blue. Normalcy reclaimed Egypt, and Hor-em-akhet the Guardian lay still and silent, staring forward, stone beneath the relentless sun.

A long moment of silent shock passed, and then, suddenly, great cheers arose. All of Giza began shouting with joy, cheering, and raising their fists toward the sky.

The thieves jumped to their feet, and rather than be beheaded, the companions found themselves ardently embraced by thieves, killers, and total strangers, all happier than they'd ever seen any Egyptian. Elaina accepted their hugs, fearful touches, and many thanks, even though she couldn't understand a word that they said; all of Egypt seemed suddenly delighted that they'd come. Countless gestures were made that Elaina didn't understand, a kind of waving upwards with both hands from their foreheads, but it was obvious that they were grateful. Apparently Hor-em-akhet didn't awaken every day … or even once every lifetime. This was a day of monumental importance and celebration … a testament to all the faithful.

Chapter 7

The Deadly Door

SISTER ASPERTINE

"God, no!"

"Please, God, no!"

"God, no …!!!!!"

Sister Aspertine fell to the ground and pressed her face to the hard-packed dirt and sand.

God can't allow this monster to live!

She prayed as never before, her soul trying to fight its way out of her body, as if she could pray time backwards, before the sphinx had come to life, and die before she'd lost her faith … and her reason for living.

The cheers of the crowd resounded her death-knell.

God save me!

Such horrors can't live!

I can't owe my life to blasphemy!

If this gargantuan pagan demon could come to life, then the rest of those impossible stories, that these blasphemers had repeatedly told, about their quest to Valhalla and the pagan Norse gods, might be true. She couldn't accept that: *she was a nun, and her duty was to believe in Christ alone!*

This can't have happened!

It can't ...!

Despite the dryness of this entire land, she kept her nose pressed into mud ... *mud of her own making.* Sister Aspertine was crying, blubbering like a child, and raining tears onto the dirt and sand pressed against her face. She couldn't rise; she squeezed against the hard-packed dirt as lowly as she could. Perhaps, if she prostrated herself entirely, deeply enough to bury herself in her final grave, then God would tear out of her mind the memory of the horrible statue, her sight of the monstrous demon Hor-em-akhet coming alive, speaking to her, and hearing his Hellish voice scald her ears and pollute her mind.

She was poisoned! Contaminated! Filthy!

Ruined by a devil-statue!

Nothing lives in defiance of God ...!

But it had lived ... in defiance of God ...!

Please, for my faith, end my life, but spare my soul!

Sister Aspertine had no clue if she'd shouted, whispered, or silently mouthed her prayers. Before the arms of the giant stone blasphemy, upon the cursed ground it rested upon, she tasted its pagan dirt on her lips; *perhaps that's why God ignored her pleas.* Still upon her knees, slowly she stretched out, prostrate, until she was flat upon the ground, and sobbed her prayers to the mud and the ears of any saint that would heed her.

A hand reached down and tried to pull her up, but she pushed it away with a foul curse that she'd never uttered before, and whoever it was let her be.

Loud cheers and celebration surrounded her; she heard Karl order Alarika to tell the crowd, all of the Egyptians, their whole story, and then silence fell except for Alarika's heavily-accented voice calling to her people. Sister Aspertine didn't understand a word of Egyptian, and tried to ignore her, to focus on her prayers, but as Alarika spoke, long and clearly, a silence fell over the crowd, which held its breath upon every word. Sister Aspertine glanced up to see Alarika point to her former army of thieves, who seemed unhappy about their unexpected notoriety; they looked down as if troubled, and then Alarika pointed toward the desert.

Ignoring them all, Sister Aspertine pressed her face back upon the dirt; Alarika was a pagan as bad as the witch … and the sorceress … and the demoness.

How had she expected to stay pure while traveling with pagans …?

A hand touched her again; she recoiled.

"Sister …?" Nate's voice whispered. "Sister, are you hurt?"

Concern filled his voice; of all of their company, Nate was the only true Christian, the only companion that she trusted. His hands closed upon her arms, pulled her upwards, and she relented.

God wasn't listening to her prayers.

Never had she wanted to rise less. Upon the dirty ground, she didn't have to face the smiles painting every face, companion and Egyptian. Roselyn was one step closer to becoming a Valkyrie again, her grin beaming. Eloise and Elaina seemed delighted to have experienced magic of a level that Sister Aspertine prayed never existed. Karl, Phil, and Henry just seemed glad that the thieves hadn't killed them. Alarika was commander of her army again, and the thieves seemed to consider themselves some sort of honor guard; many stood shoulder to shoulder between the companions and the Egyptians, protecting them from the silent, frozen

Egyptians paying rapt attention to Alarika's every word. Alarika was pointing at Eloise and whirling her hands in the air as she spoke; she was telling them about the sandstorm ...

It didn't matter. *Nothing mattered anymore.* Sister Aspertine had spent her life serving God ... and now she wondered if God was even real. He certainly wasn't the only god; God wouldn't breathe life into a pagan statue, no matter how big ...

No mortal could bring the monstrous sphinx to life ...!

That meant that ... some other god ... it could only have been a god ... had breathed life into this horror.

Karl and Roselyn ... where all else failed, their strange lover's poem had worked. The ancient Egyptian story of two lovers separated by death ... impossible as that was ... could only have worked if their bizarre story of Yggdrasil was true. This thought stabbed; Roselyn and Elaina worshipped northern gods, and Eloise was a priestess to her evil goddess, and Alarika worshipped a pantheon of Egyptian gods ... from a civilization that was ancient when Jesus walked the Earth.

Was God in Heaven real ... or one of many?

How could they all be true?

Nate's face swam into her vision, his expression anxious, and his thumbs brushed the drying sand from her cheeks; Sister Aspertine hadn't even noticed the tears blurring her vision.

Where could she find relief?

How can faith be bandaged?

Suddenly his strong arms were around her, and she was pressing her face against his hard mail, her arms clutching him tightly. She needed someone to hold onto ... or she'd lose her mind.

Without faith, what was she?

Who was she?

Nate lifted a wineskin and forced her to drink despite her refusals. One arm around her, Nate held her while Alarika continued speaking, and from her words Sister Aspertine caught the name of the oasis that'd saved them from the blistering heat of the Deshret: el-Daklha. She stood listening, probably because it was easier than contemplating the impossible. Without Nate, Sister Aspertine was certain that she'd fall and never arise ... both in this world and the next.

The least that God could do is kill me now ...!

Eventually Alarika pointed to Elaina and mimicked dancing, Sister Aspertine realized where she was in the story. Although the unknown words were lost to understanding, the rest of Alarika's gestures were obvious: poling down the river, and the arrow that had slain Samuel, and their sadness for their loss, and then she pointed at Sister Aspertine, and mimicked folding her hands in prayer. Normally Sister Aspertine would've objected; it was blasphemy for a pagan to mock prayer, but so much blasphemy had happened here that this retelling seemed trivial.

Sister Aspertine didn't know what to do ... and she had only one source of support; she tightened her arms around Nate and clung to him. A strange smile glowed on Nate's face, but Sister Aspertine was too preoccupied to worry about it.

Alarika finished her story, gesturing to the great sphinx. The crowd cheered, and many shouted gladly at Alarika.

"They ask for our pleasure," Alarika announced to the companions. "They say that they exist to serve the beloved of Hor-em-akhet."

Karl sighed and shook his head.

"We need food and rest," Karl said.

"We can't afford to waste time!" Roselyn snapped.

"We can't enter a 'crack in the world' unprepared," Karl shook his head. "We need to be rested and supplied, and unlike the last time, we need to know where we're going. We don't want to get lost again."

"I can tell you as much as anyone," Alarika said. "But it's a long tale; let's find a place out of the sun."

After speaking to the thieves, Alarika led the companions in a grand procession through Giza, and every Egyptian rushed out to see them parade by. Countless blessings heaped upon them, shouted from all directions, and many seemed honored just to reach out and touch them. Roselyn walked stiff-shouldered, shrugging off any hands that dared touch her black armor *(was it really the armor of a pagan goddess of death?)*, but Sister Aspertine ignored them, and their fingers brushed against her soiled, ragged habit as if these pagan blasphemers would be forever blessed by touching a Bride of Christ. Behind Sister Aspertine, Nate seemed to enjoy their sudden popularity; he held his arms out to both sides, welcoming the touches of these unbaptized strangers. Elaina and Eloise walked doing the same, and Karl, Phil, and Henry seemed unperturbed by the unfamiliar touches; they marched as if unseeing the exuberant crowd.

The thieves led them to a luxurious patio roofed with a high wooden lattice interwoven by long, leafy vines, heavy with young purple grapes, and the companions were seated at a splendid table upon which servants piled many breads, oranges, dates, raisins, nuts, bananas, pitchers of water, and bottles of irep. The companions ate with relish and drank freely. Cheers from the vast crowd escalated, their numbers so overwhelming that the crowd packed the street, encircled the patio, and surrounded adjacent buildings. Every face seemed blissful, boisterous, and filled with joy.

Proof of their pagan gods had come during their lifetime.
What person of any religion wouldn't celebrate such a blessing?

Sister Aspertine ate a few bites and drank some irep, and then she asked for a place where she could be alone. With Alarika translating, two servants led Sister Aspertine apart from the others, to a small, dingy room with only a high, thin window, a narrow bed constructed of a bamboo framework and a mattress of woven reeds. Sister Aspertine hurried inside and pulled the door-curtain closed behind her, and then she fell onto her knees and burst into tears.

"God, Jesus, Holy Spirit, spare me or take me!" Sister Aspertine begged of the shadowed ceiling of her room.

No reply came.

God wasn't listening …!

"Sister …?" Elaina's whisper asked, and a soft hand touched her shoulder. "Sister, wake up."

Consciousness crawled out of a pit of despair and opened weary, bloodshot eyes. Her head was leaning over the edge; she must've crawled onto the bed, but she couldn't remember. Sister Aspertine looked upwards, seeing an expression which her blank, empty soul no longer recognized.

"Sister …?" Elaina asked. "Are you ill …?"

Sister Aspertine rolled away from her.

"You … you've ruined me," Sister Aspertine said with great difficulty. "God … has cursed me …"

"I, too, was born a Christian," Elaina said. "I, too, have had my faith tested."

"That ... horrid statue ...," Sister Aspertine shuddered. "Go. Leave me ..."

Elaina's weight settled upon the creaky bed beside her.

"How can you quit ... when you're so close?" Elaina asked.

"Close ...?" Sister Aspertine asked. *"Close to damnation ...?"*

"God didn't send you here to kill your faith," Elaina said. "Master Sir Rafe has the strongest faith of any man I've ever met, and he not only traveled to the realms of Yggdrasil, he met other gods ... talked to them ... and his faith never wavered."

"That ... that's ... not ...," Sister Aspertine mumbled. "That can't be ...!"

"It's true," Elaina said. "I've seen it in my dance, and I've never lost my belief in God."

Sister Aspertine shook her head.

"Witch ...!" she accused, but her voice had no strength left in it.

"There are two ways to embrace faith," Elaina said. "You can hide behind what you know, and call everything that refutes your knowledge witchcraft, or you can accept that God knows more than you ever will, and open your eyes to all of His glories, and to the grandeur of the entire universe, and trust that someday either you'll come to understand it all ... or that He'll explain it you on the other side of the Pearly Gates."

Sister Aspertine raised her eyes and looked at Elaina.

"Do ... do you really believe that?" Sister Aspertine asked. Elaina smiled.

"All but one word," she said.

"Which word?" Sister Aspertine asked.

"*'He'*," Elaina smiled. "The universe is too grand to have been born of a man."

Sister Aspertine lowered her head again.

"That's blasphemy," she said.

"The Bible is the Word of God written by men," Elaina said, "and I've never trusted men as much as I trust women."

Elaina rose from the bed, vanished, and then returned with a bowl of warm water and a clean towel. She washed Sister Aspertine's face and hands, took off her crumpled wimple and combed her long, wheat-gold hair, and then she shook out her wimple and smoothed the wrinkles in her torn habit as best she could.

"Where ... where are we going ...?" Sister Aspertine asked.

"We sail back south, upriver, almost as far as the Temple of the Kings, to a place called Abydos," Elaina said. "There we'll approach a sacred site: the Temple of Osiris."

"Where we'll call upon Osiris ... the child of Geb and Nut," Sister Aspertine said, and she sighed as if she'd expel her soul.

"You've listened well," Elaina said.

"My faith's dead, not my ears," Sister Aspertine said.

"Your faith is far from dead," Elaina said. "Metal must melt in the forge before it can be shaped into a sword."

With no more will to resist, Sister Aspertine allowed Elaina to pull her to her feet and lead her out to join the others. Eloise was sitting beside Alarika, Henry, Nate, and Phil at a table laden with food and drinks, relaxing under the canopy of fresh leaves hanging down between the wooden lattices. At least three servants stood on each side of them, holding plates of purple grapes and brown

breads, and pitchers of water. At the door to the street
stood a dozen of Alarika's thieves, guarding the entrance,
with a much-quieter crowd of people surrounding their
borrowed dwelling. Yet they rose to their feet and
cheered when Elaina and Sister Aspertine emerged.
Elaina waved at the cheering crowd as she escorted Sister
Aspertine to the table and made her sit and drink some
tart irep.

Sister Aspertine looked up; the distant, horrible head
of the great sphinx, visible through the leaves and
wooden lattice, dominated the sky. Behind it rose the
even-taller pyramids. She looked away, cursing the pagan
icon that'd stolen her faith.

Karl and Roselyn emerged arm-in-arm to thunderous
cheers, and only Eloise turned her head and looked away.

Supplies were brought, mostly carried in the arms of
children, who were allowed to enter the patio and deposit
woven platters and baskets of food, strange stools that
Alarika called camel-saddles, reed mats to rest upon,
white wool blankets, and thick clothing such as only the
richest Egyptians wore. At Alarika's suggestion, they all
changed clothes, even Roselyn, donning white robes and
turbans. At Elaina's insistence, Sister Aspertine relented,
and gave up her dirty, scuffed and torn habit for a clean,
white robe and scarf.

If God still cares for me, he won't forsake me because of my garments.

Several local leaders came, so honored that they were
accorded almost as much awe and respect as the
companions, and they spoke briefly with Alarika, and
then had to shake hands with each of the companions.
Finally one of them made a speech, at which the crowd
cheered, although Sister Aspertine couldn't understand a
word of it.

Soon Alarika announced that they were ready to
depart, and a grand wagon arrived, pulled by four massive
camels, to carry them back to the river. Every thief of
Alarika's former command lined the path to the wagon,
and after they mounted, and all their weapons, gear, and
armor were loaded, the thieves rode their horses and
camels surrounding the companions, most of whom
stood in the wagon and waved to the cheering throng.

They disembarked the wagon before an ornate vessel
to pale even Al-Hassim's red ship with gold sails. All of
the provisions that they'd been given, enough to feed
Alarika's army for days, were piled aboard their ship, and
Alarika hand-picked a dozen of her guards to sail with
them, while two dozen were ordered to sail in other
boats. The remainder would ride alongside them, on the
shore, bringing all their horses and camels.

The people of Giza cheered and bowed before them.
Phil, Eloise, Elaina, and Alarika remained at the rail,
waving to them as the Egyptian sailors pushed off, and
the crowd kept cheering until their ship sailed upriver and
out of sight.

Those who could boarded other boats and followed
them.

The owner of their boat, one of the wealthy patrons
of Giza, an old man with a bald head and a long, thin
beard, insisted on being introduced to each one of them.
As always, boats sailed slowly upstream. Phil suggested
that Eloise could speed their voyage if she could summon
a strong breeze, but Eloise refused to ever tempt the
desert winds again; her last attempt had almost killed her.

Alarika's guards lounged about, and tossed some food
to their companions on the other boats, and at sunset
their ship stopped at a rickety dock to pass some food to

the guards on horseback, who labored to keep their horses fed and watered and still keep pace with the ships.

The other cities apparently hadn't heard of the sphinx awakening. As sailors aboard other ships shouted to them, looks of shock and disbelief masked their faces. Yet the companions ignored them, and Sister Aspertine sat silently in the shade of their sail.

"Sister ...?" Nate's voice interrupted her.

She looked up at his face, into his puzzled expression.

"Is something wrong?" Nate asked her, lowering his voice to a whisper. "You haven't spoken all day."

Sister Aspertine bit her tongue and lowered her head. *What could she say?* Misgivings plagued her mind, but she didn't want to ruin the faith of her one faithful companion.

A friendly, comforting hand rested on her shoulder, and she looked up into the only kind face that she knew outside of England.

"I'm all right," Sister Aspertine whispered to Nate. "I ... I appreciate your ... solidity."

"I'm always ready to comfort you," Nate said, and he sat beside her on the deck.

Sister Aspertine bowed her head and said nothing. Her gratitude for his presence was greater than she could say. Nate was the one companion that she could count upon. Often she caught his eyes watching her, while everyone else was distracted; he was her staunch protector, always standing guard over her. Nate was the gift that God had given her on this journey. Sister Aspertine would be glad to say good-bye to the others, but Nate's company she'd always treasure.

As they sat, Nate's hand absently rested upon Sister Aspertine's knee. She flinched slightly, unaccustomed to familiar touches, but Nate was looking out over the rail, at the sandy shore dotted with palm trees and the riders struggling to keep pace with them. Nate seemed unaware of it, and Sister Aspertine was reluctant to push him away; with doubts and recriminations tormenting her mind, the touch of a friendly hand felt strangely comforting.

Several days later, nearing sunset, after an exceptionally hot afternoon, they reached the city of Abydos, a wide, palatial city of many shrines, and they disembarked with fanfare rivaling the speeches in Giza.

Alarika and Roselyn argued; their host wished for them to rest in the nearby mansion of a friend, and Alarika liked this notion, but Roselyn wouldn't be gainsaid, and she insisted that they'd wasted enough time, and that they had to proceed straight to the Temple of Osiris.

After much discussion, to which Sister Aspertine paid scant attention, Karl decided that they could ask Roselyn to wait no longer, and their wealthy host summoned carts to carry them and their baggage to the Temple of Osiris. However, Karl forced Roselyn to agree that, if they didn't find a 'crack in the world' right away, then she'd come with them to the home that their host offered. To this stipulation Roselyn agreed. They mounted the carts, which were much smaller and less grand than their procession in Giza. At Alarika's command, their drivers drove them inland under a sky whose endless blue was deepening over their heads.

The Temple of Osiris was large and ornate. It rested on a wide, level ground, surrounded by a low wall and two courtyards, with several smaller, outlying buildings. The sun set as they entered a nearby dwelling and donned their armor again; in case they did find a 'crack in the world', Roselyn insisted that they be ready for it. Sister Aspertine refused her crumpled, smelly habit, unwilling to surrender the clean, white robe that she'd enjoyed since Giza. Elaina and Eloise also remained in white. With servants carrying their supplies, they passed through the gate and crossed both courtyards, where huge, dark doorways opened to each side, and they walked up the long stairs. Great stone blocks and artistic palisades stood before massive square columns, upholding a thick ceiling, and they stepped through a dark passageway walled with relief carvings of ancient kings and gods.

The sun dipped below the horizon, and the desert sky darkened to violet as they entered the magnificent temple.

A huge crowd followed, led by their wealthy host, who insisted on walking between Alarika and Karl. Inside, the temple was even more magnificent. The torch-lit interior was intricately decorated, and they passed double rows of huge, round columns, between tall, squared blocks, to find triple rows of the same round columns, each of which the whole company could hide inside, if the vast stones were hollow. They stopped before the doors to an ornate chapel. Sister Aspertine stared at the thick columns and high ceiling, wondering how such stones could be shaped and stacked without the help of the divine.

Yet this ancient temple was pagan, an evil tribute to devils that had deceived mankind before Christ came to drive them out. Sister Aspertine stopped when the others did, the last of the company, disgusted by everything that she saw and felt.

Here was more proof that pagan gods existed.

Only Nate, standing beside her, offered her a dim trace of goodness in this palace of unholiness; Nate made the sign of the cross. Guilt rained upon her; once Sister Aspertine would've felt the need to enlighten these poor, hopelessly-lost souls, but now her own faith was quavering ... on the brink of oblivion.

"We're here," Roselyn said to Alarika. "Now, open the portal."

"I know the chant," Alarika said, "but we'll need a sacrifice."

"Sacrifice ...?" Karl asked. "What kind of sacrifice?"

"Didn't you know?" Alarika said. "My father was called the Mad Hermit, and had to flee to the Valley of Thieves to escape the sentence of death ... for his child-sacrifices."

"Children ...?" Karl gasped. "We can't sacrifice children!"

"How many?" Roselyn asked.

"No!" Karl argued. *"We're not ...!"*

"You promised!" Roselyn said coldly.

"I never promised to murder!" Karl shouted.

"Sacrifice isn't murder," Roselyn said. "A sacrifice sends its victims straight to their gods ..."

"We're not sacrificing anyone!" Karl declared.

Sister Aspertine glanced up, seeing Karl and Roselyn facing each other like combatants, eyes glaring, and the rest of the company drew back, seeming unwilling to interfere.

"This is why we're here," Roselyn said to Karl. "I go this way, even if I walk alone. If you'd betray your oath, then leave."

"I'm not a murderer," Karl said.

"A few years in Valhalla will change that," Roselyn said. "After you've died a thousand times, you realize how pitiful one death is."

"Then I won't be going to Valhalla!" Karl said angrily.

Roselyn stiffened, gripping her sword.

"Say that again and I'll slay you now," Roselyn said, and she laid her hand across the long hilt of Hel's sword and deepened her voice. "I became a Valkyrie, and I've ruled in Valhalla for eight years, awaiting the day when you'd join me; *you will not disgrace me …!*"

"Peace!" Elaina said, gesturing for Roselyn to restrain her swordarm and her rising anger. "We should discuss this …"

"The 'crack in the world' to Yggdrasil opened only at a deadman's touch," Roselyn said. "What made you think this 'crack' would be any different?"

"Sacrifices aren't uncommon in our religion," Alarika said. "These are our lands … our gods …"

"*I don't murder innocents!*" Karl said.

"*Obey your oath!*" Roselyn said. "I'll perform the sacrifice …"

"*You will not!*" Karl said, and fast as a striking cobra, Roselyn drew Hel's sword and pointed it at Karl's heart.

"*No one stays a Valkyrie!*" Roselyn warned. "If you'd try, then draw your sword …!"

"*No!*" Elaina cried, and she stepped between them.

"Alarika, is there any way to open the portal without killing someone?" Karl asked.

"My … my father said that a sacrifice was essential … and so did the sphinx," Alarika said.

"*The life of an innocent, shed in the holy place, may open a portal,*" Elaina quoted. "Those were the words of the sphinx, and I suspect that he spoke the truth; why would he lie to us?"

"*No,*" Karl said.

Roselyn ignored him, and glanced at the crowd.

"*No!*" Karl repeated. "If you do this, you do this alone!"

"*I'm a Valkyrie!*" Roselyn shouted.

"Then …!" Karl started, but he caught himself, and lowered his voice, but not his seriousness. "Roselyn, if you do this, we're through …!"

Roselyn stared at Karl with all the fury of a battle-maid.

"Will you abandon the Seer, your former companion, as you've abandoned me?" Roselyn shouted, and each word rang like a death knell.

Karl looked doubtful, but turned away.

"I won't be party to murder," Karl said.

"If I didn't need you on the other side of this portal then I'd slay you now," Roselyn's words sliced through them, but Karl ignored her. Finally he turned to Eloise.

"Wife, what say you?" Karl asked.

All eyes fell upon Eloise. She took a deep breath, then replied in slow, clear words.

"Husband, I've no desire to see a sacrifice, or enter another 'crack in the world'," Eloise said. "But … I have a duty to the Lady. The Seer serves the master of Roselyn and my mistress, and forsaking him would be a great disservice to Her. I'd prefer to go home, with my husband, and raise our children together, but … friendship has ever sustained us, even when all hopes failed."

"What about murder …?" Karl asked.

"Druids perform sacrifices," Eloise sighed. "Only those of deep faith understand."

Elaina came over and rested both her hands on her daughter's shoulders.

"I concur," Elaina said. "I won't slay the sacrifice, but I'll enter the 'crack in the world'."

Karl glanced at Nate and Phil.

"This squire follows you," Phil said to Karl.

"I obey my knight," Nate said.

"This goes beyond duty," Karl said to Nate. "I give you both choice."

"We grew up on stories of Yggdrasil," Nate said. "If a 'crack in the world' opens, I'm going through."

Phil nodded. Karl glanced at Henry.

"We hired you to sail us here, not to enter …," Karl said.

"Since we left England, I've seen too much to doubt anything," Henry said. "I can't go home saying that I feared to follow."

"We might not make it home," Karl warned.

"Never daunt sailors," Henry said. "We brave the sea every day. Besides, I made a promise to Lord Sir Rafe …"

Karl nodded, and then he turned to Alarika.

"I've spent my life hoping to open this door," Alarika said. "This was my father's dream …"

Finally Karl turned to Sister Aspertine; she slowly shook her head.

"Sister, you can't stop now …!" Nate pleaded.

"Let her decide …," Karl said.

"Sister Aspertine, you'll never know peace … if you refuse," Elaina said. "The proof that you need, proof of God's supremacy, only lies through the 'crack in the world'."

"I … I don't know," Sister Aspertine said.

"My faith has never wavered," Nate said. "Meeting witches and Valkyrie hasn't changed me. Foreign gods won't change me. Don't abandon your soul, or mine, to despair. We need you, there … more than ever …!"

Sister Aspertine looked up into his eyes, so golden brown … beautiful, as if Nate was glowing inside with the radiance of Heaven.

Slowly she nodded.

Suddenly one of Alarika's thieves shouted at them, and the crowd murmured behind him.

"He wants to know if he can come with us," Alarika said. "All of these people ask the same thing."

Karl looked at Roselyn, who shrugged.

"We go through first," Karl replied. "Anyone who wants to follow us … can."

Alarika translated, and everyone, from their wealthy host to Alarika's whole army, to the priests of the temple, the commoners who just happened to be there, and the servants carrying their supplies, all gave a loud cheer.

"Warn them," Elaina said to Alarika. "Warn them how dangerous it'll be."

Alarika spoke again, but the only response was scornful laughter.

"The last time we entered a 'crack in the world' we almost died within minutes," Roselyn said. "I've passed through two other 'cracks in the world', and in one I almost lost my life, and in the other I almost lost my soul. I welcome all who'd join us; their death-cries may give us important warnings."

"If another green sea-dragon protects this 'crack', then I doubt if many will enter," Karl said.

"We need a sacrifice," Roselyn said to Alarika. "Ask for a volunteer … or I'll choose one from the crowd."

With a grim stare, Alarika turned to the crowd and spoke to them, and their gasps of shock and dismay also needed no translation. Many dark eyes glared at them, and all smiles vanished.

Suddenly there was a disturbance and a young voice cried out. Several voices were raised, and a man came forward, pulling a young boy, who was resisting as best he could. Sister Aspertine noticed that the boy had only one full arm, his other was half missing. The man pulling the boy spoke loudly in Egyptian.

"He says that this boy is a slave, a thief, and an orphan," Alarika translated.

"He'll do," Roselyn said.

"Roselyn ...!" Karl shouted, his voice brimmed with his worst temper. "Not Reginleif, Valkyrie, or Queen, ... Roselyn ... please: reconsider, if you can. *If you kill this boy, you kill our love ... irreversibly ... and forever!"*

Roselyn glared at Karl, and then she raised her weapon, the great sword of Hel.

"I ... am ... Reginleif!" Roselyn shouted.

With the speed worthy of a queen of Valhalla, Roselyn whipped Hel's sword around and stabbed right through the chest of the terrified boy. He never screamed, but Sister Aspertine and others did, taken aback not only by the inhuman brutality of the murder, but by its unexpected suddenness. The young, one-armed boy merely looked surprised, as if unable to comprehend what'd just happened, and then complete emptiness shrouded his open eyes. He stared down at his impaled body ... and then his empty shell collapsed to the ground.

"So be it," Karl said with finality.

Alarika stepped toward the boy's limp corpse as Roselyn pulled Hel's sword from him, and let his body lay flat upon the stone floor.

Raising her arms to the ceiling, palms upward, Alarika prayed in her own tongue, and when she was finished, after glancing about to see that nothing had happened, she repeated her chant in English.

> *"Hail to thee, Prince of Amenta,*
> *Osiris, Lord of Nifura, grant that I*
> *may advance in peace towards Amenta,*
> *and that the Lords of Tasert*

may receive me and say to me,
'Salutation! Salutation in Peace!'.
Let them make for me a seat
by the Prince of the Divine Powers.
Let the two Chenemta goddesses,
Isis and Nephthys, receive me,
in the presence of Unneferu the Victorious.
Let me be a follower of Horus in Re-stau,
and of Osiris in Tattu. Let me
assume all forms for the satisfaction
of my heart in every place
that my Ka wisheth."

Again, the companions glanced about, but nothing unexpected presented itself.

"Murder … for nothing!" Karl snarled.

"Karl," Eloise warned. "Heed the words of the sphinx: *The life of an innocent, shed in the holy place, may open a portal where the living may enter. Recite his prayer, call upon Osiris, and jump into life."*

In her white robe, Eloise stared at each of them, and then stepped to straddle the dead boy's body, one foot on each side, atop his pooled blood. Suddenly she raised her voice to echo throughout the many-pillared hall.

"Osiris …!!!"

Thunder crashed outside, and a lightning flash illuminated the dark doorway. Hearing the rumble, the crowd drew back, gesturing signs of protection, yet the companions stood unmoving, glancing apprehensively. A distant, rushing roar of wind echoed from the desert, and the chamber around them suddenly grew chill, and every candle and torch extinguished, as if all warmth was drawn off by an unseen breath. Darkness enveloped them.

Every voice fell silent, every heart swelled, and all hands trembled. Even Alarika's fierce army of thieves paled, and the wealthy patrons and the crowd stepped back.

From the corpse of the sacrifice, lying atop its own pool of crimson blood, came a soft glow, dim, but arresting the eyes of every watcher. Eloise stepped back, away from him, as his light grew. A small whirlwind enveloped the boy, and his dead body moved, blown by the wind, lifted, and rose into the air. Sparks and fire emanated from his glowing corpse, and slowly he rose toward the ceiling. Suddenly his eyes popped open, and his arm and half-arm flew outwards, straight from his sides, as if snapped like feeble whips. Sparks and fire consumed him with a screech like a wounded vulture, but he didn't diminish. The light grew brighter, blinding, until a tiny shining sun radiated from his silent chest and burned their eyes.

Sister Aspertine fell to her knees, too horrified to pray.

Her companions had murdered ...!

Had they really opened a 'crack in the world'?

Would this be worse than the stone monstrosity that'd stolen her faith ... and if so, what would she lose next ...?

The shape of the boy, now engulfed in yellow light, started to grow, and to slowly roll backwards, and finally turned completely over, head over heels. No boy flipped before them, only a giant shape of pure golden light, shimmering too brightly for their eyes to look at directly. Staring through their fingers, everyone, even the companions, were forced back as the fiery shape grew ever larger, and finally threatened to grow too great even for the enormous Temple of Osiris.

An earthquake struck, so hard that everyone, peasant, patron, thief, and companion, was hurled to the floor. The walls, pillars, and ceiling shook. Just as Sister

Aspertine cried out, certain that the walls would fall and the ceiling collapse upon them, the thick pillars beside them, round and square, began to move ... as if alive. The columns slid upon the floor. The crowd screamed and ran to keep from touching them, or being crushed by them, as the columns slid away from the growing light.

Temple walls cracked apart at the seams, crunching like stones breaking, separating from the floor and the ceiling, evenly, as if they'd been secretly built to come apart. The entire stone ceiling lifted off of them, floated, and flew upwards into the starry sky, making room for the glowing golden shape to expand, its bottom end just brushing the floor before them, and yet it kept turning, flipping backwards in slow revolutions.

Sister Aspertine looked up and gasped: *the shape of the golden light resembled a cross ... a Gnostic cross!*

Every pillar and wall, entire sections of the temple, rose from the floor, and the massive stone sections of the temple slid slowly apart, in all directions, and began to spin in circles around the outside of the temple. Evenly they floated, massive stones, never touching, but increasing in speed, until they were all trapped in a whirlwind of huge flying blocks, moving outwards, making room for the growing, glowing cross of light.

Pale with terror, it took only one man's flight to begin the rush to escape, and then horrified voices cried out as the onlookers ran away. The crowd fled first, running under the swirling stone-storm, the wealthy patron with them, and Alarika's thieves hesitantly followed ... with many fearful backwards glances. Last fled their servants, taking their supplies with them. Phil shouted at them, but they ran off, heedless.

"Is this expected ...?" Elaina cried to anyone who could hear her.

"Expect anything!" Karl shouted back at her.

"Those peasants had our supplies ...!" Phil shouted.

"We can't chase them now!" Karl shouted, staring up the huge, growing shape of light.

"It's a cross!" Nate shouted.

"It's an ankh!" Alarika cried.

"The Egyptian symbol of life!" Eloise exclaimed.

"Life!" Roselyn shouted. "The sphinx said ... *jump into life!"*

"There!" Elaina shouted, pointing upwards. *"Look! Inside the loop of the ankh!"*

Too frightened to resist, Sister Aspertine looked up. The top of the giant golden cross, now taller than the mightiest tree, had widened into the symbol of the sandal-strap, the Egyptian icon of life. The insanity around them flowed awash within the spiral whirlwind circling faster and faster, a dizzying blur. The ceiling of the temple of Osiris had risen so high into the starlit sky that it could barely be seen. Yet, through the wide gap in the top of the massive, glowing ankh, they spied a vastly different land: a dark sky, lit only by a few dim stars, lay over a quiet, still land of shadowed, sandy dunes, unmoving amid the chaos.

"That's it!" Roselyn cried. *"That's the other realm! The 'crack in the world'!"*

"Wait for it!" Karl shouted. "Take hands, and try not to look into the light! When it inverts, when it comes close to the floor, jump through it!"

"Are you mad?" Alarika exclaimed.

"Trust us!" Karl shouted. *"We've been through this before!"*

"Here it comes!" Nate shouted.

Sister Aspertine lifted her head from where she lay sprawled, hurled to the floor by the shaking ground. The massive golden ankh, now towering over them, was turning upside down again. The wide, teardrop loop was descending toward them, about to brush the ground. Through the loop, the quiet, still lands looked calm and peaceful compared to the magical chaos around her, but Sister Aspertine feared that peace worse than the magical ankh, the monstrous stone guardian, and all of the ungodly horrors she'd witnessed since joining these blasphemous companions. Now she could see clearly: through that mystical portal lay the lands they sought, the realm of the gods and goddesses of ancient Egypt, and to pass through that portal, to enter that accursed doorway, would be the final death of all she believed in, the murder of her faith, and the end of her life.

"Get up!" Roselyn shouted. *"Get ready!"*

The companions struggled to stand, the floor beneath them still trembling, but they managed to rise; Karl, Roselyn, Eloise, Elaina, Nate, Phil, Henry, and Alarika … all but Sister Aspertine.

"Follow me!" Roselyn cried, and with a mighty leap, she jumped through the portal and vanished into the land beyond.

"Go!" Karl shouted, and he grabbed Eloise and Elaina, and together they jumped, over the golden edge, through the inside of the golden loop. Alarika followed them, jumping as high as she could, to swan dive through, and Henry followed her.

"Nate, come on!" Phil cried, and suddenly Sister Aspertine felt hands seize her from behind.

"Sister! We must go!" Nate shouted.

But Sister Aspertine couldn't enter that terrible portal. *She couldn't prove to herself that God was false …!*

"Nate! Now!" Phil shouted.

Nate pulled with all of his might, and half-lifted Sister Aspertine, but she pushed against him and tried to pull away, fighting to stay in the only world that she knew. Suddenly more hands seized her around the knees; Phil's hands, and with his help, the brothers lifted Sister Aspertine despite her struggles.

"*No!*" Sister Aspertine screamed. "*I don't want to ...!*"

With matching leaps, both squires jumped backwards into the glowing loop, into the heart of the mystical portal, and fell through the 'crack in the world'.

Sister Aspertine screamed as she was flung helplessly up into the air, vainly clawing her way back to her world, but both boys landed onto their backs, and with the grunts of their impacts still exhaling their breaths, Sister Aspertine crashed down atop them. Then she rolled off their chests, over their heads, onto rough, gritty sand.

Jesus forgive me: the sands of another world ...!!!

She looked up, and saw the huge loop of the great golden ankh rise away, taking with it her last view of God's world, with its whirlwind of sand, temple walls, and huge pillars moving higher, farther away from her with each second. Her opening to sanity rose into the sky as the giant ankh righted itself again. Then the ankh glowed brighter than ever, and arose higher, seeming to swell, to fill the starry sky.

As it reached its full height, radiating like a new sun across a dark land, the ankh suddenly exploded with a crashing thunderclap. The great golden ankh, shining brilliantly, blasted apart into fiery sparks that streamed across the sky, drowned the dim stars, and snaked down in every direction, illuminating the dark dunes and echoing with the hisses of a thousand serpents.

Slowly, the last of the fiery sparks fell to the ground, striking not only the sands near them but bouncing off the tops of nearby hills and vanishing behind distant dunes.

An unexpected darkness and silence assailed them, more threatening than any visible challenge.

The ankh, the only portal back to their world, was gone. The alien world around them looked like deep desert at night ... save that only a few dim stars glowed in the endless, cloudless blackness above their heads, not the countless points that had shined overhead as they rode smelly camels across the Deshret.

Roselyn jumped up, raised the sword of Hel over her head, and howled a jubilant warrior's cry of challenge and triumph.

Sister Aspertine stared, disbelieving. Like it or not, she'd passed through the portal, through the 'crack in the world' ... *and now she was trapped in a pagan Hell.*

Chapter 8

Forbidden Darkness

ELAINA

Elaina bounced and rolled upon the alien gray sands with practiced ease. With her dancer's dexterity, she flipped to her feet while her young companions struggled, still on the ground; only Roselyn had regained her footing, if indeed she'd ever lost it, and Elaina watched, impressed, as Roselyn raised the sword of Hel and shouted a challenging war-cry to this strange, new universe. Karl and Eloise lay sprawled upon their knees, Alarika and Henry near them, all gaping up at the nearly-empty sky where the brilliantly-glowing golden ankh had hovered ... before it exploded in cascading showers of sparks. Then she spied a struggle; Sister Aspertine was repeatedly beating Nate and Phil with her tiny fists.

"*Why?!?*" Sister Aspertine screamed as she struck. "*Why did you bring me here ...?!?*"

Neither boy seemed hurt, only surprised. Farmboys turned squires, trained to fight by Karl, Rafe, and

Roselyn, the weak nun's fists couldn't bruise them. Still, out of habit, both raised their hands to shield their faces.

Elaina turned away; whatever Sister Aspertine's newest complaint was, Elaina wouldn't let it bother her. *She was in another world!* From Norway, Elaina had watched, in her dance, as her daughter and her companions had sought the 'crack in the world' to Yggdrasil, but her vision of them had ended once they'd escaped from the Guardian Dragon of the Underground Lake. Elaina had danced as hard as she could, but no trace of her daughter could be detected while she traveled in the realms of the Norse Gods. Once Elaina had detected that her daughter had returned, she'd been delighted to hear the music of their tale repeated all over England. Relieved that her daughter had survived, Elaina had soon realized that she envied their journey, meeting the Norse gods with whom she'd often tried to commune, but never succeeded.

Now Elaina had equaled their greatest accomplishment; she'd passed through a 'crack in the world'; *she couldn't be happier.*

Karl jumped to his feet and drew his sword, glancing around apprehensively.

"This … is … *bad,*" Karl said warily.

"What …?" Elaina asked, looking about, but seeing only dark sands.

"Danger haunts every 'crack in the world'," Karl said. "Better a deadly attack … than one we don't see."

Roselyn brandished her sword in unspoken agreement, staring around with narrowed eyes.

"*Bastards …!*" Sister Aspertine shouted, still hitting both boys. "*Vile blasphemies of …!*"

"Enough of that ...!" Karl shouted so forcefully that Sister Aspertine seemed shocked to find him standing, prepared to fight. "Boys, why did you bring her?"

"Nate ...," Phil began, but then he faltered. "I was ... just helping."

"Lord Sir Rafe sent her to help us," Nate said.

"Yea, she's been a big help so far," Karl sneered.

"I didn't want to come ...!" Sister Aspertine shouted.

"You should've left her behind!" Roselyn agreed. "What good is she?"

"She helped us survive the prince's palace in Italy," Nate reminded them. "We're facing the gods of Alarika's faith. We have a Valkyrie, a seeress of Odin, a sorceress of the Lady, and a nun of Christ; *we might need all of them.*"

"We're not here to find gods," Karl said. "We locate the Seer, then leave."

"The power of the Lady can take us home," Eloise said.

"The Seer couldn't sense the Lady until we'd brought her to the Well of Mimir," Roselyn said. "Unless the Lady's been in this realm before, her power is probably separated from him."

"That may explain why he didn't return to her ... or to Odin," Karl said.

"He's still a powerful sorcerer," Eloise said. "He tricked Hel and Loki, outside Utgard, before the Lady arrived."

"There's no point in seeking a way back until we find the Seer," Karl said. "Boys, watch our backs. Elaina, can you dance ...?"

"Gladly," Elaina said.

"Maybe we should seek shelter first," Phil said. "Our last venture through a desert almost killed us, and dawn can't be far off ..."

"He's right," Karl said. "Dance to find shelter. A cave would work best ... and a source of water would help."

"Give me a moment," Elaina said, still looking around. "I've never danced ... in another world."

Would dancing reveal anything in this world? Elaina didn't know, and only trying would prove success or failure. First, she had to hear the music. *Would it be an entirely new song?* Elaina hoped that it would. Slowly she turned around, searching for clues, examining everything. The dim stars in the dark, cloudless sky seemed lonely, as if the celestial endlessness of the sky was dying, empty of the countless stars she was accustomed to seeing. *How could stars vanish from one world but remain in another?*

"I'm ... really here," Alarika said softly, amazement beaming from her face. "I ... *I can't believe it!* Father ... *was right!"*

"You may wish that he was wrong before long," Eloise warned. "Now hush; Mother needs to concentrate."

The dim starlight overshone a land of peculiar sandy dunes, not the usual white sand of northern beaches, nor the pale, yellow sands of dry Egypt, but gray sands, like crumbled slate, which looked oddly blue in the starlight. Miles of uneven dunes stretched as far as the eye could see, crumbled, as if neither wind nor water had touched them for centuries. Low mountains rose in the distance to one side, and to the other side the horizon shined with a faint glow, a lessening of the darkness that consumed the rest of the sky; dawn was coming.

Shelter; Elaina recalled their miserable days crossing the Deshret, escaping from Alarika's army of thieves. The endless heat and angry, relentless sun had burned her fair skin so badly that she'd feared that she'd die of exposure.

Elaina closed her eyes and listened, but all that she heard was loud crunchings of sand.

"Please, hold still," Elaina said to her companions. "I need to hear this land."

Their crunchings lessened, but didn't vanish. Even if her companions could stand perfectly still, they were loud breathers, and as Elaina reached out, she could almost hear their troubled hearts beating. Of the company, she alone knew how to stand perfectly still and silent, but she also knew how to ignore distractions. Elaina listened deeper, seeking the odd sounds of this unknown land.

Nothing came right away, but Elaina knew to be patient and kept listening.

Minutes passed slowly by. *Where was the music?*

Not a sound came to her. Not a whisper of wind blew. Not a grain of sand shifted, apart from those under her companions' feet. The silence of this land was alien to her. She turned slowly, facing each direction, but not an echo or tremor could she detect. Everything was quiet ... *as silent as a grave.*

Elaina swallowed hard, a bitter taste on her tongue. The sounds of her universe were gone: wind, water, fluttering leaves, waves crashing, voices laughing, animals, people, and hearts sharing the joys of lovemaking ... the sounds of life. The only harmony of this land ... *wasn't music.* The gods and goddesses of Egypt lay trapped in their Winter, unlike the season of Fall that the gods of Yggdrasil and the Lady of the Druids endured, or the bright Summer, in which ruled Christ of Heaven. The gods and goddesses of Egypt were trapped in unending Winter, which few pantheons survived ...

This land was dead. *The only music here ... would be a funeral dirge.*

Elaina tightened her dancing muscles, which she usually strove to loosen. She faced the dim light on the distant horizon, the approaching dawn, and raised her arms to the sky. This world held no music: *the dead didn't sing.* Elaina stretched her arms wide, and then froze, as motionless as the world around her. She'd heard a song once ... at a funeral ... very long ago ... of sadness and loss: *music of the grave.* Graveside music wasn't made by the dead. *Graveside music ... funeral music ... was made by ... and for ... the mourners ...!*

Elaina lifted her chin, looked up at the stars, and began to sing.

Her first note was soft, barely audible, a plaintive plea for life. Eternal as the endless sands, each note reached the extent of her breath and died awaiting the next. She stood poised, ready to move, awaiting a reaction. Her yearning melody slipped hauntingly over the empty land, the dark sands, the still air, cool with the desert night ... and the gentle radiance of the few stars.

Elaina's song became her music. Without hesitation, Elaina began to dance.

Sands swirled under her lithe feet. Elaina climbed a rise, and fell into the music of her own song with amazing ease, as if this silent world were hungry for melody. She wove and spun, wrapped her arms tightly about her shape, then jumped from a dune-ridge, extending her reach to its farthest, like a flying swan sliding gently down the sands to its base. Sensations swarmed her, echoes of ancient fears, barely perceptible, before they vanished and were replaced. Brief visions appeared: a towering scarab, like a monstrous beetle, looming over wide lands, blue and white flowers blossoming, sweating camels pulling a long caravan of covered carts, a starlit, giant cat, its pointed ears hovering amid a black sky, quietly watching all of Egypt. A strange box glowed, painted with mystic symbols, with two holes, like pupils, in the side of the box, with stylized eyes painted around them. Block by block, pyramids arose, built by tiny figures laboring under whips. A dead body lay hidden inside a tree. Two giant gods fought, one with the head of a hawk, the other with the head of a snake, both determined to slay the other; *their hatred burned like an angry sun.*

Elaina's movements swayed with the precision of a sundial. Never had Elaina danced so deeply, lost in harmonious abandon, a new universe about her. Yet this wasn't her world; incongruities swarmed her. She fought against distractions, and tried to focus, to remember her purpose: *shelter!* Yet the harder that she visualized her need, the more insignificant her efforts felt.

Finally a wide mountain of sand shook, and from it rose a great box, heavily-decorated, a coffin, an ornate sarcophagus, rising into the air. The lid lifted, slid aside … and Elaina looked in …!

"Eeeeeeeeeeeeeekkk……..!"

Consciousness came unwillingly; Elaina writhed and pushed back the hands holding her.

"Mother, stop fighting …!" Eloise shouted.

Starlight in a mostly-barren sky … *where were the countless stars?*

"Let her sit up," Karl said, and many hands assisted her.

"No, I'm all right," Elaina gasped.

"What happened?" Eloise asked.

"Dancing … here … is different," Elaina said. "Never felt … anything like it …"

"Did you learn anything?" Eloise asked.

"No," Elaina said. "No shelter ... but I saw many things, ancient things ..."

"What made you scream?" Karl asked.

"Something ... horrible," Elaina said. "A ... god, cut into pieces ... stitched back together, wrapped in rotting linens ..."

"Osiris, the dead god," Alarika said. "He's our ruler, the wisest and most powerful god of all."

"In this land ...," Sister Aspertine said absently.

Everyone frowned at this comment, and Karl looked up to see Phil and Nate exchange glances.

"Draw your swords!" Karl snapped at them. "I told you to watch our backs! We could be attacked by anything ...!"

Both boys looked shocked, but obeyed, drawing their swords and facing opposite directions.

"We won't be attacked," Alarika said. "This isn't the Norselands; our gods want their people to come to them. This land is welcoming."

"It doesn't look welcoming," Karl said. "In ten hours, we'll be burned and blistered again. Boys, climb the hills; let me know if you see anything."

Phil and Nate hurried off in different directions, climbing the tallest dunes and staring out, then proceeding to the next tallest dune.

"Alarika, do you know where we are?" Karl asked.

"No idea," Alarika said. "The legends say that the dead appear in the Field of Wheat."

"Wheat ...?" Eloise asked.

"Wheat can't grow in sand," Karl said. "Even if it did, a desert sun would cook it on the stalk."

"I saw no wheat in my dance," Elaina said.

"We've no camels or sunshade," Henry said, "… and little water."

"What's the Field of Wheat?" Eloise asked.

"Father called it the Field of Dreams," Alarika said. "There, the spirits of the dead could have anything."

"We should go there," Karl said. "We want the Seer …"

"*River …!*" Phil shouted, standing atop a distant dune and pointing toward the dimly-lit horizon. "There's a river over here!"

Hesitating only long enough to help Elaina to stand, they wasted no time. Nate ran to join them.

"Nothing in that direction," Nate said, pointing behind them.

They helped each other climb up the steep, shifting, sliding sands to join Phil atop the tall dune. There they looked out over a bleak landscape, unbroken gray sands with deep, wind-blown ravines snaking between tall dunes. Behind them loomed dark, distant mountains, and before them, in the distance, stretched a long, winding river, on the edge of the horizon, visible only by reflected gleams of starlight.

"How far do you guess …?" Karl asked.

"Maybe … ten miles," Henry said. "Over level ground, we could be there in three hours … if we hurry."

Elaina frowned at the twisting ravines, cutting like a maze between the dunes.

"Without God, we'll be dead before we get there," Sister Aspertine said.

"Can magic shield us from the sun?" Karl asked Eloise.

"The Lady's power doesn't refute nature," Eloise said. "I've never been able to create shadows, and even if I could, it'd only be an illusion."

"Illusions won't stop sunburn," Elaina said.

"We'd best waste no time," Henry suggested.

Surrendering to the inevitable, they began walking. Quickly they found themselves stuck in a ravine, forced to go in another direction, following the terrain. They climbed the dunes, where they could, but often the steep hillsides crumbled when they tried, and they ended up digging the hillside steeper more than progressing upwards. Frustrated, they marched along the twisting passages. Nate proved the best at climbing, and he scaled the dunes, then pointed out the best routes. Hours they walked, watchful of the few gleaming stars that lit their way.

Twice Elaina and Sister Aspertine had to stop for rests. Elaina felt guilty, knowing how badly the sun would bake their skins, but fear sapped her strength. Never had she known such agony as her scorched northern skin while crossing the Deshret; she wasn't sure if she could survive it again.

Hours passed. Nate kept pointing them, and reported that he could see the river clearly. Yet the stars remained undimmed.

"We must've arrived right after sunset," Karl said.

"I don't think so," Eloise said.

"I agree," Elaina said. "It's been hours. The stars are unchanged, neither moving, brightening, nor dimming."

"Is ... is it possible ... that the sun doesn't rise here?" Henry asked.

"That's impossible," Sister Aspertine said, but her voice was heavy with weariness.

"This is a land in Winter," Karl said. "Theologically, a dead land."

"Egypt was once the birth and center of civilization," Alarika said. "You saw our monuments; we dominated all life, and our gods and goddesses ruled supreme."

"In my dance, I saw the dead god, stitched together," Elaina said. "Maybe they're all dead."

"Osiris was dead, but Isis brought him back to life," Alarika said.

"Heresy ...," Sister Aspertine mumbled.

"I think we'd best take another break," Karl said. "Drink well; we'll be at the river soon."

They ate sparingly of their only bag of food, but drank from their few skins, knowing that water lay ahead. Soon they began marching again. However, eventually Elaina and Sister Aspertine lagged again, looking exhausted.

"We'll have to sleep soon," Henry whispered to Karl.

"Let's get to the river first," Karl said. "There we'll have water ... even if we don't have shade."

"That's true," Henry said. "But if anything's alive in these lands, it'll be at the river, too."

The river gleamed in the dim starlight, flowing slowly but steadily, along shores of wet sand, without a trace of weed or stalk, nor a single blade of grass. Phil and Nate hurried forward to get there first. At its edge, Nate bent to cup the water in his hand, to drink from it, but Phil seized his shoulder and flung him backwards.

"Hey ...!" Nate complained.

Phil said nothing, just stared at the water. Nate jumped up and made a fist to punch his brother as the others caught up.

"Why did you ...?" Karl began.

Suddenly they all fell silent, save for Sister Aspertine's muffled scream. Looking into the river, they saw human bodies floating just under the surface ... Egyptians ... wafting in the slow current ... downstream.

"The River of Death," Elaina gasped.

"Best not drink from it," Phil said.

The river was sparsely filled. Every few moments another body appeared, a young man, an old woman, a boy with one arm ... stabbed through his chest ... still bleeding ...

"They're like ... the newly-dead in Niflhiem," Eloise said.

"A river to carry the bodies," Roselyn said. "That must save a lot of wandering."

"We've almost emptied our bota bags," Henry said.

Karl sighed and shook his head.

"We can't fill them here," Karl said. "We've escaped one deathtrap: the sun would've risen by now, if it were going to. Thirst is our next ..."

"I could try dancing again ...," Elaina offered.

"We won't find any streams here," Karl said, shaking his head. "We need to get to this Field of Wheat ... and dream of fresh supplies."

"If that's where these dead are going, then we should follow them," Eloise said.

Walking beside the dead river was much easier; the dunes leveled out beside its bank, and they weren't forced to take detours. The river flowed slightly faster than they could walk, drifting the corpses along. Elaina watched the grim, silent bodies, mindful of what they were ... and wondered where they would lead.

Chapter 9

Dream Lover

NATE

Step after step, long hours passed, with barely a mouthful of water for each companion, and finally their bota bags hung empty. Nate felt disappointed: the stories of Yggdrasil that had thrilled his youthful imagination disgraced this boring land. Endless sand and floating corpses paled beside meeting Loki and being chased by Hel. He felt cheated, yet he hid his sullen mood and kept walking.

Where were the trolls, giants, and dragons? What good was coming to another world if all they found was sand and a dead river?

The stars never dimmed, the sun never rose, the river never veered, and the dead never stopped floating by. These sights quickly grew stale. Nate's eyes darted about, watching whatever he could, but the only changes floated silently past them. Men mostly floated on their chests, hiding their faces, but women and young children generally floated on their backs. As they walked across the crunching sands, a beautiful woman, stark naked, came floating past. Nate paused to admire her former beauty ... only to be knocked flat as Roselyn stormed past.

With no sunlight, they couldn't count the days, but they slept four times, and were plodding along, dying of endless thirst, when Phil suddenly cried out:

"Wheat ...!"

On the horizon, a line of gold glistened.

Thirst made stopping unthinkable. They marched another hour, unwilling to stop, watching the golden color spread out before their eyes. As they approached, the river banked suddenly away. Onto a wide beach, the whitest, finest sands they'd ever seen, the dead bodies washed up, and then they awoke. Each head rose, looked about in surprise, and then they jumped up, looking delighted, ran uphill, and disappeared into the tall stalks of wheat. As the companions got closer, a young dead girl squealed excitedly and ran from the water's edge, her arms splayed wide. Then, as she pushed into the thickly-growing golden stalks. Suddenly she vanished, not behind the stalks; she simply disappeared.

"Where did she go?" Henry asked.

"It doesn't matter," Karl said. "If there's water there, we go."

No bodies washed up for a while, and then seven figures came bobbing down the river, simultaneously awoke upon the beach, and each jumped up and ran into the wheat.

"What's drawing them?" Nate asked.

"Friends and family," Alarika answered. "Their dreams."

As they reached the white sands, a gurgle of splashing water drew their attention: just inside the wheat sprayed a tall fountain of clear water. They couldn't wait; they ran forward, into the golden stalks. The tall, stiff wheat stalks brushed their arms with comforting familiarity: real, growing wheat, with long, flopping fronds like dry grass, and stiff stalks, each stalk topped with a cluster of ripe grains. They grew from a ground of moist sand, firmly packed, and out of that sand spewed the streaming fountain of clean water, sloshing just over their heads only to splash back down. Nate, Phil, and Elaina stopped, looking at it warily, but Karl, Eloise, Roselyn, Henry, Alarika, and Sister Aspertine ran straight to it and began gulping water.

"What if it's poisoned?" Elaina demanded.

"It's safe or we die of thirst," Karl said.

"Whatever awaits to kill us here, I doubt it will be a fountain," Henry said.

"If God wills we die, so be it," Sister Aspertine said between gulps.

"None of us would dream of a poisoned fountain," Alarika said.

Nate and Phil exchanged a glance, then started forward.

"Excuses may not save us next time," Elaina said, but she joined the others and drank.

The refreshing water bubbled and sprayed, and they took their time, slaking their parched throats. Eloise and Elaina washed their bare arms, and when everyone stepped back, Phil stuck his face right into the upwards stream. Unexpectedly, the fountain suddenly stopped.

"Hey ...!" Phil complained.

"Look!" Nate almost shouted.

Behind them stood a wide table of stained English oak, like the tables in Castle Bristlen, laden for a feast. Roast fowl, mutton legs, and beef ribs lay cooked and steaming beside bowls of barley and vegetables, loaves of bread, bowls of honey, bottles of irep, and tankards of henket. The companions stared at the feast, dumbfounded.

"Someone should test ...!" Elaina said.

"*I will!*" Nate and Phil shouted together.

Nate tore off a leg of pheasant and bit into it while Phil drank from a henket tankard, then sank his teeth into a hunk of steaming, heavily-spiced meat that turned out to be lamb. Karl and the others waited only a moment before rushing forward to join them.

"*That's not long enough!*" Elaina shouted, but no one stopped eating. Finally, Elaina scowled and stepped forward, taking a goblet of irep. "Well, it's not like I'll survive here alone."

"Eat as much as you can, and then rest," Karl said. "We'll eat again before we leave, and carry off as much as we can."

Nate couldn't remember food ever tasting so good. The pheasant fell off its bones, the beef flavorful and dripping with juices, the vegetables steaming even half an hour later, after their stomachs strained to hold more.

Nate looked around; he couldn't see the river anymore; the wheat field stretched as far as they could see in every direction.

"Which way do we go?" Nate asked.

"Sleep first," Karl said. "Worry about direction when we need to leave."

Nate frowned; *why should they ever leave? If they could have their dreams here, where else would they go? What else could they want?*

As he lifted his henket tankard again, not surprised to find it refilled, Nate glanced at each of the others. Karl was tearing a mutton bone clean with his teeth, Phil scooping a spoonful of honey onto oat gruel, and Alarika was feasting on a fresh loaf. Roselyn downed the last of a bottle of a strong irep and set it down, and then waited for it to magically refill. Henry, Eloise, and Elaina had finished, and were resting on thickly-cushioned beds and chairs that had appeared, the ground beneath them covered with a thick, new carpet.

Sister Aspertine was kneeling on the carpet, her head bowed in prayer. She seemed troubled, and Nate set his tankard back onto the table and approached her. As Nate stepped close beside her, he noticed that Henry, Eloise, and Elaina were sound asleep.

"Sister ...?" Nate asked, and she lifted her tear-streaked face to meet his.

"Field of Dreams ...," Sister Aspertine wept. "I've prayed ... my dream is to meet God, to know what He wishes of me ... and ... *nothing!*"

"Perhaps God can't ... I mean, won't come here ... to this world," Nate said.

"I can't believe that," Sister Aspertine said.

"That's why we need you," Nate said. "Your faith never wavers."

Sister Aspertine paused, stretched her lips into an unwanted smile, and looked up into Nate's eyes.

"You strengthen me," Sister Aspertine whispered, and then she quickly looked away.

"Sister ...?" Nate asked.

With a fearful glance at him, Sister Aspertine jumped up and ran away, pushing through the wheat.

"Sister ...!" Nate shouted, and he chased after her.

They ran far through the golden field, Sister Aspertine becoming lost in the tall sheaves. Nate followed, spying her path only by waving fronds. She ran fast, and lithely, but her thick, white robe tangled in the wheat. He ran slower, his armored weight crushing the stalks before him. Yet she tired first, and when he caught up with her, she'd fallen amid the sheaves, and lay sobbing into her hands.

"Sister, what ...?" Nate demanded.

"Go away!" Sister Aspertine hissed. *"Please ...!"*

"Why ...?" Nate asked.

"For my faith!" she cried. *"Before I ... I ...!"*

Sister Aspertine looked up at Nate, her tear-filled eyes drilling into his confused expression, and suddenly she rose and threw her arms around him.

Sister Aspertine kissed Nate hard and passionately. Astounded, he held her, more out of shock than desire. Yet her lips pressed softly against his, her kisses ardent, her breath fevered. Willingly Nate yielded to her advances, amazed that his orchestrated flirtations were actually bearing fruit.

Her fingers dug into his thick hair, and he squeezed her thin frame against him, his fingers melding into the delicate curves and indentures of her back.

He'd done it! Abstinence only exists amid a curiosity of what's missing, and Sister Aspertine couldn't resist curiosity anymore. She was beautiful, young, and fresh, a budding flower begging to be picked, hiding desires every woman needed fulfilled. He slid his hands into the long, plush hay-gold of her hair, so like the wheat-gold around them.

Hands explored, and not a single touch was repelled or pushed back. Sister Aspertine's sweet lips left his mouth, traced his cheek, and dove onto his neck, planting more fervent kisses.

Thoughts assailed Nate; Sister Aspertine was a nun: *he shouldn't be doing this! She shouldn't be doing this!* But she was young, so pretty, and God himself mightn't be able to see them here; *this was her only chance to experience being a woman!*

No longer was this a rivalry between him and his brother; Nate wanted Sister Aspertine as desperately as her kisses seared his skin. *Blasphemy!* echoed shouts from the back of his mind, but his flaming desires responded to her urgent and willful indulgences and deafened him to naysayers.

Slowly they separated, drawing back to look at each other, to face what they were doing.

"Sister ...," Nate fumbled.

"No," Sister Aspertine whispered. "This sin fills my heart, and the greatest sin would be to deny what God placed there." She paused, spreading her arms. "No man has ever seen me undressed. Nate: undress me."

She waited, imploringly, as Nate struggled within himself. His hands trembled, his certainty that he was violating a sacred covenant at war with his desire to explore her soft, shapely form. Sister Aspertine was inviolate, forbidden, and tender. No Roselyn or Eloise; they were strong and firm, while she was gentle and delicate. She wanted and needed him, and without him, her youthful beauty might be wasted forever.

She was still wearing the white robe that she'd been given in Giza. Nate reached out, pulled her bow until the belt freed, and loosened her knot. The front of her robe gapped enticingly. Sister Aspertine smiled, a truly happy grin, and she reached to pull upon a leather strap on his vambrace. Nate smiled, but removing armor was difficult for anyone unfamiliar with it, and easy for novices to hurt themselves upon, so he began helping her, and soon his armor, gambeson, and tunic lay flung upon the sheaves, which spread out like a living mattress beneath them.

With her cheeks blushing pink, Sister Aspertine took Nate's hand and lifted it to her shoulder, and then slid it down. The wide collar of her white robe slipped down her arm, exposing her bare, perfect shoulder, whose pale skin glowed like polished ivory, and her loosed hair tumbled freely. Nate had never seen anything so beautiful, but then she pulled his hand free and shifted it to her other shoulder, and Nate repeated his revelation of her pale, soft essence.

Kissing, they meshed, long and deeply, lost in ecstatic passion, words unneeded or desired. Perfection thrilled every touch, and paradise swelled every kiss. Nate couldn't think any longer; thoughts swirled, unimportant, in the hazy unreality of fleshly desires.

Nate gently pushed, both thumbs catching fabric, and her robe fell away. Radiant, angelic, Sister Aspertine stood reveled in a freedom she'd never known: her physical perfection shined, matched only by her smile: she was loved, her beauty appreciated, her every inch desired. Slowly her supple arms rose in exultation, and she flexed before him, her small but ample breasts mesmerizing, letting her pale body feed his ravenous eyes, destined to ever remain hungry for more. She threw herself into his arms, embracing to never let go.

God be damned! Nate pushed against his trousers as they rolled together, writhing on the sheaves, and somehow his legs pulled free. Both clung, naked, and kissed again, lips roving lower and more desperately.

Moans and gasps exhaled in increasing fervor as lascivious expectations flamed into carnal culmination. Sister Aspertine yielded to Nate's every direction and embraced every opportunity. Never was any invasion more welcomed, more desired, or more demanded. Aspirations worthy of eternal devotion spun their heads with pounding cravings that Nate had rarely dreamed of, and eagerness expounded unrepressed. Appetites expanded and fulfilled, ardor overwhelming reason and restraint. Serpentine they enwrapped each other, entwined in boundless ecstasy.

Feral, fleshy pleasures escalated and exploded in their minds, spirits, and souls. Ambrosias of indulgence spawned a transcendency of contentment, sublime and paramount, swelling every sense. The grandeur of their final climax extinguished all reservations of culture and decorum; in their consummation, the universe righted itself around their perfect joining, a communion with infinity greater than dancing or magic.

Ribs flexing beneath tingling fingers, long they held each other. Nate clung desperately, disbelieving but unable to deny the pounding emotions awash in his brain. To him, Sister Aspertine was Heaven herself, more perfect than any woman or goddess from story or song. Nate couldn't believe that he'd ever pursued her for any reason except the holy essence of all that she was, the culmination of all that he'd ever desired. He loved her, worshipped her, and would gladly give his life for her. He didn't care what any of the others thought, or what God desired; *Nate would spend every minute of the rest of his life loving Sister Aspertine.*

Chapter 10

Hell's Revenge

SISTER ASPERTINE

Sister Aspertine's head spun, her thoughts pounding harder than her heart, awash in a swirling tide of new and overpowering emotions. Inconceivable sensations flooded her, pleasures that she'd never known existed, alien and inexplicable. She wondered where she was. Briefly the thought flitted through her mind that she was floating, drifting underwater in an endless river of life, completely unlike the river of death that they'd followed.

Yet slowly, reality wedged itself into her realizations, and she felt dry stalks of wheat pressed beneath her with uncomfortable intensity. A strong, unfamiliar warmth wrapped around her, a telltale coolness of the soft breeze blowing over her, and an unimagined satisfaction blanking her mind, seeping from a warm, moist, and lathering suffusion.

Someone was holding her tightly. A firm hand was grasping her upper ribs, rough fingers in her bare armpit, clinging to her. An finely-haired and muscled arm lay draped over her. A head, brown hair, and a familiar face nuzzled her shoulder; *Nate was holding her.*

Sister Aspertine tensed. Worry troubled her. *Why were they sleeping so close?* She lifted her head ... and spied her own ... naked nipples, stomach, and legs ...!

Her scream exploded. Sister Aspertine jerked away from his violation of her purity, his unclean nakedness so close to her own.

What had he done to her ...?
How had she become naked ...?
How had they come to be alone ...?

Seeming to burst from sleep, Nate startled and tried to cling to her, his eyes wild, raving incoherently. Violently Sister Aspertine pushed and kicked him back, scrambling away from him across the flattened stalks, her screams never ceasing. Nate was naked, even below his waist; Sister Aspertine screamed and shut her eyes; *never before had she looked upon a naked man!*

Yet, as her eyes closed, visions swam; *she had seen Nate naked before!* She'd watched, with longing and anticipation, as he ... *bared himself before her, as she gave herself willingly ...!*

Sister Aspertine screamed again, her shrieks merged with his shouts of shock and dismay. Confusion transcended both voices, unequaled, as treason excelled the sudden awareness avalanching upon her senses.

What had she ... they ... done?
How had she allowed ...?

Incoherent screams intermixed. Haunting memories swelled, unwanted, irrefutable:

Fleshly delights ...! Carnal rushes ...!
Forbidden pleasures ...! Sin ...!

Unreality stabbed and slashed impossible memories against inviolate principals. *Was this real? Had she dreamed sinful thoughts? Had the devil pervaded her nightmares and invaded her most-holy privates?*

Her hands struggled to cover herself. *Why was she and Nate naked …?*

Voices! Cries of alarm! Footsteps pounded, crashing through growths of wheat. *Others were coming!* Roselyn's eyes, Hel's sword held high over hear head, appeared, staring at her.

A bright cloud flew over her; her white robe, the one that she'd been wearing, was flung overtop her nakedness from Nate's fingers. *Why did he have her dress?*

Others ran up behind Roselyn as she kept screaming: Karl, Henry, Alarika, Phil, Elaina, and Eloise.

Why were they all staring at her …?

What had happened …?

Sensations spiked her frightened thoughts, forcing feelings that couldn't be real.

Her fingers kneading Nate's naked flesh …!

Her hands grasping his …!

Sister Aspertine screamed again.

No …! It couldn't have happened …! She'd never …!

All were eyeing her and Nate. *She and Nate were both naked!* She didn't want them looking at her. She raised her hand to block their view. *She wished they would go away, stop looking at her …!*

The wheat suddenly grew taller and thicker, blocking her view of their faces. The field expanded, shoving a mile of wheat stalks between them. She saw the others slide rapidly backwards, moving away from her.

Nate's hand seized her raised arm.

"What are you doing …?" Nate shouted.

Sister Aspertine had no idea what he meant. *She wasn't doing this …! This was impossible …!*

Everything that had happened since she'd come to the Field of Dreams was impossible!

... Field ... of ... Dreams ...?

The field of wheat stopped growing. She and Nate stopped sliding farther from the others, and the trembling ground beneath them stopped and became stable again. The others were far off, and she and Nate sat staring at each other.

He was still naked, his clothes and armor cast aside ...!

"Get dressed!" she screamed, and she waved her hand at him in a gesture of rejection.

Like magic, Nate's clothes and armor flung itself at him, and he cried out in pain. Suddenly he was fully covered, but incorrectly; one vambrace was under his tunic, one strapped upside-down on the outside of his tunic, and his mail coat on backwards. His trousers were on right, but his gambeson lay wrapped around his waist like a skirt, and one of his boots balanced on his head.

"How ... how did you do that ...?" Nate screamed, staring at his confused coverings.

"How did you ... make me ...?" Sister Aspertine screamed.

"Make you ...?" Nate screamed. *"What are you talking ... that...? You wanted me ...! You made me ...!"*

"I never ...!" Sister Aspertine screamed, but she stopped. Her memories conflicted. *She'd never have done that! She didn't have carnal desires!* But yearnings haunted her; *she remembered wanting him, needing his touches, as if she'd die without them ...!*

"You made me!" Sister Aspertine shouted. *"Your filthy, disgusting dreams ...!"*

"What ...?" Nate shouted. *"You kissed me! We ...!"*

"We did what you dreamed I'd do!" Sister Aspertine shouted. *"You awful ... perverted ...! This is the Field of Dreams! You dreamed it ... and it happened ...!"*

Both fell silent ... staring in disbelief.

"I ... dreamed ...?" Nate asked.

"You violated me!" Sister Aspertine screamed. "I'm a nun! My virtue is sanctified! *You raped ...!"*

"I never raped anyone!" Nate shouted.

"God avenge me!" Sister Aspertine shrieked. *"God, punish this defiler!"*

Thunder crashed, and white clouds split apart, spewing streams of golden, Heavenly light. Angelic choirs arose singing. A wise, radiant face appeared, strong, white-bearded, eternal, with eyes that blazed like exploding stars. Flying about him floated the smiling heads of babies, each fluttering on six wings, singing *"Praise to hosanna!"* The Heavenly face glared down upon them with godly disapproval.

"He did it!" Sister Aspertine screamed, pointing at Nate. *"He ...!"*

An irresistible force seized Nate and pulled him upwards to hover, helpless in the air. Sister Aspertine smiled wickedly, gleeful, with righteous indignation before the sacred arm of justice. Then Nate's sword rose, and its belt and scabbard fell away; his naked blade bared itself and rose higher. Sister Aspertine's face beamed, shining with holy vengeance.

With a sudden thrust, Nate's sword flew forward, its point pierced his chest, and stabbed clean through Nate's mail, chest, heart, and out through his back. Blood spewed forward and behind. Nate cried out ... and then he slumped, his corpse floating in midair.

Sister Aspertine screamed. Her hands clutched her hair, shrieking, and she trembled all over. The clouds darkened, the golden light and angelic voices dimmed, and the face of God vanished. Nate crashed limply to the ground, still impaled with his own sword.

Sister Aspertine fell back against the sheaves, vainly trying to crawl her way backwards. Nate's crumpled body lay in a twisted lump, red blood pouring from his chest and back. His sword lay drenched, his motionless body impaled. Nate was dead ...

God Himself had killed him!

Or ... *had He?* This was the Field of Dreams! His dreams had raped her. *Had God really come ... to avenge His muddied bride ... or had it all been a dream?*

Her dream ...?

If so, then ...!

Evil laughter erupted all around her. A great pit opened; she scrambled away from its growing edge, screaming as she fought to keep from falling into its infernal depths. Flames arose from the furnace below, Hellfires, bursting into black plumes, and waves of blistering heat rose before her. A great, wicked man's shape rose from the thick, acrid fumes, massively horned, with a whipping, forked tail behind him. Satanic teeth gnashed, threatening sadistic fury, as flaming eyes devoured her.

"Murderess!" Lucifer cried in a voice of pure wickedness, shaking a monstrous pitchfork high over his horns, huge wings of darkness unfurling behind him, with a flaming finger of guilt pointed straight toward her.

Sister Aspertine screamed.

The glare of ultimate devilry stared down upon her: *her master, her jailor, her torturer for all eternity. She deserved it! She'd murdered ...!*

No! Nate wasn't dead! He couldn't be dead! She'd only dreamed it ...!

But he'd dreamed of having sex with her, and Sister Aspertine couldn't deny that they'd had sex, that she was no longer virginal ...!

Did that mean that Nate was really dead ...?

Was everything here a dream ... or did the Field of Dreams make everything they dreamed real ...?

Sister Aspertine rolled onto her knees, reaching out to support herself ... and she realized as her white robe fell off that she was still naked. With a whim, she wished herself fully dressed, and her old, ragged habit instantly clothed her. Yet she didn't like ruined clothes; with a forceful wish, Sister Aspertine wished for her habit repaired, and suddenly her crumpled habit transformed into perfect newness ... and her ironed wimple again crowned her head. She glanced at her new garments astounded; her new habit was clean and stiff, as if previously unworn ... *and she'd gotten it with only a wish!*

But ... was it real? Any more real than the devil come to drag her to his lakes of lamentation?

Sister Aspertine clasped her hands and squeezed her eyes shut. Ardently she prayed, directly to God, to banish these dreams, to make everything false go away. The laughter of Lucifer filled her ears, but she ignored him, blotting out all but her devotion to God, her subservience to His will.

The evil laughter died. Sister Aspertine kept praying, but finally she opened her eyes and looked: *the huge devil was gone.* The infernal pit was gone. Even the white clouds were gone, the normal dark sky with its few dim stars lay shining above her. She was surrounded by a field of golden wheat, kneeling on a bed of crushed stalks, and behind her ... *Nate was still dead.* He lay unmoving, ghastly, his blood dripping, soaking into his clothes and the sand.

Jay Palmer

Sister Aspertine hesitated. At the end of Nate's dream, she was still naked, her virginity broken. Unless God had repaired her, she was still violated. *Could she restore herself?* She pushed the thought aside; Nate was dead, and if she didn't save him before her dream ended, then she'd truly be his murderer. *How could she explain that to the others?* Well, Roselyn might understand, but the support of a pagan demoness wouldn't relieve her guilt. Even if they let her live, her murderess' soul would be forever banned from God's Heaven.

Yet ... *to bring the dead back to life? How could she do that? Only God could perform such miracles! How could she blaspheme against His just providence ... and still expect mercy upon her traitorous soul ...?*

She was damned either way!

She had no choice. *She wasn't a killer.* In her stiff, new habit, Sister Aspertine stood, faced Nate's corpse, and raised her arms.

"Arise!" Sister Aspertine commanded, and his limp form, bulging eyes unseeing, floated up, lifting off the sheaves. She waited until he rose above her, back to the position that he'd held before she'd willed God to impale him. All of the starlight seemed to shine solely upon him, hovering dead, and Sister Aspertine clenched her jaw, determined not to muddle this chance.

"Sword: out!"

The red sword slid from his chest and fell to the sheaves beneath him. Yet Nate didn't react, and his misplaced armor remained in place.

"Armor: off!"

She didn't know much about armor, but she couldn't imagine it'd be conducive to healing. His tunic was still drenched in blood.

180

"Clean!" Sister Aspertine shouted, and the blood vanished. A rip still remained in his tunic, but she felt that she was pressing her luck and being too picky ... purposefully delaying the command that she feared to give. Yet it was now or never ... *she mustn't trial God's will.*

Sister Aspertine swallowed hard and stared at Nate. *"Heal ... and live!"*

Nate's eyes closed, then popped open, and he gasped, his expression horrified.

Sister Aspertine crossed herself, stunned by her own audacity. Miraculously, it'd worked; *Nate was alive ...!*

Unaware if she was consciously wishing it or not, she floated Nate down toward her ... and right into her tightest embrace.

"You're alive!" she whispered, squeezing him tight. *"Thank Heaven!"*

Nate pushed against her grip, struggling to free himself, staring up at the dim stars.

"Wha ... what happened ...?" Nate gasped. "I ... I thought I saw ... *Him ...!"*

"Well, ... never lust after His bride!" Sister Aspertine scolded.

Nate's face paled, and he kept looking up at the sky. Sister Aspertine released him and turned away to hide her troubled smile.

"But ... m-m-my sword ...!" he stammered.

"It's right there ... on the ground ... drenched with your blood," Sister Aspertine said, still slightly trembling with shock, and at her own audacity. "If you want to keep it out of you, keep your mouth shut ... about whatever transpired ... here ... or anywhere else!"

"I will ...!" Nate promised. "... I ... I'm sorry!"

"We'd best get back to the others," Sister Aspertine said.

"I mean it," Nate said. "I'd never ... force ...!"

"God's will is ... forgiveness," Sister Aspertine said firmly, although the lump in her throat almost gagged her. "Speak of it no more."

Chapter 11

Divine Revelations

ELOISE

Nate … and Sister Aspertine …?

Eloise gaped at Nate and Sister Aspertine, both naked on the sheaves, staring back at them with wild expressions. Suddenly they slid magically away, faster than human legs could chase.

"*Nate …!*" Phil shouted, pushing aside the stalks.

"*How …?*" Karl asked.

"Where are they going?" Elaina asked.

"*Eloise …!*" Karl shouted angrily.

"*I didn't do it!*" Eloise defended.

Karl hesitated, then looked at Elaina.

"I couldn't do it!" Elaina said.

Karl frowned, but then he glanced at the others. Henry looked horrified, Alarika and Roselyn amused, and Phil looked stunned beyond belief, still staring at the distant point where his naked brother and equally-naked Sister Aspertine had vanished.

"Squire, ignore what you just saw …," Karl said.

"She's a nun!" Phil shouted. *"How could he ...?"*

"She's a woman ... finally," Roselyn smirked, lowering Hel's sword. "Perhaps now she'll be more tolerable."

"B-b-but ...!" Phil stammered.

"Do we go after them?" Elaina asked.

"No point," Karl said. "Neither of them can shift the ground. We'll give them some ... privacy."

"Time is wasting ...!" Roselyn snapped.

"We found the 'crack in the world'," Karl said. "We're not leaving without the Seer."

"I'll dance for him," Elaina offered, and both Karl and Roselyn nodded.

After they walked back, Eloise looked about, worriedly, at the thick, countless stalks of wheat. *How could Elaina dance in this?*

Suddenly a huge circle of wheat liquefied before them, and they all drew back. Golden stalks melted, dripped into a pool, and flowed into a molten lake of rippling gold. Its surface stilled and solidified, and became hard, cold metal.

"Who did that?" Karl demanded.

"I didn't," Elaina said.

"Someone ... else ...?" Eloise suggested, looking around. "Maybe we're not alone ...?"

"Alarika ...?" Karl asked.

"I wish I could ...!" Alarika started.

"Not you," Karl said. "Which Egyptian god could do this?"

"Our gods can do anything," Alarika said.

"You said your evil god was Set," Karl said. "Is Set here?"

"This is their land ...," Alarika started.

"No, I mean: *here!*" Karl said. "Before, it was Loki; he brought us to Yggdrasil ...!"

"I know nothing of your Loki," Alarika said.

"If Set were here, would we know it?" Karl asked.

"If Set were here, we'd be dead," Alarika said.

"No one knows how gods think," Eloise said.

"I do," Roselyn said. "I've lived with them ... as practically one of them."

Eloise glared, but Roselyn ignored her.

"What do we ...?" Karl began.

"Ignore them," Roselyn said. "Gods don't care about humans, and it's wasteful to worry about them."

"Should Elaina dance?" Karl asked.

"We don't know who made this dance floor," Eloise warned.

"Whoever it was, they could've melted us just as easily," Karl said.

"We must find the Seer ... *at any cost!*" Roselyn argued. "He'll have the answers."

"*Yes, he will!*" Eloise snapped.

"Enough, daughter!" Elaina said. "You, too, Roselyn ... *if you want my help ...!*"

Both girls startled, but Elaina ignored them, slipped off her shoes, and stepped barefoot onto the cold golden circle. With her usual grace, she tested its smooth, shiny metal surface, sliding her toes across it. Then, suddenly music erupted all around them: harps, flutes, drums, and trumpets sang a loud and lively melody, bursting from the very air around them.

Eloise frowned. Someone powerful was giving them everything that they wanted; water, food, a place for Elaina to dance, and now music. *But beings with power didn't give gifts without expectations ....!*

The smooth, golden floor proved perfect for dancing, and Elaina never danced better. A flame couldn't have flitted more gracefully, or steam hotter, or puff of breath more lightly. She leapt as if wings lifted her, and spun as if she'd drill herself into the ground. Eloise wished that she were as nimble ... or half as mesmerizing ... as her mother. Yet envy couldn't overpower her immense pride; *her mother was magnificent!*

However, after several incredible flips, kicks, and a dazzling rising spiral that left all the men breathless, Elaina ended her dance without a smile.

"I ...," Elaina began, her voice was weak. "I don't know ... what happened. He was ..., I mean, he wasn't ..."

"*Wasn't ...?*" Roselyn asked.

"Wasn't there," Elaina said. "I saw him, the Seer, but he was ... hollow."

"*Hollow ...?*" Roselyn demanded.

"More like ... transparent," Elaina said. "I called to him ... but it was like .... he couldn't hear me."

"Does that mean anything ... to anyone?" Karl asked.

Eloise, Roselyn, and Alarika all shook their heads. Henry looked helpless, and Phil seemed oblivious; he kept glancing back in the direction of his brother and Sister Aspertine.

"Do you know where the Seer is?" Karl asked, and he sighed when Elaina shook her head. "We still haven't rested. Get some sleep; we'll head out once we're refreshed."

"What about ...?" Phil asked.

"We won't leave without them ... or the Seer," Karl said.

"Come, husband," Eloise said. "Let's rest ... in private."

Until this moment, Eloise didn't know if Karl would come with her. He hesitated, then stiffened, walked toward her, and held out his arm. Eloise took her husband's arm and strode at his side, pushing together into the tall wheat. Just before they'd opened the 'crack in the world', Karl had warned Roselyn that he'd never again be with her if she murdered that innocent child, and then she'd sacrificed the boy. Now he'd proven that he'd meant it.

Eloise had her husband back!

She felt happy as a queen!

Suddenly Karl stopped, before they'd taken three steps into the stalks, and his arm jerked, as if to pull free. Eloise looked at him worriedly, but he was looking at her even stranger.

"Where'd that come from?" Karl demanded.

Eloise wondered what he was talking about, and then noticed that he was looking at her hair … *no, something else!* Eloise lifted her hand and felt … on top of her head …

"What … is it?" Eloise's voice trembled.

"It's a crown," Karl said. "A jeweled crown!"

Eloise examined it with her fingers, and then lifted it off her head; a high, thin silver crown encrusted with perfect rows of diamonds, emeralds, rubies, and sapphires. Never had she seen a crown so beautiful or masterfully made …! It was priceless …!

"It's her!" Roselyn shouted.

"What …?" Karl asked, glancing back at the others.

"Sister Aspertine floated away," Roselyn said. "Well, we all wanted that, and the food and water, and her mother needed a place to dance, and music to dance to … but only Eloise would put a crown upon her head …!"

"No, I didn't …!" Eloise argued.

"It might not be conscious," Elaina said. "Try something."

Eloise spread her arms helplessly, disbelieving that they could believe her responsible for all the strange happenings.

"Wife, what have you always wanted ... but we couldn't afford?" Karl asked.

Eloise shrugged, and suddenly a comfortable softness draped over her: Eloise was wearing a beautiful, perfect ermine cloak.

"See ...!" Roselyn said.

Eloise ignored her, experimentally waving her hand ... and showered them all with golden rings, jeweled necklaces, and silver bracelets ...

"Enough!" Karl said. "We don't need treasures. Bring Athelwynne here ... to us."

Eloise hesitated ... and the last of her jewelry rained onto the wheat. She glanced at it, then strode out onto Elaina's golden dance floor, trying to feel determined. Since her first attempts to cast a spell, she'd dreamed of being able to master powerful magics like the Seer. Yet she'd never done it, not even on the Magic Isle.

Could she do it here?

Did this land grant unlimited power?

Eloise lifted her hands, her fingers trembling with anticipation. *Athelwynne could help her ... if anyone could! He knew the Lady better than any Druid, and he'd insure that Karl could enter the Elysian Fields ...!*

A soft prayer to the Lady whispered from her lips. She squeezed her eyes shut, summoned all the strength that she had, and reached for the magic.

As easily as a wish, Eloise felt the myriad worlds: Magic. Emotion. Spirit. Reality. Godly. Sensations. All the essences of the universe that her mother communed with, half of which blended together until most humans couldn't sense their differences. Other worlds, seldom felt, appeared before her, more distinct than she'd ever sensed them. Eloise was a goddess, simultaneously comprising every level of being. Just seeing all the worlds open before her filled her with wonder, unfamiliar sensations that she'd never dreamed of, and understandings that she'd never achieved, all of which she'd never forget.

This must be how Athelwynne casts spells!

Yet she couldn't lose herself in amazement; Eloise focused ... and willed her magic into fruition.

Overlapping waves of myriad universes churned and shifted at her slightest whim, and a new glow arose and expanded: a bright, solar light erupted, blinding them.

"*Seer!*" Roselyn shouted.

Eloise opened her eyes, stunned by the ease of her casting. Athelwynne the Seer stood before her, alight, shining with a bright white luminescence, his very skin aglow.

She'd done it!

"*Athelwynne ...!*" Eloise called.

Yet the Seer didn't move, didn't even acknowledge her or Roselyn. He stared blindly, not reacting at all.

"What's wrong with him?" Karl demanded.

"His body's here ...," Elaina said. "Where's his soul?"

"*His soul ...?*" Roselyn demanded.

"*Quiet!*" Eloise shushed them.

She stared at Athelwynne, his handsome, familiar face, his iron-black hair and eyes, identical to the friend that she'd last seen before the Gates of Valhalla. This wasn't her first spell that hadn't fully worked. Whatever part of him was missing, she'd find it ...

Eloise concentrated, and visualized several levels of existence about her, and willed them together. Every world reappeared, bowing to her determination. She couldn't fail; whatever magics had empowered her, she'd use every ounce of strength that she had to restore the Seer. *Everything depended on him ...!*

Yet nothing happened. The Seer remained, glowing like a lantern, but not blinking or displaying any sign of awareness. Eloise strained, concentrating to her utmost, and finally she fell back, exhausted. *She'd failed.*

"My turn," Roselyn said, and she strode forward, drew back a hand, and slapped Athelwynne right across his glowing cheek. *"Wake up!* We came for you, and we can't go back without you!"

The Seer's jaw fell open, and a voice emerged from him, but it wasn't his deep, snappish tone; unheard since they'd left Her at the Well of Mimir, the beautiful voice of the Lady of the Druids channeled through him.

"Help Athelwynne, my dear friends!" the Lady of the Druids' soft, sweet voice urgently implored. *"His soul's been stolen! Trapped ... in a box ... with eye-holes!"*

"My Lady!" Eloise screamed, and she fell to her knees.

"No!" the Lady of the Druids cried. *"They're taking him back! Beware Anubis! Beware his box!"*

As She spoke, the Seer's light momentarily dimmed, and slowly Athelwynne faded like a vanished dream. In an expanding smoke ring, the Seer dissipated until he was gone ... and Her voice faded with him.

"Lady ...!" Eloise screamed.

"Seer ...!" Roselyn screamed at the same instant, but both screeched in vain.

Roselyn waved her hands through the space that the Seer had stood in, now empty.

"Damn!" Karl cursed.

"A memory box ...!" Alarika exclaimed.

"What ...?" Elaina asked.

"An Egyptian memory box," Alarika said. "There're old, and brightly decorated, sometimes with tiny gems. One, or sometimes two holes are in it, positioned like the pupils of eyes amid the decorations, so that people can look inside and see their dearest memories. Legends talk about cursed memory boxes, capable of capturing the Ba and the Ka."

"Ba and Ka!" Karl exclaimed. "You told us about those!"

"And Anubis was a god, wasn't he?" Henry asked.

"Anubis is a god," she corrected him. "A fell ... and powerful god ... with the head of a jackal ... conceived, born, and raised in the House of the Dead."

Roselyn lifted Hel's sword, fury in her eyes.

"I'll sever that jack...!" Roselyn began.

"No!" Karl shouted. "Say nothing about their gods ... especially nothing to anger them!"

"At least we know that the Seer's here ... and alive," Phil said.

"We know why he couldn't escape," Roselyn said.

"And the Lady knows that he's here," Eloise added.

"We know what's trapped him," Elaina said.

"And who owns the box," Henry said.

"And we know where he is," Karl said. "The Lady said *'They're taking him back!'* No commonplace sorcery could've tricked Athelwynne, and he's been taken by more than one ...."

"We have to seek ... the Egyptian gods ...!" Eloise said.

"But ... what will we do ... when we find them?" Elaina asked.

"We bow to their will," Alarika said. "Every mortal combined is nothing before the power of our gods."

"We've fought gods before ... and won," Eloise said.

"These are *my* gods!" Alarika protested.

"Nobody's fighting anyone ... not if we can help it," Karl said.

"We just need to free him," Eloise said. "Restore his soul; he'll do the rest."

"Loki would've defeated us, had Athelwynne not fought with us," Roselyn said. "Yet Loki bested him outside of Niflhiem; that's how he got here."

"And he won't be facing just one god, but an entire pantheon ...!" Alarika added.

"Impossible odds have never deterred us," Karl said, glancing at each one of them. "We'll deal with whatever we must, when we must ... and do ... *what Eric Bjornson would do.*"

He faced each companion, and didn't shift to the next until they'd nodded to him. He came to Alarika last.

"I won't fight my gods," Alarika said.

"No person of faith would," Elaina said. "We just need your help to reach them."

Slowly Alarika nodded.

Standing so close to each other, Eloise looked up at Roselyn, and the glare that exchanged between them was hard, defiant, and filled with silent enmity. Sadly, Eloise turned away first; her spellcasting had tired her, too much to face a former Valkyrie wearing divine armor and carrying a goddess' weapon ... even in the Field of Dreams.

"Come, my husband," Eloise said softly. "As you commanded, let us rest."

Frowning, Karl held out his hand, and as she took it, he led her deep into the wheat, away from the others.

Finally he pushed back a thick row of wheat stalks, and laid on them to flatten them, and then he held out his hand to her.

"You and Roselyn are rivals no more," Karl said warningly. "She and I are through. We can't afford another war between you two."

"Valkyrie never stop fighting," Eloise reminded him. "Valkyrie avenge ..."

"No vengeance ... from her or the Lady ...!" Karl said.

"I won't ensorcell Roselyn ... as long as she helps find Athelwynne," Eloise said.

"Roselyn wounded a youth before we entered Yggdrasil," Karl said. "You weren't there. After we'd escaped from Eorl Sir Guldwin's camp, Roselyn shot a camp-boy ... to spare us from having to kill two dozen children. But only Reginleif ... the Valkyrie ... could've murdered that boy to open the 'crack in the world'. I never loved Reginleif."

"And I've never loved you more," Eloise said, and with a wave of her hand, Karl rose, and the wheat stalks beneath him became a wide, sturdy bed, covered with thin blankets, and the stalks around them grew ten feet high to encircle them with privacy.

Eloise kissed Karl lovingly.

She had her husband back!

Jay Palmer

194

Chapter 12

Backward Dreams

KARL

Karl smiled: *Eloise was still the most talented lover that he'd ever known!* She'd do anything, and constantly managed to surprise him with new tricks. Karl often suspected that Seren shared with Eloise her professional secrets of how to please men. Having spent most of her life working in a brothel, Karl suspected that Rafe was the only man in England more satisfied than he.

They awoke entwined, as they hadn't awoken in years. Although the mother of his children, Eloise's mysteries had separated them, even while they'd shared the same bed. Yet those days were ended; Karl knew her secrets now, and while he'd never approve of her having a secret life, or of her being a Druid, he felt certain that she'd revealed all that she'd formerly hidden.

Besides, learning Druid magic couldn't have been easy; *she couldn't have had time to do all the things that he'd feared she'd been doing!*

He watched Eloise's eyes flutter open, and tried not to notice how much fuller her cheeks were than when he'd first met her. He rarely noticed; she hadn't filled out as much as he had, and he usually saw her exactly as she'd looked the first night they'd made love, in the Silver Swan Inn in Madrone, pert, youthful, and glowing with pale skin and wanton desires. She was the perfect wife … and mother of their children, and now there'd be no more unexplained absences.

Her eyes found him, only seconds before her lips did, and Karl was soon gasping with pleasure again.

Eventually the heaviness of his armor replaced his lightness of culmination; Eloise loved to leave him reeling. Then she'd tried to magic herself a new dress … and failed. *Would her magic return?* Karl didn't care. The Seer was with the gods of Egypt. Alarika knew where they had to go, and soon they'd leave this crazy Field of Dreams.

Over her white robe, Eloise put on her ermine cloak and her new, priceless gem-studded crown; apparently creations didn't vanish when the magic passed from their creator. She took his arm, and together they walked to find the others.

As Karl and Eloise pushed through the sheaves, Roselyn snapped to face them, one hand on Hel's sword. Seeing them, she frowned, then laid back down upon the carpet where she'd been sleeping. The others didn't even awaken. Phil and Henry were snoring not far from Roselyn, and on a cloth between them lay a pile of the gleaming jewelry that Eloise had rained upon them. Alarika and Elaina were sleeping close to the table, some stalks heavy with boughs of grain hanging over them.

"Well, look who's returning!" Eloise smirked.

To Karl's delight, Sister Aspertine and Nate slowly wandered back, wading through wheat up to their chests. Both were fully-dressed, and neither smiled; Karl was glad that they didn't have to go looking for them.

As they got closer, Karl noticed that Nate looked downcast, and walked rigidly, absently plowing his path, knocking stalks aside. Sister Aspertine appeared as lithe as Elaina, skirting around the clumps and pushing back stalks with her hands, but she also kept her head bowed. Her white robe was gone, and her deep blue habit appeared to have been washed and mended, but her cheeks were blushing pink, and her eyes glared. Neither she nor Nate looked directly at anyone.

Karl didn't know what to say; *he was Nate's knight, not his father.* Farmer Tiller would deal with his son's forbidden indiscretions with a nun; Karl had enough women-problems for one journey. Yet Eloise hailed them, and her laughing voice awoke the others.

Phil jumped up, and at first sight of his brother, he frowned. Nate saw Phil's expression and stopped, hanging his head and approaching no closer. Henry stood more slowly, pausing to tie up their pile of jewelry inside the cloth.

"Good morning, Sister Aspertine," Elaina said as she got closer. "So nice to see you ..."

"... dressed ...," Roselyn added with a smirk.

"We were ensorcelled by the magic of this godless land," Sister Aspertine said.

"I didn't think that nuns enjoyed magic," Eloise said.

Sister Aspertine's eyes flared, and she started to reply, but Alarika cut her off.

"This land isn't godless!" Alarika snapped, and then she turned to Eloise. "Leave her be. Women should claim what we want, just like any man."

"You'd make a good Valkyrie," Roselyn said to Alarika. "Come, we're gathered; let's start."

"Start ...?" Sister Aspertine inquired. "I thought we were going to rest ..."

"Rest ...?" Karl asked. "What have you been doing for the last eight hours ...?"

"Eight hours ...?" Sister Aspertine asked, and Nate looked plainly surprised. "We've only been gone ... well, less than an hour."

"We need to go," Roselyn said.

"Very well," Sister Aspertine said. "Rested or not, we must leave at once. It's a blasphemous land."

"Which way?" Alarika asked.

"I'll dance," Elaina offered.

"Good," Karl said. "We know why it didn't work before; the Seer's been separated from his soul ..."

"What ...?" Sister Aspertine gasped.

"The Lady of the Druids contacted us," Eloise told her. "Athelwynne looked into an Egyptian memory box of Anubis, and it stole his soul. We need to find that box ... and free the Seer."

"Mortals dare not defy Anubis," Alarika warned.

"Valkyrie don't fear gods," Roselyn said.

"We won't take any risks unless necessary," Karl said. "First, we've got to find them ... and him."

"Eat first," Phil said, still glaring at Nate. "Pack supplies."

"Agreed," Karl said, and he turned to the table.

Nate stepped forward, and Phil angrily grabbed his arm, as if about to hit him. Nate didn't resist, only looked down, his expression sad. In silence, he reached for a henket.

Their feast had returned, fresh, steaming foods covered wide platters and filled their bowls, and tankards and pitchers brimmed. Eloise described everything that had happened since they'd seen them *'enjoying each other's company'*. With a smile, she described Elaina's dance and her failure to locate the Seer. Then Eloise explained how she suddenly wielded powers as great as any god, and used her power to summon Athelwynne. She recited the words of the Lady of the Druids precisely, and related what they believed that Her words meant.

"Can you still do magic?" Sister Aspertine asked Eloise.

"I wish!" Eloise laughed, and she pointed to the table and waved ... yet nothing happened.

"I didn't think so," Sister Aspertine said as Eloise looked startled. "Nate got his ... dream ... first, and then I got mine. But mine's over, thank God, and obviously Eloise had hers."

Henry experimentally stretched his hand out over the table and wiggled his fingers, and nothing happened.

"It's not me," Henry said.

"We shouldn't be trying!" Sister Aspertine said. "Each person's dream makes puppets of the others; we should leave here now ... before this ungodliness curses us!"

Alarika waved her hands mystically: nothing. Phil tried next, and then Roselyn ... without success.

"Stop that!" Sister Aspertine ordered, but none minded her.

Karl shrugged, held up his hand, and suddenly his favorite drinking horn, which he'd left behind in Castle Bristlen, materialized in it. Karl staggered, and almost dropped it, but then he held it firmly, concentrated, and it filled with clear liquid. Karl eyed its clear contents, and then tasted it.

"The Water of Life ...!" Karl smiled. "It's real!"

"No, it isn't," Sister Aspertine said. "Can't you see? These … things … are deceptions … trying to tempt us."

"Can you fetch my dresses … from Castle Bristlen?" Eloise asked Karl excitedly. "Sister Aspertine restored her habit; I should've done that!"

Karl shrugged again, and with a wave of his arm, a dozen royal gowns appeared, laying atop the sheaves. Eloise laughed and ran to gather them.

"Begging your pardon, I could use newer boots," Henry said, and Karl obliged, transforming his old, worn boots into stiff new ones.

"Only God should have such powers!" Sister Aspertine scolded. "Rafe sent me to warn you: men shouldn't play with powers like this! It's blasphemy, and will corrupt your souls …!"

"It's just dreams," Karl said.

"It's not that simple!" Sister Aspertine said. "This table appeared when we got here; we all wanted it, but Nate must've made it, and it's still here!"

"Permanence is best," Henry smiled, examining his new boots.

"Would you say that if you'd just lost your virginity?" Sister Aspertine demanded. "Not because it was given, or taken, but because someone dreamed it away? Every second that we remain here, we're Karl's puppets. He can kill us … and bring us back to life." She glanced at Eloise and Roselyn. "We live … and love … based on his dreams, even if he's not consciously willing it!"

Eloise and Roselyn exchanged a worried glance.

"I notice that you two aren't fighting anymore," Sister Aspertine said to them. "Is that willingly … or Karl's dream?"

Eloise and Roselyn startled, and then both looked at Karl.

"I didn't do anything!" Karl said.

"How do you know?" Sister Aspertine asked. "Can you control ... your dreams?"

Karl looked momentarily worried, and Roselyn and Eloise both frowned.

"Eat up!" Karl said. "Pack whatever we can. We're leaving."

Everyone started gathering their things; Eloise grabbed a clean dress and slipped behind a growth of wheat. Soon she emerged in her favorite red gown, long and flowing around her. The rest of them stood ready.

"I need quiet," Elaina said as she pulled off her slippers.

Upon the golden dance floor, Elaina danced again, wonderfully, and Karl turned away ... so that he couldn't watch. Karl enjoyed watching Elaina dance, and admired her grace and beauty ... more than he should appreciate his wife's mother. Her mature dancer's figure couldn't help but stimulate, and he forced thoughts of her from his mind. He was glad to be back with Eloise, although he regretted breaking faith with Roselyn; he didn't know how he'd get over his feelings for her. She was physically as lovely as the first day that he'd seen her in Castle Bristlen ... unchanged, while the rest of them had aged eight years. Yet Reginleif wasn't Roselyn; she was powerful, willful, and dominant, a queen worshiped as a goddess by millions of Yggdrasil's warrior-elite. While he'd struggled to meet impossible royal demands and raise his children, Roselyn had learned to expect her every wish willingly-granted. If only she'd remained as sweet as she used to be, so soft and gentle ...

"Karl ...?" Roselyn whispered.

Karl turned to find Roselyn looking at him while the others watched Elaina.

"Reginleif …," Karl replied, and she winced.

"I deserve that," Roselyn said. "I pushed you, but … please understand; a few years of fighting in Valhalla will change your opinion of what I did."

"You murdered that boy," Karl said.

"What murder …?" Roselyn asked. "All those Egyptians that you call dead … they live here! Millions of Norsemen live in Valhalla. Niflhiem holds countless more. The Seer describes the Elysian Fields as endless gardens filled with happy people … Druids who died. We both know what Heaven is. Murder is nothing but a transition; no Valkyrie can change that."

"People with the right to choose their faith shouldn't suffer others to choose when their life ends," Karl said.

"You're right," Roselyn said. "I'm sorry. But things can work out; I didn't choose to be killed by Loki, but I wouldn't take it back. The only thing I'd take back … is you."

Karl smiled, and Roselyn smiled back, and they leaned forward to kiss.

"Karl …!" Eloise screamed.

Karl looked over; Elaina's dance had ended, and every companion was standing … watching Karl and Roselyn reunite.

Eloise looked furious, and she raised her arms …

"Don't …!" Sister Aspertine shouted. "This isn't real! It's just a dream!"

"What …?" Roselyn asked.

"Listen to what you just said!" Sister Aspertine shouted to Roselyn. "Valkyrie don't apologize … except in Karl's dream!"

Roselyn gasped, and then she turned to face Karl, murder in her eyes.

"Are you … manipulating …?" she demanded.

"*No!*" Karl shouted, and he stepped back, looking at them. "*I'm not ...!*"

The others all glared disbelieving.

You think this is my dream?" Karl shouted. "*I don't want to be here! My dream is going back home! My dream is all of us ... in England, in Castle Bristlen, holding my children in my arms, and laughing with Rafe and Seren. I never wanted to come to Egypt, and I don't want to be here now! I want to be home!*"

A brilliant light shined down from above and blinded them. After days of dim starlight, the bright sunlight gleamed, making them blink and shield their eyes. They heard a terrible rumble, like saws grinding, and someone was hammering metal, and then voices shouted in surprise, and cheers rose. Between his fingers, Karl's eyes adjusted to see several dozen workers throwing down their tools and rushing to greet them.

"*Karl ...!*" Rafe shouted. "*Eloise! Roselyn! You're back!*"

Karl's eyes focused on the impossible ....

He and all the other companions were standing ... inside the courtyard of Castle Bristlen ... in England ...!

They were home again ...!

Chapter 13

Unwanted Returns

ROSELYN

Staggered, Roselyn glanced about, hearing distant seagulls crying in the cool, moist English breeze.

Was this real?

Workers stood, stopped in their tracks to stare at them, all around the courtyard of Castle Bristlen. The once-great gate had been their center of activity; the ruins of the old gates lay stacked aside, leaving its wide entrance open. Logs were laid out, men with saws and adzes had been shaping new beams to replace the old. Dogs were barking, the blacksmith hammering, and the familiar low, gray clouds of England dotted a bright sky rich with seagulls.

"Karl, what have you done?" Roselyn gasped. *"Where are we?"*

"Daddy!" shrill voices shrieked, and two little kids ran forward, arms spread wide.

"Eric! Roselyn!" Karl exclaimed, and he knelt and opened his arms, and both kids jumped into his embrace.

Rafe's heavy arm seized Roselyn in a loving hug; *no einherjar would've dared touch her so!*

"How …?" Rafe demanded, and then he reached out one hand and grabbed Phil's shoulder, shaking it gladly. "It's wonderful!"

"No!" Roselyn shouted. *"We're not here! We can't be!"*

Rafe looked confused, but his other hand grabbed Eloise, and he pulled her in close.

"W-w-what happened?" Eloise stammered.

"We're home!" Nate exclaimed.

"It's a dream!" Sister Aspertine shouted. "Karl's dreaming of Castle Bristlen …!"

"We made it!" Henry shouted, and he greeted several workers with friendly waves.

"No, this can't be …!" Eloise said.

"Mistress!" screamed Edith's young voice. *"Mistress Seren, there're back!"*

Roselyn pushed free of Rafe and seized Karl's shoulder.

"What about Athelwynne …?" Roselyn challenged. *"Why did you bring us here …? How am I going to get back into Valhalla …?"*

Karl looked up at her, still hugging his children, his expression perplexed.

"Take us back!" Roselyn ordered. *"We're not done: take us back!"*

"Stop it!" Elaina shouted, seizing Roselyn's arm, which was grasping Karl's. "Don't make it worse! We need to know what's real … before we do anything!"

Roselyn released Karl, but maintained her frown. Everything looked familiar; she knew the dirt that they were standing upon. She knew these stone walls. Seagull-cries filled the familiar breeze over the Atlantic Ocean. Rafe's face was slowly healing, no longer covered by a bandage, but his slash still pink and tender-looking. Everything looked like it should've, if they'd been gone for months. Yet Roselyn wasn't an expert on healing; in Valhalla, Odin's rainbow healed every bump and scrape.

"Eloise!" Seren cried. *"Karl! Roselyn!"*

Limping on a cane, with Edith supporting her other arm, Seren came down the short steps, and hurried toward them as best she could.

"Everyone, stay calm," Elaina said. "We'll figure this out ..."

"I hope we are here," Sister Aspertine said.

Greetings were warm but hesitant. The companions didn't know what to think. Roselyn scowled, but she couldn't refuse to hug Seren, who had joyous tears in her eyes. Nate and Phil hugged their little sister tightly, and Rafe sent a page in to set out drinks and have the cooks start dinner.

"We're not in debt anymore!" Rafe beamed at Karl. "When we went to see Eric, I filled all six bota bags, and I've been selling them ... the Water of Life ... at exorbitant prices!"

"Athelwynne safe?" Seren asked.

"We didn't ...!" Roselyn started.

"We saw him ... kind of," Karl said, standing with a child on each arm. "Perhaps ... we should explain ... inside."

"But ...?" Roselyn started.

"If this is a dream, then we'll wake up soon enough," Karl assured her.

Roselyn scowled, but she allowed the others to lead her inside. She touched the doorframe heavily, examining it with her fingers: the scratched door of the keep, which still had several arrowheads embedded in it from the siege, was rough, and promised splinters for those careless enough to risk them. Roselyn felt the wood's grain, its damaged textures: *no dream was this realistic!*

Karl appeared to be so delighted that Roselyn wanted to punch him. Besides making her say all that nonsense about *'murdering innocents'*, he'd almost kissed her ... *with everyone watching* ... after he'd spent the night having sex with Eloise ... *with everyone trying to not listen.* In Valhalla, a legion of einherjar would've spent a year torturing any man who offended a Valkyrie, and Karl deserved no less.

Smiling servants brought tankards of ale ... and then plates of food. Little Athelwynne seemed delighted by his mother's familiar arms, and Eloise hugged and clutched him warmly. They sat around their huge, familiar table, set before their baronial thrones, with no pretension of formality. At Karl's command, Nate told their story, and most of Castle Bristlen stood listening, mesmerized. A few knew the three sailors that'd died, and Rafe promised that a requiem mass would be said for each of them, and that Rishard would be welcomed and cared for, when he returned. Sister Aspertine told Rafe where they'd left him to convalesce, and Rafe promised to send a messenger to the nuns at that Italian hospital right away.

Nate told their tale even better than he'd told it to Alarika's army of thieves, as no translator was needed. Every listener gasped and thrilled at Nate's dramatic recitation, and every belly was filled before they reached Elaina dancing in the Field of Wheat.

"So ... are ... we ...?" Rafe asked.

"We real," Seren said.

"The Field of Dreams projects illusions better than Utgard-Loki," Phil said.

"There's only one way to know for sure," Roselyn said. "Karl, wish us back."

Every face frowned.

"We have to rescue Athelwynne," Eloise agreed.

"No," Karl said.

"You promised ...!" Roselyn shouted.

"We can't leave him soulless ...!" Eloise argued.

"Must save Seer!" Seren agreed.

"... And you two are going to get us killed before we get anywhere near Athelwynne!" Karl said to Eloise and Roselyn. "Your ... jealously ... you never should've made me choose!"

"You chose long ago ...!" Roselyn said.

"When you married ...!" Eloise agreed.

"I don't know if this is a dream or not," Karl said. "It's the best dream, if it is. But we can't live the rest of our lives not knowing. We go back, but until we return here again, no rivalries ..." Karl turned to glance at Nate and Phil, "... between anyone!"

Roselyn, Eloise, Nate, and Phil all nodded.

Karl took little Athelwynne in his arms, held and kissed him, and then handed him to Seren. Then he hugged and kissed little Eric and little Roselyn, and sent them to their Uncle Rafe.

"Sister Aspertine, you're doing a wonderful job," Rafe said.

"T-thank you, sir," Sister Aspertine stammered.

"The same goes to you, Henry," Rafe continued, and Henry nodded. "Alarika, it was a pleasure to meet you, and the hospitality of Castle Bristlen will always be open to you." Alarika nodded. "The rest of you, come back safe. Take no chances: *do what Eric Bjornson would do.*"

Karl offered his hand, and Rafe shook it.

"Dream or not, I pray you go with God," Rafe said.

Karl nodded, and then he picked up his ale horn and drank before speaking.

"Let this dream be ended!" Karl shouted loudly and clearly. "We're back in the Field of Wheat!"

Every person waited expectantly, eyes darting from face to face.

Nothing happened.

"Try again," Roselyn said.

"It's over!" Karl commanded, his voice raised, looking at the ceiling. "We're not in England! Take us back to Egypt, though the 'crack in the world', to the Field of Wheat!"

Again, nothing happened.

"Are ... are we really here?" Alarika asked.

"If we are here ... then we're not in the Field of Wheat anymore," Elaina said. "Our dreams are ... just dreams."

"*No!*" Roselyn shouted. "*I must be a Valkyrie again!*"

"Give it time," Karl said. "No matter how powerful the dream, eventually you wake up."

Two days later Roselyn mounted the battlements. Alarika stood upon that high perch, where'd she'd spent much of her time, mesmerized by the sea.

"It's incredible," Alarika said, looking out at the endless waters. "So cool here ... and so many trees! I've never known anything but desert."

"Wait until the rainy season," Roselyn said. "Or ... don't. I need to go back. I'd like your company."

Alarika frowned.

"I don't have much worth going back for," Alarika said. "I'd hoped to find my father, but having felt the power of those dreams, I'm sure that he's happy."

"I'll never be happy here," Roselyn said.

"I know," Alarika said. "I've debated going back. I'll be the hero who walked in the lands of our gods."

"I've got to reenter those lands," Roselyn said. "I'd ... appreciate your company."

"I'll ... think about it," Alarika said. "These lands are beautiful, but ... what would I do here?"

"My problem exactly," Roselyn said. "In Yggdrasil, I'm a queen. Here, I'm nothing."

The next day it rained ... which astounded Alarika. She stepped out into it and just stared upwards, her arms wide, until she was drenched.

Farmer Tiller and Sarah arrived in a covered cart, and Nate, Phil, and Edith spent the morning with them. At midday, Karl and Eloise feasted them, and work on the new gate was delayed. Yet Roselyn only scowled.

Two days later, cries of dismay erupted suddenly from the courtyard, and Phil came running inside.

"Countess Roselyn!" Phil shouted, disrupting every conversation. *"Come quick! The Valkyrie fly!"*

Everyone ran outside, where they found every eye looking skyward. Amid the windy blue and scattered clouds flew great beasts, huge horses with vast, flapping wings. They dove and banked towards them. Roselyn cheered, as did many, for these shield-sisters had saved all of their lives, but most of the peasants drew back, silent and fearful.

Eloise and Edith came running out of the great hall, and Karl and Rafe left their tools upon the half-assembled gate and approached.

"Fetch ale!" Rafe shouted to the servants. "Tankards and pitchers! Tap several fresh kegs!"

Roselyn's breath caught, tangled in her nervousness. There was only one reason why her shield-sisters would return ...

Could it be true?

No, she couldn't believe it ...!

The cry of Göll reached their ears, although they were still too distant for any other voice to reach them. Reginleif smiled; up close, Göll's shrieks could blow over strong warriors ... or deafen them.

Her sisters had come!

Delighted, Roselyn ran to the gate. Outside Castle Bristlen, Hrist the Ground-Shaker landed first, and then Mist, enveloped inside her eternal fog, Skeggjöld, wielding her deadly axe, Hildr, their fiercest warrior, Prudr the Mighty, Göll the Shrieker, Herfjötur the Mistress of Bondage, and Hlökk, before whom all men scream. Then came Geirahöd, her long, magical spear-quiver over her shoulder, Randgríðr carrying her great, invulnerable shield, dark, devious Róta, the Wrecker of Plans, and Skögul, the friendliest of the shield-sisters, but whose temper raged like the fires of Muspell.

Roselyn bowed before them.

"Reginleif!" Skeggjöld cried. "The Lady of the Druids contacted Odin, and told him that you located the Seer. The gods of Egypt have agreed to release him, for fear that the Horned Hunter should invade their lands and take him back. Odin has declared your mission accomplished, and we are sent to greet our sister and return her to her duties!"

"No greater happiness could fill my heart!" Roselyn said, smiling so brightly that tears leaked from her eyes.

"Come!" Skeggjöld said. "We feast in Elvidner!"

"May we not offer hospitality?" Karl asked, coming up behind Roselyn.

"Nay, mortal, although we're grateful for the offer," Skeggjöld said. "The Valkyrie celebrate; not all the alehouses of England could drown our thirst."

Roselyn turned just in time to be enveloped in Seren's loving hug, which she gladly returned.

"No be stranger!" Seren whispered in her ear, and Roselyn kissed her wrinkled cheek tenderly.

Rafe hugged her next, and he blessed her, wished her happiness, and promised to pray for her. Roselyn kissed his lips and left him smiling.

Phil came forward, pulling his brother, and both bowed deeply before her. Roselyn smiled upon them, and promised that she'd keep an eye on them, should they ever desire Valhalla. Elaina's hug was hesitant, and Alarika shook hands with her, although her wide eyes seemed affixed to the winged steeds of the Valkyrie.

"Until now ... I wasn't sure ...," Alarika confessed.

"Sisters, this lady is Alarika, who serves the gods of Egypt, but if ever a Valkyrie-worthy maid walked the desert, it is she," Roselyn said, gesturing to her, and all of her sisters examined Alarika closely.

Eloise stepped forward, but she could come no closer.

"Eloise, I return to Valhalla," Roselyn said. "I wish you long life ... and eternal happiness in the Elysian Fields."

Eloise nodded warily.

Then Roselyn turned to face Karl.

"Lover, this Valkyrie waits no longer," Roselyn said. "Choose now; Eloise ... or me."

Karl glanced between them, his wife and the Valkyrie, and shook his head.

"I love everyone here, and none more than my loving wife," Karl said. "Yet, all are safe; my duties here are complete. It's time that I join Eric Bjornson, my brother einherjar."

A brief scream came from Eloise, and Karl knelt before her.

"Wife, you married me knowing … until death we part," Karl said.

"*I love you!*" Eloise sobbed.

Karl rose and kissed her. "I'll love you forever."

Without another word, Karl embraced her, and then each of them, Rafe and Seren the longest, and finally his three children. Then the Valkyrie quickly mounted, Mist behind Skögul, and Roselyn took Mist's stallion. With composure worthy of the attention of every Valkyrie, Karl mounted behind Roselyn, and she spurred hard. Her horse galloped across the wide grass to the edge of the cliff over Demril and leapt out into midair, spreading its wings. Behind her, Karl clutched her tightly, and behind them the other Valkyrie followed, flying up into the sky toward Bifrost, whose rainbow bands shone down to welcome them.

Roselyn smiled; *she was Reginleif again!*

And … Karl had chosen her, and he would be hers forever!

Chapter 14

The Perfect Dance

ELAINA

Elaina wrapped her arms protectively around Eloise as she cried. Sadly, the prediction of Skafti, her long-dead mystical teacher, had come true a second time. For almost a decade, Elaina had avoided her only daughter's company to delay this misery, but now all lay in vain. Karl was gone; *Eloise would know nothing but unhappiness forever ...*

... or was he?

Elaina wondered what really existed around them. Some things seemed odd, but others so real that she couldn't deny their existence. Yet, since they'd passed through the eye of the golden ankh, what the others called the 'crack in the world', how certain could they be of anything? Since entering the Field of Wheat, and becoming subject to each other's dreams, how much reality existed?

Nate's erotic dream had subdued Sister Aspertine, but her reaction, between when the companions had spied her naked and screaming and when they'd returned quiet and peaceful, seemed discordant. Time seemed to have passed differently while they were apart. Eloise's dream of claiming sole right to Karl had come true, and her dream of wielding ultimate magical power had summoned the Seer, and their mutual affection must've reached the Lady of the Druids ... *but how could that have happened?*

Was it all just another dream?

Karl's dream had restored calm to the company, but only until his love of Roselyn had threatened to destroy it, and then he'd brought them back to Castle Bristlen ... *if they were really here.* Then Roselyn had gotten ... *forgiven by Odin, remade into a Valkyrie, and Karl departed with her ... to be hers forever ...!*

Elaina lifted her hand and willed it:

'Glow!'

Brilliance shined from her hand. It radiated like the Seer had ...

"*Eloise* ...!" Elaina whispered.

Eloise looked up and gasped.

"Mother! You're doing magic ...!"

"No," Elaina said. "I'm dreaming."

"What ....?" Eloise asked.

"It's my turn," Elaina said. "Nate, Sister Aspertine, you, Karl, and then Roselyn got their dreams ... and if I hadn't tried to make my hand glow, I might never have known."

"What are you going to do?" Eloise asked.

"Dance," Elaina said. "Dance as I've never danced before."

Elaina waved her hand before her, and suddenly the two of them stood in a beautiful hall, a huge ceiling hanging beautiful golden chandeliers overhead, each shining with a hundred candles. An angled framework of thick beams held up a spotless ceiling from high walls, upon which ornate windows shined from colored glass surrounded by gold. No columns blocked the wide, spacious wooden floor, so smooth and polished that reflections stretched across it.

"Wow!" Eloise mused. "I wish our feast hall looked like this."

"This is the hall I've always dreamed of," Elaina said.

"But, if we're still in the Field of Dreams, then this is just a dream, too," Eloise said.

"Dream of treasures ... and your wealth fades when you awaken," Elaina said. "Dream of wisdom ... and you keep it forever."

Elaina clapped her hands, and a dozen minstrels appeared on benches, Frenchmen, by their dress, their instruments at the ready. As one, the musicians began to play.

"Will you join me?" Elaina smiled.

"Of course," Eloise said, and she rose as her mother did.

"I've always dreamed of dancing with you," Elaina said.

"Are you forcing me to dance?" Eloise asked.

"Who can tell ... inside a dream?" Elaina asked.

Elaina loved the spritely music that her musicians were playing, a lively piping of flutes, the strumming of lutes in perfect tune, soft horns, and the drummers set a perfect beat.

Eloise matched Elaina's first slow, nimble step, balancing with practiced poise, and mimicked her arm movements. They spun into a coordinated routine with exact synchronicity. Elaina knew that she was dreaming; to her knowledge, Eloise had never danced before, never mastered a flowing balance, and knew no exotic poses or how to hold them.

Masterful melodies played, a spiraling tune of precision and artistry, music of saintly harmonies seldom heard by human ears. Elaina tried to ignore that her dreams were enhancing everything she saw and heard; she needed to master the Field of Dreams, not become deceived by it. She poised on her left foot's toes, Eloise upon her right foot, and together they raised their arms and pirouetted.

The ultimate dance: Elaina had always dreamed of it. The goal of every true seer was to fully connect with the universe, to completely become one with it, and to know and understand all. This was her chance, and she thrilled at the opportunity. Elaina and Eloise kicked high in unison, their toes brushing each other.

Elaina pushed aside her awareness of this chance, and her hopes, and even thoughts of her daughter. Elaina and Eloise passed by each other, closely, their bodies swaying, their arms uplifted to the ceiling. Thoughts disturbed seers, so she closed her consciousness and opened her heart to the pure emotion which drives true dancing.

Elaina spun, and she and Eloise joined hands, and together they pranced the length of the hall and back, circling each other in the bliss of the love that they shared. Mother and daughter, torn apart and then reunited, never to be separated again, parted, and then linked hands. Elation effused every leap and turn, each step and bounce.

The music amplified, filling their souls, matching the majesty of perfect dancers joined forever. Their dance became freer, arms extending farther than ever before, legs stretching high, toes pointed, as if they could lean forward and step onto the moon.

The swirling unison of their movements became a cycle of symmetry. Joy filled Elaina, but the true power of a seeress wasn't the knowing of feelings within her, but sensing the feelings outside of her skin.

Elaina felt the smooth, strong floorboards of her dance hall flex as she and Eloise stepped as one. She felt their rapid heartbeats, their matching breaths, their elation as they frolicked awash in the delights of dance. Elaina was spinning free, reveling in her expansive suffusion of sensory ranging.

She sensed startled amazement in Eloise, exposed for the first time to the freedom of dancing, the wondrous power of body and emotions flowing in perfect synchronization. Most people never grasped the enchantment of uninhibited dancing, unbridled and candid. Yet dancing wasn't good for retrospection; contemplation came after the dance.

Dancing is always an experience of the moment. Heart and spirit underlied the unifying aspects of the universe, the bindings that joined all life. By freeing her heart, opening her mind to every sensation, Elaina joined its awareness, the universal sharing of spirit. She felt changes in the winds ruffle her wings and tail feathers as she flew over the cliffs of Othar. Between her teeth, the tough grasses crunched and ground as she chewed her cud in the field. She was sitting on her bed, her strong arm around Seren, comforting her wife, and soothing her distress over the departure of Karl and Roselyn. She was sweating in the courtyard, her bulging muscles leaning into the saw, and then pulling it back from what would be a main crossbeam for the new gate. She was hiding behind the stables, trembling as a handsome young page, whom she loved above all things, laid his hand upon her breast for the first time; she desperately wanted more, but feared that her father would kill him if he suspected …

Sensations from all over Bristlen flooded Elaina, overwhelming, and she staggered. Eloise's dancing also stuttered; she stumbled, and barely caught herself before she fell. Yet Elaina recovered with practiced ease, danced to her daughter and circled around her, her arms like willow wands brushing, softly grazing, her smile assuring her that everything was all right. Eloise was everything that Elaina had ever prayed for her daughter to become, but her magic was limited, unable to maintain the dance moves that Elaina had mastered long before. She sensed that Eloise understood, and Elaina kissed her daughter without disturbing the flow of her dance, which had to be constant, matching the eternal movement of all things.

Elaina spread her arms and leapt into independence. With Eloise resting, Elaina was free to perform miracles of dance that her younger, less-flexible daughter could never attempt. She danced as she'd only dreamed of, reveling in meter with the pulses of every heartbeat in England. The notes of the musicians blended with the tempo and melody of creation, and Elaina felt everything.

Yet … worlds beyond dance existed … and she intuited more …

Sensations stronger than she'd ever felt, more tangible, filled Elaina, on the fringes of her reach. Beyond the worlds she knew, foreign feelings wafted, countless emotions, stretching her awareness. Her old, familiar servants on her isle above Oslo Bay danced and sang in her absence, and from the distant West, across the Atlantic, came tremulations of peoples that she'd never sensed before, lands unknown … stretching to another strange, massive ocean. Thoughts and emotions of whole populations, vast empires that she'd never touched upon swelled, and at a whim, her exploration revealed countless lives stretching west, and then south, to an entire continent which no European had ever mapped.

The vastness of Earth came to her in one overpowering rush, blinding her in her dream hall, deafening her to the minstrels. Elaina had never considered the world as a sphere, eternally twirling, yet suddenly it was a living ball in her arms, and she held it protectively, as she'd once mothered Eloise. Elaina swayed with the world, rocking with its waves, its turnings of night and day, and the pull of the moon circled her as she pirouetted, awash with oceans of joy, struggles, heartbreak, and contentment. Elaina experienced the world as no mortal ever had ... and shared with it all that she loved.

Yet holes appeared in her feelings, gaps leaking sensations for which she couldn't account. Powerful, infinite emotions, stronger than any mortal's, whispered through points all over the globe as she and the world danced together. The strongest feeling she recognized as Bifrost, the Rainbow Bridge to Yggdrasil and the realms of her Norse gods. Another sensation felt equally familiar; the Temple of Osiris, the doorway to the afterlife of the Egyptian Gods. Others dotted all over her living sphere, more 'cracks in the world', each leading to lands and pantheons of gods unknown ... more than she'd expected.

Every continent on Earth held doorways to immortal lands!

Elaina reached out. So many 'cracks in the world', so many other realms ... surely there was unification, a greater understanding to be had.

She danced in a miasma of kaleidoscope images, of infinite realms and divinities, stretching beyond comprehension. She saw other realms, like countless, floating bubbles, moving, shifting, yet eternally connected. Other doors, other 'cracks in the world', opened upon realms outside of Earth, planetary spheres so far apart that only divine realms could connect them, but to which Elaina, with cosmic awareness, could travel at will.

Yet, as Elaina danced across the dark sky amid countless stars of all colors, she knew that this endless series of worlds, these infinite realms, couldn't be connected by accident. Something deeper existed, some force that had created them all, and Elaina dreamed of seeing it, of becoming one with the ultimate truth.

Elaina probed deeper. She dreamed of seeing the source of all worlds and merging with the eternal consciousness of creation. Stars exploded and were born anew. Eternities flitted past barely noticed. All creation opened itself to her in a fountain of hopeless longing, unexpected fulfillment, and enticing desires.

Fire!

Destruction!

Explosions of death and violence!

Elaina staggered in her dance as the very music of reality changed. Drums of planets colliding echoed from a single thunder, so deep that only a blast of creation, destroying all that previously existed, could evoke it. Eons tortured her, chockfull of gulfs to swallow countless realms, followed by stars crashing together as cymbals of ultimate devastation. Dark, evil hungers rose in the centers of all things, ravenous holes, consuming with endless gluttony. Shooting stars pelted her, disturbing her steps, leaps, and gyrations. She shifted her dance; from flowing, swan-like fluidity, Elaina stomped, punched at the air, and snarled in bitter fury. She danced with cruel abandon, forceful, domineering, and demanding, lost in tumult. Chaos surrounded her, a universal reality older than worlds, existing without framework or reason. Accidents and happenstance ruled, and death alone held dominion, for no life existed in the Land of Ultimate Chaos.

Hatred arose, hatred for her; Elaina had invaded its realm of mindless desolation, a being of harmony dancing through an eternity of infinite wreckage. Life held no jurisdiction here, and her orderly presence offended its nature.

Debris struck her from every direction.

Elaina screamed. She tried to force her way back to sanity, to anywhere, back to any realm that she'd already visited; anything to escape the agony murdering her. Damaged too greatly, Elaina fell before chaos, which nailed her to destruction, riddling her very nature, sucking her spirit-corpse into the maw of infinity. Her thoughts dimmed, doomed to fade and be lost.

Elaina couldn't escape back to a former world… and she couldn't remain.

Could she go on …?

Deeper …?

Into the deepest …?

Even chaos must come from somewhere!

Go farther! Push harder! Drive into the deepest depth …!

Pain vanished, relief filling its wake. All around her lay chaos, overshadowed by infinite realms, one of which was Earth. Her friends lay there, in England, and sleeping in the Field of Dreams.

But how could this be …?

Because they'd dreamed it!

Elaina gasped, slowing her dance to gentle flexes of lithe muscles. Sensations needled her, so subtle that she had to reach for them, but when she extended her hand, they dispelled like smoke beneath her failing grasp.

Where all thought existed, the unthinkable seemed alien. The harder that Elaina tried to grasp anything, the faster her comprehensions slipped away. Time didn't exist here, neither a beginning nor an end. Elaina had finally found a universe where nothing permanent existed. Everything was ethereal, wispy, just beyond reach.

Some billows of mist bore hazy shapes, moving, changing, but nothing clear, nothing defined. Misperceptions echoed in her dancing; her weight seemed difficult to shift, her balance uncertain. Elaina fell through a cloud, buoyant and softly resistant, yet infinitely powerful. As if she'd dived into welcoming arms of those that loved her, Elaina felt soft, warm steams lift her, raising her spirit.

One cloud gravitated toward her. Elaina's eyes widened; the image in the mist was her reflection, as if she were looking into a steamy mirror. She was dancing her perfect dance in the hall with Eloise, prancing across smooth, polished boards, her bare feet sliding, fluttering, full of glee and longing … and she danced on a golden metal floor surrounded by tall stalks of wheat. Her images danced as she did, purposeful, both seeking …!

Here!

She'd arrived exactly where she'd wanted to be. Yet it wasn't what she'd dreamed …

Dreams!

Each reality of hers … was a dream!

Each dream of hers … was a reality!

All of the glowing clouds around her … were her every dream!

> *Finding the perfect lover …*
> *Happiness for her daughter …*
> *Living the life she wanted …*

No wonder everything seemed so flimsy and insubstantial!
Here ... *dreams were everything!*

But why ...?

Elaina knew only one to learn the secrets of the
universe: *she drew a deep breath ... and began to dance again.*

Elaina plunged into dreamy fogs, winging like a dove,
swimming through air, dancing on clouds. No direction
limited her; Elaina spun and flipped, flexed, and flowed.
Music such as she'd never imagined erupted, not from
outside sources; her soul burst forth a symphony with a
rapid, excited beat, and the sprung-tinkles of a harp
welled up as if plucked upon her own heartstrings.
Trumpets blared in harmonious cadence, breaking the
stately medley with staccato cadences. Perfect dancing
became her reality, she and the universe, together as one.

Dreams!

The essence of the universe was ... dreams!

With unexpected clarity, Elaina understood.

Dreams start everything. Without dreams, chaos
dominates. Dreams check entropy, and begin the
processes of planning and creation. Without dreams,
nothing organizes, designs, or imagines. No plan comes
to fruition unless it's first dreamed.

Chaos occasionally assists, yet chaos destroys more
than it creates. Dreams foment order and lay the
stepping stones to accomplishment. All realms, even
those of the gods themselves, began as dreams. All
goodness started as dreams, and the best became reality
only through the unwavering efforts of dreamers.

Elaina understood:

The Field of Dreams was a reflection of truths, not of lies.

The motives of the Egyptian gods became obvious;
the Field of Dreams gave to their faithful a glimpse, not
of themselves, but of the essences of all things.

Jay Palmer

Elaina swayed in the ultimate Core of the Universe, the Realm of Dreams, and yet she was also dancing upon a wooden floor in England, watched by Eloise, and upon gold in the Field of Wheat … because all were dreams.

Karl and Reginleif were in Valhalla, rediscovering the love that they'd allowed to fade by absence, but only partly; both were also staring into each other's eyes amid golden sheaves.

Sister Aspertine had returned to the Abbey of St. Dunstay … and she slept among the sheaves … and stood before the Gates of St. Peter … holding hands with Nate, because she was dreaming.

Nate, Phil, and Alarika were in Castle Bristlen, and Henry had returned to his family in Demril. Yet all also stood in the afterlife of the Egyptians, gathered together, missing much of themselves.

Because dreams were the basis of reality!

Dreams could exist in multiple places … simultaneously!

However, none were whole. Each of the party lay sundered, broken and divided. The curse of Skafti had claimed upon all of them: *none would know aught but unhappiness and eternal suffering.*

Elaina couldn't allow that. They'd each had one shared dream, and she couldn't let their individual dreams tear their souls apart. She was also in a dream, dreaming a different dream, *but couldn't anyone, even mortals, change their dreams?*

Elaina spun, pirouetting, faster than eyes could see. All universes spun with her. Then Elaina stopped, grasping command of every universe with more willpower than a goddess.

"We are back in the Field of Wheat!" Elaina shouted.

Chapter 15

Small Dreams

PHIL

Phil set his tankard back onto the table ... and it fell straight through the vanished boards. He topped backward ... his bench was gone. He smashed into crackling stalks, blinded by long leaves, and grains of wheat rained upon him. He collapsed onto his butt, grasping for balance, and then glanced around, wondering what had happened.

Wheat in his hair... on his clothes ...!

He was back in the Field of Wheat!

Phil scowled; *when was all this going to end?*

He heard similar gasps, and Sister Aspertine and Alarika screamed. He climbed to his feet to find Elaina standing poised, as if having just finished dancing upon the golden floor. Eloise stood not far from her, looking stunned, her empty hands grasping ... nothing. Eyes wide, Nate was also climbing to his feet, and he lifted up ... a half-eaten hunk of cooked pig still on a long bone, now layered in sand. Alarika pushed down her skirts, which had been up over her knees; she blushed like she'd just finished in the privy. Henry was holding his arms as if he'd been hugging someone. Karl and Roselyn both cursed, and instantly they dashed into the thickets of wheat, their pale buttocks flashing.

"What in Niflhiem ...?" Karl demanded.

"My apologies," Elaina said, and she waved her hand at them both, but no clothes appeared upon them. An expression of surprise crossed her face. "My dream has ended."

"What ...?" Karl shouted. *"What do you ...?"*

"I brought us back," Elaina said.

"Without asking?" Karl demanded. *"Why ...?"*

"We need to free the Seer," Elaina said. "But first, I think ... some new clothes are needed."

"Hurry!" Karl shouted.

"Who's dreaming now?" Elaina asked. "Henry, Phil, and Alarika have yet to dream."

Alarika waved her arms dramatically, fingers splayed, but nothing happened. Shrugging, Henry pointed at the ground and waved one finger, but to no avail.

"Phil, dream me some clothes!" Karl ordered, and Roselyn elbowed him with a glare. "Us ...!"

Phil hesitated, fearing; *what would happen ...?*

Phil waved his hand at Karl and Roselyn, but nothing happened.

"You can't just gesture," Elaina said. "Dreams power this land; dream of Karl and Roselyn dressed in clean clothes."

Phil grimaced, and tried to picture Karl and Roselyn in clothes, but he couldn't decide which outfit, and when he finally waved, both Karl and Roselyn stood in white Egyptian robes, as they'd been given after awakening the sphinx.

"That's the best that you can dream?" Nate derided.

"It's fine," Karl said. "Elaina, why're we here? Have we been here the whole time?"

"No, and yes," Elaina said. "I used my dream to dance the perfect dance, and visited realms beyond imaginings."

"We've experienced too much imaginings," Karl said.

"Am I still a Valkyrie?" Roselyn demanded.

"You've always been a Valkyrie," Elaina said.

"We escaped from here!" Sister Aspertine burst shrilly.

"No, we remained," Elaina said. "We were at Castle Bristlen, and St. Dunstay, Valhalla ... a dozen other places ... and here ... all at the same time."

"That's impossible!" Karl said.

"Nothing's impossible in dreams," Elaina said. "I'd thought so, too, but I was wrong. We can't escape from reality into dreams; dreams are the heart of reality."

"That's crazy," Alarika said.

"That's what you said about England ... before you saw it," Elaina said. "I'm not asking for trust; I used my dream to delve into secrets that few gods know. I saw that we'd never be complete, any of us, until we finished our task ... and that we could only do here."

Karl fumed, and Roselyn scowled.

"You could've waited ...!" Roselyn snapped.

"... until you could finish ...?" Eloise snarled, staring daggers at both of them.

"Daughter, enough!" Elaina said. "You and Roselyn have been as fickle as Karl, and we can't afford jealousy. We've a long way to go, and no one's sleeping with anyone until we're done."

"Why bring us here?" Sister Aspertine demanded. "Why not dream us to where this ... Seer ... is, and save us the trip?"

"Dreams are fulfilled by actions," Elaina said. "We can dream anything, well, Phil can, but we're not the only ones dreaming. The Egyptian gods also dream, and where our dreams conflict with theirs, theirs are likely to prevail. They dreamed this realm, and to reach them, we have to cross it ... in reality, not just in dreams."

"What now?" Karl asked.

"Everyone who enters the Field of Dreams experiences their fantasies," Elaina said. "Normally, the dead enter individually, so their dreams don't overlap. But we aren't dead; we came as a group. We're trapped here until we've all had our turn."

"If I don't make it back into Valhalla ...!" Roselyn snarled at Elaina.

"You had your dream," Elaina said. "Ask Phil to dream you back there, if you want, but part of your soul will remain here ... forever."

Roselyn scowled and turned to Phil.

"I need my armor ... Hel's armor ... and her sword!" Roselyn said. "And a barrel of the Water of Life!"

Phil quailed under Roselyn's stare, and cautiously concentrated as best he could. When he opened his eyes, a barrel stood before Roselyn, and Hel's armor, sword, and quilted clothes lay scattered about the bent sheaves.

"I'd like my stuff, too," Karl said, and a moment later, his garb and armor lay beside Roselyn's.

"We should equip ourselves," Alarika said. "We could be facing anything, even deep desert."

"No point dreaming for what we can't carry," Karl said.

"Dream camels and carts," Alarika said.

Frowning, Phil spent the next five hours struggling. He seldom dreamed, even in his sleep; Phil saw no point in dreams. Life consisted of orders: orders of birth, levels of ability, and ranks of status. Dreams caused nothing but chaos. Elaina's explanations were just words; Phil suspected that she'd just imagined it, that visions held no more substance than stories or daydreams. Her claim that all worlds were built out of chaos and dreams made no sense at all.

Everyone wanted something. Alarika made Phil create a dozen camels, four pulling two large, sturdy carts filled with supplies. Karl insisted on stallions, one for each of them. Eloise made him create a matched pair of horses pulling an elegant, delicate wagon with a wide cloth roof over it … and a dozen new dresses. Nate wanted a dozen waterskins filled with the Water of Life, and he drank greedily as soon as they appeared. Karl wanted twice that many, enough Water of Life to last for weeks, and spare weapons, extra food, blankets, rope, and cooking gear.

Sister Aspertine asked to be sent home, but Elaina overspoke her.

"You must stay, nun."

"Why?" Sister Aspertine demanded.

"You've seen too much," Elaina said. "Your faith will fail … unless you see the rest."

Sister Aspertine actually cursed, and then, surprised, she clapped a hand over her mouth.

"You sound almost human," Roselyn laughed.

"Reverend Mother Agatha threatened to cast me from the abbey," Sister Aspertine said.

"When you return, she'll listen to you," Elaina promised.

"How can you know that?" Sister Aspertine demanded.

"Because, once you've met other deities, you'll understand God better than any reverend mother," Elaina replied.

Sister Aspertine paused, then made the sign of the cross.

Elaina had Phil create a spare habit for Sister Aspertine and dresses for her, and she stored them on one of the wagons.

Nate came back for more ... and complained that Phil wasn't making it right. Phil revised Nate's dream twice before he realized that Nate was toying with him, and Phil loudly wished for a bucket of water to dump over his head.

Roselyn and Alarika laughed.

Phil created everything else that they asked for, yet he didn't enjoy it. He was a farmer turned squire, and he was a fighter, perhaps someday to be a knight; it wasn't his place to wave his hand and create things. The Field of Wheat was a curse, a violation of the natural order to which all things belonged. He didn't want power like this.

No one should ...!

Suddenly Elaina's face blocked his view.

"You're the unhappiest man I've ever seen getting everything that he wishes," Elaina said.

Phil scowled, nodding to their supplies. "These aren't my wishes."

Elaina smiled at him.

"You may never get this chance again," she said. "Wish for something ... anything!"

"That's just it," Phil said. "I could wish to be knighted, but I'd know it was false."

"Karl certainly would ... after your dream ends," Elaina said.

"I'm not a dreamer," Phil said. "I ... like things ... real."

"Then allow me," Elaina said. "I wish ... for a marvelous suit of armor, that fits Phil perfectly, as strong as Hel's, but studded with emeralds ... and trimmed with gold."

Phil half-smiled, and spread his fingers wide. The suit of armor appeared, the most splendid armor that he'd ever seen, riveted mail and plates rimmed with gold bearing rows of glistening green stones, all polished until they shined. The helm for which he'd tossed his brother overboard would've looked shabby beside it, and Phil nodded approvingly.

"That's it?" Elaina puzzled. "Just a nod ...?"

"It's just a dream," Phil muttered.

"No, it isn't," Elaina said. "When you leave here, this armor will still exist."

Phil looked at the new armor more appreciatively, but still askance.

"What would happen ... if I wished to be someone else?" Phil asked.

Elaina looked surprised.

"I don't know," she said. "Why would you want that?"

Phil looked up into Elaina's face, wondering how much he dared say. She was older, wiser, and noble. She was a powerful seeress. Normally, boys like him didn't talk to ladies like her.

"It's not my place to say," Phil said.

"You can't tell me?" Elaina asked. "Because I'm nobility?"

"Yes," Phil admitted.

Elaina laughed.

"I was born in The Bent Hook, and only because the tavernmaster didn't have the heart to throw my birthing mother outside into the snow," Elaina said, and Phil's mouth dropped.

"But ... you're ... Eloise's mother ...!"

"True nobility comes from deeds, not birthright," Elaina said. "I seduced a baron's son, and taught myself to rule wisely. I made Skafti teach me the magic of dancing. Afterwards, King Ólafr Haraldsson gave me Skafti's island and financially supported me and my servants ... as payment for secrets that my dancing revealed. But my mother was ... just like Seren ...!"

Phil reeled, gasping at the unthinkable. *Could it be true ...?*

"I never knew ... you were so ... mercenary," Phil whispered.

"Think twice before you dream yourself into someone else," Elaina said. "You might dream yourself into someone who's miserable ... because they dream of being you."

"I ... don't have dreams," Phil said, and Elaina smiled.

"Only those who fear dreams don't have them," Elaina said. "Plenty of young girls must dream of you. But there must be ... some small, tiny desire that you've had ... something that you liked ...?"

Phil thought hard, but other than beating his silly brother at everything, and drinking good, strong ale, he didn't have many likes, yet he struggled to name something.

What had he seen that he liked ...?

"I like ... watching you dance ...," Phil said.

Elaina's eyes widened, and laughter burst from her lips. Phil paled ... and then he blushed scarlet.

"*I stand corrected!*" Elaina grinned wickedly. "*You have ... monumental dreams!*"

With a merry chuckle, Elaina turned and walked away ... and Phil couldn't resist appreciating her perfectly swaying hips ... and then he blushed deeper.

Chapter 16

Restoration

HENRY

Henry said nothing, but turned away, biting his lip. He'd been back home, holding his three year old daughter in his arms, and then suddenly she was gone. *Did his daughter fall?* No notice had warned him that he was about to fade. *What would his wife think?* Her shriek of delight when he'd walked through their door still echoed in his ears, and his whole family had smothered him in hugs and kisses.

Yet it hadn't been a joy. He'd walked alone all the way down the rugged cliff-side trail, switching back and forth, watching Demril grow as he descended toward it. Before going home, he had to visit the houses of his closest friends ... where he told their wives how their husbands had died.

Thorkel's wife had allowed him inside, but she was crying before he even spoke. She was a wise woman, her children grown, and all were sobbing as he muttered his fateful message. He'd explained their mission, and told them of how they'd been attacked in Italy while guarding their boat. He stopped then, for they had no need to hear of the remainder of their misadventures ... which had ended in failure; *they'd returned without the Seer.*

Dennel's wife was young, pretty, and unable to understand. Twice Henry had to repeat the story of the attack and theft of their boat, and still she seemed doubtful, as if Dennel would walk in at any minute and contradict Henry. Her children, the oldest of which was six years old, collapsed and cried upon their floor, and still their mother stood speechless, uncomprehending.

Samuel's wife was older, smarter, and stronger. She made Henry sit, served him beer, and made him describe every detail, asking rabid questions that Henry struggled to answer. She made him tell her all about Italy, their foundering boat, the pirate's ship that they commandeered, their visit with the grand visor Ptah Shabaka, and of their arduous escape across the desert. When he described how an arrow had slain Samuel, she paused, bowed her head, and recited the Lord's Prayer. She didn't let him say another word; she thanked him, and saw him to her door; he stood outside her closed door only seconds before the sounds of her sobs curdled his soul.

Rishard wasn't married, but his parents, brothers, and sister were horrified to hear of his stabbing, although glad that he was alive. That they'd left him in a hospital seemed an act of kindness, and they praised both Karl and Eloise as worthy lieges. They thanked Henry for bringing them news, and bowed their heads when Henry told them of the three from their village who'd not lived to see a hospital. He left troubled, for he'd said nothing of Eloise's healing spells, knowing the trouble it would cause.

Now he was back, past Egypt, through the 'crack in the world'. Five they'd been, all sailors, and only he remained. He was facing dangers unknown from Egyptian gods: the last sailor ... *expendable.*

Henry knew how these stories went. Karl was a baron. Eloise was his baroness and a druid witch. Roselyn was a Valkyrie. Elaina was a sorceress of divination. *They'd be spared ...!*

Nate and Phil were farmboys made squires ... and good fighters. Alarika was an Egyptian, the font of all that they knew about the gods of this land. *They lived in danger.*

Yet Henry was just a poor sailor, of no special ability, and the last of five hired, unremarkable men. *He was doomed.*

He'd been so excited when they'd returned to Castle Bristlen; Henry hadn't expected to ever see England again. He knew his odds were the worst, that he'd be the one sacrificed, when next the Wyrd chose a companion to die. Arriving in Castle Bristlen, he'd thought that he'd escaped his fate ... *but that's why they called it fate!*

And fate had drawn him back ...!

Long he'd watched Phil invent supplies as a magician might conjure demons, disgusted by his own creations. Finally Elaina walked up to speak to Phil, and Henry didn't wait to hear her words. He wasn't stupid; no man could dream two dreams at once, and their company had entered this magical land together, walking, not floating down the River of Death. Only two companions hadn't explored their dreams: Alarika ... and him.

They had enough supplies. They didn't need him. Henry strode away, uselessly pushing back the thick stalks as he waded through them. The stalks closed upon him like a vise ... *like the clutches of fate.*

Finally, Henry found a clump of tall wheat growing almost to his shoulder, and there he sat, on the sand between the stalks, leaves brushing him, hidden from view from the others. Some of his companions had been furious at being taken from the Field of Wheat, and others furious to be brought back. Henry didn't believe for a second that they had any control over it; destiny was decided by beings far greater than mortal.

Yet he'd been unhappy. They'd returned to Castle Bristlen whole and healthy, with the addition of a beautiful young desert woman. He'd returned to Demril, only one of five close friends.

How long he sat upon the sand, surrounded only by wheat, Henry couldn't guess, but slowly his thirst grew. Henry wished he'd brought some henket, but not so badly that he wanted to go back and face the others.

Finally heat and dryness tightened his throat, and Henry's thirst couldn't be denied. He started to rise, but on a whim, he waved his hand … and a pitcher of henket appeared.

At first Henry startled, but he'd expected it. *Yet … what now?* To sit and idly dream was pleasant, but to have ultimate power, as the others had shown: *what should he do?*

Henry knew what he wanted to do, but the claws of rationality raked his mind in denial. Priests in churches preached of modesty and humility, but he'd also attended the moon dances; that was where he'd met his wife, and where he suspected that his eldest child had been sired. He'd seen what the others had done with their dreams, and suspected that he could also do anything.

But … dare he do such a thing …?
Dare he not …?
How could he live with himself if he didn't try …?

Life wasn't fair, Henry thought. Some lucky few were born noble, or with great strength or wit, and the world seemed to turn around them. He'd lived a shadowy existence, barely noticed by the important. Baron Karl was also peasant-born, but he'd been one of the luckiest men alive, tall and handsome, and had won the hearts of Baroness Eloise and Roselyn the Valkyrie. Men like Karl welcomed him, perhaps even befriended him, but he'd never be like Karl, and most of the nobility wouldn't even acknowledge his existence. Few would remember him after he died, and a few years afterwards even his name would be forgotten.

His fellows had already paid for living as shadows of Karl, and he doubted if he'd be as lucky as Rishard. His price was yet to be paid … but he knew that payment would be demanded … *soon.*

Henry took a deep breath, summoned all of his courage, wished with all of his heart, and slowly he waved both of his hands.

"Come back to me …!"

To his delight and amazement, Thorkel, Dennel, and Samuel appeared.

For a moment they all sat, staring at each other, dumbfounded. Thorkel and Dennel looked startled, staring confused at the tall, golden wheat stalks surrounding them. Samuel looked horrified, staring at Thorkel and Dennel as if every devil in Hell were staring back at him. Henry sat flabbergasted, half unsurprised that it'd worked … and half terrified because it had.

"Where are we?" Dennel asked.

"Where's Rishard?" Thorkel asked.

Samuel started to scream, but Henry gestured him silent with such urgency that they all obeyed.

"Quiet!" Henry whispered. *"And don't stand up!"*

After a moment's hesitation, Dennel whispered, "Why not?"

Henry exchanged a warning glance with Samuel.

"H-h-how …?" Samuel whispered.

"You won't believe what we've been through … or where we are," Henry said.

"Where's our boat?" Thorkel asked.

"Where's the sea?" Dennel asked. "I can't even smell it."

"At least a hundred miles from here … well, beyond the 'crack in the world', at least," Henry said.

"You found it?" Samuel asked.

"I went through it," Henry said to Samuel. "But … *you … didn't …!*"

Samuel stared at Henry, then glanced at Thorkel and Dennel. His aged brows furrowed.

"You mean …?" Samuel whispered, nodding to their companions. *"I'm … like … them …?"*

"What'd you mean … *'like us'?"* Dennel asked.

Samuel waved him silent, and sat thoughtful.

"I was shot," he remembered. "I took an arrow … in my back … it hurt …"

Samuel examined his side, pulling open his shirt, and reaching around to feel his back with his hand, incredulity on his face.

"What's your last memory?" Henry asked Thorkel and Dennel.

Thorkel and Dennel exchanged confused glances, then shrugged.

"Wait!" Dennel said. "We were attacked, some men on the wharfs …"

"That was back in Italy," Samuel said.

"What?" Thorkel asked. "We are in Italy …!"

"We're in Egypt," Samuel said.

"We were in Egypt," Henry said. "We're nowhere now ..."

"That's crazy!" Dennel said. "Why, just a few minutes ago ...!"

"That was a month ago," Henry said.

"Where's Rishard?" Thorkel demanded.

"Am I ... I'm dead ...?" Samuel asked.

"Not exactly," Henry said. "You need to be silent; I'm going to show you some magic ..."

Thorkel laughed ... but broke off when Samuel shushed and gestured at him.

"Say nothing loud ... and by all means, don't shout," Henry said, and he waved his hand. A bottle of brandy appeared before each of them. The others startled, but Henry seemed unperplexed, so they didn't scream. "Samuel, you'd better start ... tell them what happened ... from the day that we landed in Italy."

Soon they were all drinking, aghast, as Samuel described how they'd found their knarr stolen, found Rishard mortally wounded, and presumed that Thorkel and Dennel were slain. Eyes stretched wide and bulged.

"Don't fret," Samuel told them. "I ... died, too ... *didn't I ...?*"

They all looked at Henry, and he nodded.

"Don't lose heart," Henry said. "Finish your story."

Samuel hesitantly explained how Eloise had used healing magic to save Rishard, how they'd left Rishard at a Christian hospital, and he described their fight with the city guard, Roselyn descending into the gladiatorial pit, and about their misadventures at Prince Fernando's palace. He slowly got around to how they'd sailed a wreck chosen by Elaina until it sank, and then fought and killed the pirates and claimed their stolen ship, and how they'd gotten accused of thievery at the mouth of the Nile

River. Several times Thorkel or Dennel voiced doubts, but Henry waved them quiet.

"We've been trusted shipmates all our lives," Henry said. "Everything he's saying is true."

After completing the story, with horrid details of almost dying in the desert, and Elaina dancing for coins after they explored the crypts of the Valley of the Kings, Samuel explained how they purchased a ride on a wide barge, but then he stopped.

"That's where I was shot," Samuel said. "On the barge ... I don't remember dying."

"You did," Henry said. "And you won't believe what happened next."

Henry took up the story, and the three sat amazed. Dennel had seen the great sphinx before, and Henry's description of the monstrous statue coming to life terrified him. His description of the 'crack in the world', and how they'd jumped through, tested their friendship, and his explanation of the River of Death and the Field of Wheat was met with undeniable disbelief. His description of their return to Castle Bristlen, and then back, was greeted with scoffs.

"What proof would you have?" Henry asked Samuel. "A gold statue ... of your wife ...?"

With a gesture, a golden statue suddenly appeared, two-handspans tall, with the exact face and form of Samuel's wife. All three former deadmen gasped.

"So ... you ... *brought us back ...?*" Dennel asked.

"You would've done the same," Henry said. "We've been friends all our lives."

"Couldn't live without us ...?" Thorkel grinned.

"Thank you, Henry," Samuel said.

The others nodded mutely, still too stunned to fully believe. Henry waved them off.

"The question is ... what now?" Henry asked.

"What ...?" Thorkel asked. "We're here ... in a magical land!"

"You died," Henry said. "Karl, Eloise, and Roselyn didn't die ... nor will they, as long as I'm here."

"What are you saying ...?" Dennel asked. "Surely you're not suggesting ....!"

"We've known Karl since he married Eloise," Samuel said. "He's the best leader of du Harmonn since ... well, since Elaina."

"I've fought with Karl twice," Thorkel said. "I respect him, and we're together again ..."

"You know the fireside tales," Henry said. "Their journey to Yggdrasil was real ... and proves my point. Heroes never die ... but their followers ..."

"It doesn't work like that ...," Samuel said.

"If I'd died, would you three be here?" Henry asked. "Rishard is badly wounded, and he would've died without Eloise's healing ..."

"Eloise would've helped all of us, if she could ...," Dennel said. "We owe them no less loyalty."

"We swore to Rafe," Samuel said. "Our honor ...!"

"You've paid every debt," Henry said. "If we want to live ... I should wish us back home ... all of us."

"No," Samuel said. "We promised to see this through. We can't abandon Karl ...!"

"Keep your voice down!" Henry hissed. "At least, until we're decided ...!"

"I agree: we must stay," Thorkel said. "It'd be a dishonor ...!"

"I'm not leaving," Dennel said. "Henry, if you want to go, we'll understand."

"Chances are that we'll die here ... all of us," Henry said. "Is that what you want ... to die ... again?"

"I'll risk it," Dennel said.

"And I," Thorkel said.

"Our duty is clear," Samuel insisted.

"Even if it kills us …?" Henry asked.

"Go, if you would," Dennel said.

"No," Henry said. "I expected that this would be your answer. I was tempted … and I didn't trust my own judgement."

"We'll stay together," Samuel smiled.

"No, we won't," Henry said. "I told your wives … and families … that you died. I saw their faces: I won't do that again."

"You won't have to," Thorkel said.

"No, I won't," Henry said, and he waved his hand, and three large, heavy bags of gold coins appeared, each priceless bag on a loop around the necks of Thorkel, Dennel, and Samuel. All looked surprised as the precious weight pulled their heads down.

"You've done your part … and it's time that I did mine," Henry said. "Send scrolls to your families, and see that Rishard makes it back home safe. And … if I don't make it … see that my family never starves …"

"*Henry, no …!*" Samuel started to object.

"*I wish all three of you were in Italy … to take Rishard home!*" Henry exclaimed.

"*Nooooo …!*" all three started to shout … and then they were gone.

Henry sat alone, looking at the three impressions that their butts had left in the sand, and at the bent stalks of wheat against which they'd been sitting. Then he reached out and grasped the golden statue of Samuel's wife … and turned it to face him. She was beautiful, showing no trace of the sadness that he'd last seen on her face.

He'd made the only choice that he could ... the duty that he'd accepted before Rafe, with his four best friends beside him. But they'd paid their dues ... and Karl and the others didn't need to know that they were safe ... and helping Rishard. He'd given them more than enough gold to get home, and even if they cursed him for sending them back, at least they'd be alive. At least ... all but one of the sailors of Demril would make it back home.

Henry pushed the golden statue of Samuel's wife over. It toppled onto the sand. He sat and looked at it, worth more money than he'd ever have, and then he got up and went back to join the others.

Chapter 17

Betrayal

ALARIKA

Her hand waved but nothing happened.

When would it be her turn?

Alarika scowled and lifted her cup of the Water of Life, looking at the others. *What fools they were! Given their dreams, they'd only dreamed of giving up their dreams!* Yet each of them had gotten their turn, and they weren't even Egyptians. *She wouldn't waste hers!*

Phil waved his hand to create another horse, another one for his brother, but no horse appeared; he'd failed to make these northern strangers even stranger, riding horses instead of camels.

Phil seemed delighted when no horse appeared, but his brother only scowled.

She waved her hand again, wishing ardently, but to no avail. A soft growl rumbled in the back of her throat.

Alarika couldn't understand why anyone would prefer a thirsty horse to a speedy camel, but these soft people, from their chill, green lands, were bizarre. Perhaps they didn't need a mount that could travel for days without water where it rained like the sky was the sea.

Water; Alarika still staggered at the memory of the Atlantic Ocean, so vast and dark, not like the bright waters of the Nile or the Mediterranean Sea. The northern clouds ... so thick that they blotted out the sky; *Alarika had never imagined so many clouds!* The total absence of sand, save for a tiny strip by the sea, seemed unfathomable before she'd seen it. Their forests were still unbelievable.

How powerful were dreams?

Elaina's description of her vision, her visit to higher realms, troubled the others, but Alarika grasped its true meaning: the Field of Dreams made gods of mortals!

Could she bring the thick clouds and frequent rains of England to Egypt? Arrive beside the sphinx in her own flying temple of gold? Could she make herself immortal? If she did, then she'd be worshipped for centuries!

Another wave of her hand ... nothing.

How long must she endure waiting?

Elaina had taken Karl aside for a whispered conversation, but Alarika suspected that she was only doing it to keep him from Eloise and Roselyn, who were standing apart, swapping hateful glares. Alarika couldn't understand their rivalry; Karl was too smooth-skinned, too pale, and too passive. No desert warrior would stutter and mumble. If she wanted a man, then she'd take him, and the desert bleach his bones if he dared refuse her. To her, Karl seemed more a woman than a man.

An hour later, Henry came walking back, seeming to just be aimlessly wandering through the chest-high stalks. He was the only one beside Alarika that hadn't had his dreams come true. At once, she pushed into the wheat to intercept him.

"It's your turn," Alarika said, shoving back the fronds.

"I know," Henry said.

"Well ...?" Alarika asked. "What will you dream?"

"My dreams are gone ... and my blessings go with them," Henry replied.

"Gone ...?" Alarika asked.

"Time passes differently in dreams," Henry said.

Alarika paused, wondering what he was talking about, but she'd no time to waste: she lifted her hand high ... and precious rubies, emeralds, sapphires, and topaz gleamed upon her fingers, each set in ornate bands of polished gold and silver.

"My turn ...!" Alarika shrieked.

She waved both her hands widely, and created a vast, huge palace, with polished white marble walls, a high, flat roof, and great red doors encircled by and decorated with gold. Joyously she cried out as the others startled, lifting their heads to stare at her massive, new palace.

With the gesture of a single finger, the red doors opened, and Alarika strode inside. A long hallway, lined by arched doors on both sides, opened upon small rooms of opulent décor, filled with cushions and low tables. She ignored them, focusing on a tall doorway to a hall of enormous proportions, with stone pillars wider than she was tall, every surface decorated with ornate carvings and paintings, depictions of her gods and their legendary deeds. As she entered into her vast main room, she paused, frowned, and waved her hands. Massive statues of the gods of Egypt appeared, standing side-by-side upon the far wall, towering three times the height of a man. Reaching the center, facing the back wall, Alarika smiled and waved. Before the statues rose a massive gold and silver throne, the back of which bore bands arcing high like stylized wings.

She approached her throne, sat upon it, and wished herself a gown of the finest flax, the sheerest ever, practically a mist, hanging upon its arm. She wished herself a crown, tall and golden, decorated with the symbol of Ra surrounded by the snakes of Set, and she was crowned.

Alarika smiled, waved her hand again, and before her throne appeared a streaming fountain filled with the magical drink that Karl had shared with her: the Water of Life. Looking at it, Alarika grinned.

With this endless fountain splashing this godly elixir, she'd live and rule Egypt forever! She'd be their queen ... their goddess ...!

At a whim, treasures appeared in piles, surrounding her throne ... wealth to shame the treasuries of the pharaoh. *She had enough to indulge herself for centuries!* Alarika was almost ready; *she had everything that she needed ... except one thing ...!*

"Leaving us ...?" Karl's voice echoed across the chamber.

Inside the entrance to her hall, Karl and all of the other companions stood, staring at her. Alarika glared at them, at their impertinence ... entering her palace! All that she had to do was wish them outside before she left, and then she'd abandon them in this endless land of death ...!

"Fools!" Alarika shouted. *"You could've been gods! Now I ... alone ... will make my dreams real!"*

"We need you," Roselyn said. "We brought you here ... and only you can speak Egyptian ...!"

"Your quest is doomed!" Alarika said. "Now, just one thing before I wish my palace back home ... to Giza!"

The companions exchanged glances, their expressions comically frightened. Alarika laughed at their mindless loyalty, and wished for the last thing that she wanted, the one prize for which she'd helped these fools open the portal ...

"*Father ...!*" Alarika cried. "*Father, come to me ...!*"

At her wish, an aged figure appeared, dressed in a ragged red robe, glancing around as if startled.

"Father ...!" Alarika cried, smiling widely.

"*Alarika ...?*" the Mad Hermit gasped, and then he looked up at her, his eyes wide on his lined, weathered face. "*Daughter! What are you doing here ...?*"

Alarika screamed, a piercing shriek of surprise and horror.

Her father, the Mad Hermit of the Valley of Thieves, stood before her, but his features bore little resemblance to the loving face that she knew. His long beard was still gray, but his pupils were slitted, his eyes like a cat's, and two long fangs extended from his mouth. His raggedy red robe hid his body, but his long legs and arms flexed like the coils of snakes, and where his hands and feet should've been, at the ends of serpentine bodies, the hissing heads of cobras spread their hoods and stared hungrily at her.

"*The Field of Wheat ...?!?*" the Mad Hermit shouted. "*Daughter, you fool! Flee ... at once! Abandon your dreams ... now, while you can!*"

The crashes of feet made Alarika look up, and she saw her companions running forward, Karl, Roselyn, Nate, and Phil, toward her fountain with drawn swords, but she ignored them.

"*Father, what happened ...?*" Alarika shouted.

The Mad Hermit turned to look at the charging companions, who halted in revulsion when they spied his condition. His cobra-limbs hissed at them.

"Get out of here!" the Mad Hermit shouted. *"The Field of Wheat is a test, like everything else in this land! You're failing! Leave now ... before you suffer my doom!"*

"What doom ...?" Eloise demanded.

The Mad Hermit shook his head and lifted up all four of his snake heads.

"Our gods desire only the company of devout followers ... those who love them above all things ... even their own dreams," the Mad Hermit explained. "Those who lose themselves here, who care more about their dreams than joining the company of the gods, fail the test. The pit of the Duat shall open and engulf all who fail! You'll fall in ... and be trapped forever ... as I am ...!"

"I'll wish us to Cairo ...!" Alarika argued.

"While you live, only your Ka, one part of your spirit, will travel with you," the Mad Hermit said. "You'll be yourself ... for a while, but slowly your sundered soul will die ... your social life will eventually return here to rejoin your lost physical life. Your living shell shall become a vessel for demons of Set, and undo all that you wished for, delighting only in death and devastation."

"Did you die here?" Karl asked.

"No one dies here!" the Mad Hermit cursed sourly, looking at the snakes of his body. "I should've known better: three passages exist to the City of the Gods, which is the only place where mortals can be saved from my doom. Don't go the Water Route: I tried that, as it was the fastest."

"Water Route ...?" Elaina asked.

"I made a reed boat and sailed to find the gods, as it seemed the fastest way, but the waters beneath me began to boil, and I barely reached shore before my ship dissolved beneath my feet. I was badly scalded, but there I followed the shore, and crossed a land of crocodiles. Then giant scarab beetles chased me, and forced me to cross the river, whose waters had cooled, but now teemed with hungry hippopotamuses. Yet I knew the prayers, and so I escaped being eaten, until I came to the snakes of Set. I never worshipped Set; I didn't know the prayers to drive his serpents back; I was bitten. I fell, poisoned, and the ground opened up beneath me. The Duat swallowed me. Now I'm doomed, a demon, slowly to become a snake in both body and mind."

"What must we do?" Eloise asked.

"Take my daughter from here!" the Mad Hermit demanded. "Protect Alarika at all costs!"

"We protect each other," Karl said. "As long as she travels with us, she's one of us."

"Go the Overland Route," the Mad Hermit said. "Alarika knows the prayers. Find the cities, and brave the challenges. Keep moving towards the City of the Gods ... and never give up. The instant that you give up, the ground beneath you will open, and the Duat will consume you ... and ultimately make you like me."

"You said that *three passages* exist ...?" Elaina asked.

"The Duat itself leads to the City of the Gods, but no mortal can survive it," the Mad Hermit said. "A river of fire courses through it, and demons worse than I inhabit it. Even if you navigated its dangers, at its end lies Aapep, whom only Amon-Ra can defeat, and even the gods can't kill."

"*Father* ...?" Alarika shouted, but she couldn't voice her question.

"Flee, my blessed daughter," the Mad Hermit said. "You can't save me. Seek the City of the Gods ... or bitter will be our next meeting."

"We seek a friend ...," Roselyn said.

"A new light shines in the City of the Gods," the Mad Hermit said. "Rumor of that foreign glow has even reached the Duat. Seek that light ... or fall forever into darkness. Leave this place, and your dreams; they're traps ... created to distract you. Seek the gods! *Go! Now!*"

A sudden rumble erupted, shaking the floor beneath them.

"Go!" the Mad Hermit shouted. *"Abandon your dreams ... or be damned!"*

The companions turned to run for the door, but all paused to look back at Alarika.

"Daughter, wait not for me!" the Mad Hermit shouted.

"Come with me ...!" Alarika begged.

"I'll follow, to see you off, but my fate is decided!" the Mad Hermit shouted. "Run ... with your friends ...!"

"But ... F-f-f-father ...!" Alarika stammered. *"I ... awakened the sphinx!"*

"I'm proud of you, Alarika," the Mad Hermit said. "But listen: you must flee ... now! You won't get another chance!"

Suddenly hands seized her arms, and Alarika startled; Nate and Phil drug her from her throne, past her father's serpentine limbs and hissing cobra heads, and around the fountain of the Water of Life.

"Let's go!" Karl shouted over the thunderous crashes.

"Hurry!" the Mad Hermit shouted as the whole temple shook harder. *"Run ... for your lives!"*

Pulling Alarika, the squires ran down the hallway, past the tiny, opulent rooms, and out through the red doors, following the other companions. Behind them slithered the Mad Hermit, still shouting, but his cries were lost amid the deep, grinding rumbles shaking the palace. The whole Field of Wheat trembled as if it would collapse.

"Which way?" Karl demanded, pushing through the thick sheaves.

"Any way!" the Mad Hermit shouted. *"Choose the direction of your dreams! It will become the right way!"*

Holding Eloise's arm, Karl led them straight toward their waiting beasts and supplies. A step behind, Roselyn came holding Sister Aspertine's arm, helping her run. Elaina kept pace with the rest of them, Henry helping her, with Nate and Phil still pulling Alarika, who kept glancing back, unwilling to abandon her father.

Behind her, rather than run, her father slithered on all fours, his long cobra-limbs snaking between the stalks of wheat. Alarika wondered how he'd learned to do that, but he kept shouting for her to not wait for him. He stayed close, only a few seconds behind.

Karl seized the reins of a waiting horse and jumped onto its saddle. Eloise and Sister Aspertine followed his example, and Nate and Phil forced Alarika onto the white camel that she'd had Phil make, and lastly, they jumped onto their wagons, pulled Elaina aboard, and shook their camel's reins. As one, they rode off, plowing down the sheaves.

"Yes ...!" cried the Mad Hermit. *"Go ...!"*

The shaking ground thrashed, and with one sight of the Mad Hermit, their remaining mounts dashed forward, riderless. The horses galloped fastest, but Alarika's white camel caught up with Karl as the roar behind them grew deafening.

Alarika glanced back. Her father was keeping pace, sliding along behind the wagons.

"Father …!" Alarika cried.

"I can't leave!" he shouted at her. *"The dreams of the gods have doomed me! But you can escape! Plead with the gods for me, if you can! Hurry … and farewell!"*

Alarika couldn't stop watching as her inhuman father chased behind her. However, beyond his slithering form arose a sight to chill even desert blood.

An earsplitting, thunderous roar exploded, and behind them appeared a great hole in the land. A huge section of the Field of Wheat fell away … and dropped into unknown depths. Alarika's vast palace toppled into it, and vanished in a violent, crunching swirl of dust and mayhem. Amid crashing roars, she watched the hole grow wider, and more lands covered in wheat crumbled and collapsed into the smoking pit. With deafening fury, the Land of Dreams was devoured, consumed, and dropped into a black, gaping maw.

"Flee …!!!" the Mad Hermit cried.

Fast as their horses and camels could gallop, maddened by fear, they rode, but the hole behind them widened too fast. Unlike the sturdy wagons that Alarika had Phil create, Eloise's elegant, ornate carriage broke a wheel and collapsed into the pit, dragging down its matched pair of horses. The pit's edge closed upon them; the countless sheaves tumbled into the abyss faster than they could ride. The crumbling edge came closer and closer, until it trailed only paces behind.

"Alariiikaaaaa …!"

The Mad Hermit cried out, and then suddenly he toppled backwards, yanked by some unseen tether. Alarika screamed and watched as her father, his snake-limbs thrashing, flew backwards … and helplessly plummeted into the vast pit of darkness, now wide enough to reveal a wide, frightful prison filled with demons in the twisted shapes of humans and animals, divided by a river of molten rock, glowing red beneath a blackened crust and blowing ashes, which alone lit the murderous gulf of the Duat.

The Mad Hermit fell among his twisted, enraged half-animal fellows, into the Duat, and vanished from sight. Alarika cried after him, but she clung to her white camel's reins, kicking its sides for speed; *no hope of saving him existed.*

Her father, the Mad Hermit, who'd spent his whole life dreaming of coming here, had fallen ... *again.*

The crumbling edge ebbed, falling behind, while their momentum drove them rapidly onward, farther from the retreating brink, out of the golden sheaves. As Alarika watched, mesmerized by the catastrophe, the deafening roar slowly ceased. The dark pit of the Duat vanished, and the endless Field of Wheat reappeared behind them, hazy, quiet, and peaceful ... and then the whole golden land faded like the dream that it was. Endless rolling hills of harsh gray sands replaced it, empty and bleak, a dark desert stretching wide and silent under the dim, star-dotted sky.

Leading their flight, Alarika glanced around and finally heard Karl's call to halt, and the others forcibly slowed their mounts. Alarika pulled on her reins, not so hard as to throw her, and outdistanced the others before her camel slowed its pace.

Still stunned, Alarika jumped from her saddle, staring back at the distant spot where her father had vanished, fallen into the Duat.

"Father ....!" Alarika screamed, but only a distant echo replied.

She scanned every dark horizon. Behind them, not a single stalk of wheat remained, only miles of barren gray sand, empty desert stretching in all directions. They'd escaped the Field of Wheat, the unexpected torments of their own dreams, and now were trapped in the Egyptian afterlife ... with no clue as to which direction they must take to rescue the Seer ... or to find a doorway back home.

End of Book 2 of

The EGYPTIANS! Trilogy

ABOUT THE AUTHOR

Born in Tripler Army Medical Center, Honolulu, Hawaii, Jay Palmer works as a technical writer in the software industry in Seattle, Washington. Jay enjoys parties, reading everything in sight, woodworking, obscure board games, and riding his Kawasaki Vulcan. Jay is a knight in the SCA, frequently attends writer conferences, SciFi Conventions, and he and Karen are both avid ballroom dancers. But most of all, Jay enjoys writing.

JayPalmerBooks.com

Made in the USA
Monee, IL
06 February 2024

52566140R00148